Teen (Adult fiction)

Ebonics Included

Camille

-Things Get Serious-

Series 1 Book 2

Author, Publisher, & Illustrator

Kelonda Isom

To my younger self

…and to anyone

who feels they need a positive escape or distraction from life or reality, in order to make it through while avoiding the negative things and the negative people of this world. No matter how hard it gets, you'll come out on top.

The positive road you're taking will not be in vain. You do it effortlessly! Everything will turn out great! Everything will be okay. Be proud of yourself. You will come out on top. God will guide you and will never leave you. Keep your faith in God as strong as you've always had. Listen when God speaks and obey his commands.

God loves you…. he always will.

Table of Contents

Chapter 1

Sneaking Around

About two weeks after the whole boot camp fiasco, we all were finally off punishment. Me and Lashae got an extra week after admitting we were the ring leaders, and our moms did not make it easy for us at all. We cried almost every day of punishment. We really did not see the light of day and had to do a lot of different tasks as punishment like, really clean the house because they canceled our housekeeper for that entire time to make sure we cleaned. Some of the other things were extra work from school that they asked for.

I also had to look after Reci for some things like bath time and make sure she clean up her toys after playing. Lashae had to do yard work, she was picking up trash and sticks and putting them in bags. At least she was able to see outside, I wasn't even allowed by the windows. The punishment for the ring leaders was terrible. The only good thing that happened to us during this time, was that our parents got frustrated with our school. They started to suspect that the school targeted us for no reason after the school tried to accuse us of some things we didn't do. Our moms knew we didn't do them because we were not in school during this time. So they took us out of that school and signed us up for another school.

We started our new school, which was a lot more laid back and we didn't have to all be in one classroom with a private teacher anymore. We had freedom and we loved it. During this time Shaun was constantly trying to get a hold of me, but I was hard to reach since he did not have my phone number. There were a lot of people telling me that he wanted to talk to me or that he was looking for me. But I would just give them a look and not reply. It got so bad to the point where people started to tell me they saw him at our school looking for me.

I didn't believe them at first until I saw him with my own eyes waiting in the school pick up area. He looked like he was looking for someone. I couldn't believe he was actually at our school, I wondered how he even knew what school we went to. I was scared for him to see me because I didn't want my mom to see him near me, so I ran the opposite way. I hid until he walked around the corner, then I made a run for it to my mom's car. She was looking at me crazy. Maybe it was because I was breathing hard and kind of ducking behind my bookbag.

She was mad because I took so long to make it to the car. She said, "What took you so long?? You're normally out here, I've been waiting forever!" I said, "I got stuck in the school." I was still ducking, she looked at me so confused and said, “What the h*ll is yo problem? Why you acting weird?” I smiled and said, “I’m okay, it’s no problem, can we go home now?” She said, “Who you running from?” I said, “I just don’t want to be seen.” She gave me a look and drove off.

She assumed that maybe people were bombarding me with questions all day because it was a new school, so she left it alone. Thank God Shaun did not see me. I was in the clear…I thought. About 30 minutes after we got home Latoya said, “Camille, I have a meeting I need to go to. I should back in a few hours, watch yo sisters, and make sure ya’ll homework is done.” I said, “Okay.”

She said, “Do not leave this house.” I said, “Okay.” She gave us all a kiss and left. I made sure our homework was done, we had a snack, and my sisters were both chillin doing their own things. Just as I was about to go to my room and relax, the doorbell rung.

I looked through the peep hole and saw Shaun. I was taken by surprise and didn't know what to do. He kept ringing the doorbell and knocking. Eventually I said, "What do you want Shaun?! You not supposed to be here!" I was talking through the door. He said, "Camille, I need to talk to you!" I said, "No, you gotta leave!" He said, "I've been trying to contact you for weeks now and can't get a hold of you. If you don't open this door, I'ma stay out here until yo mama come home!" We had to talk loud enough for us to hear each other.

He knew my mom wasn't there because her car was gone. I didn't want my mom to pull up and see him there, I wanted him to leave so I wouldn't get in trouble. So I opened the door. When he saw me, he couldn't hold back his smile. I was looking at him waiting for him to tell me what he wanted. But all he did was smile.

I was looking confused and said, “What?” He said, “Man! I’m sorry, I’m just happy to see yo face again.” I smiled while I laughed a little. He zoned back in on me and just stared for a minute. I said, “Shaun!” He jumped and said, “Huh??” I said, “What were you gonna say?” He snapped back into reality and said, “Oh, um…to be honest, I didn’t think I would get this far. So I didn’t plan past this moment…but this moment though.” I took a breath, rolled my eyes a little while I started to close the door and said, “Oh my gosh, you don’t want nothin…” He stopped the door from closing and said, “No wait, I’m sorry. I do have something to say. I have a lot to say.”

I looked at him and said, “Okay…say it.” He looked around outside and said, “Can I come in to tell you?” I said, “No Shaun, my mom not home…” He said, “Please, it’ll just be a minute, I’ll be gone before yo mom come back.” I looked at him like I was analyzing the situation, then he said, “Please, I rather not talk about this outside. This is something we should sit down and talk about." I stood there for a few more seconds, then I said, "Alright, just for a minute." I opened the door enough for him to come in and said, "Come on." He came in and I closed the door.

He sat down on the couch while I stood up staring at him with my arms crossed. He looked at me, laughed and said, "Camille, you forgot the part where you sit down. Come on relax." I walked to the couch and said, "How can I relax, what are you up to?" He said, "I'ma tell you…sit down, please." I sat down. He was staring at me again. I stood up and said, "Shaun if you just gone stare at me, you can go…" He pulled me back down and said, "No, no, no…" I said, "You said you been trying to contact me for weeks and now that you got me right here, you have nothing to say." He said, "No, I do, I'm just nervous."

I said, "Nervous about what?" He looked down. I said, "Did I leave something at your house and your mom found it and thought I was there again? Because..." He said, "No, it's not that." I said, "Then what is it?" He said, "I miss you." I took it in for a minute, he was messing with his hands and then said, "Nothing is the same, you all I know. It's been us for the past 5 years and now it's all gone, and I don't know how to deal with that." I put my face in my hands, took a deep breath and said, "Shaun no…ugh, I don't wana do this right now." He said, "Camille, I'm sorry, I don't want us to be like this…Can you please take me back?"

I looked at him and said, "Shaun, why are you doing this?" He said, "You everything to me, I lost my girl and my best friend at one time and that sh*t killin me." I rolled my eyes and put my head back down in my hands, he said, "I'm not trying to stress you out, I'm telling you why I came here. This is what I wanted." I said, "Shaun you don't understand." He said, "Understand what? …you talking about Michelle?" I said, "Yeah." He said, "I get yo point but it wasn't like that at all, I've been trying to tell you…" I said, "Shaun, I don't want to hear it again." He said, "This is why you don't understand, we can't ever talk about it." I said, "It hurts, it still hurts, okay? …can we agree to just pick this up later when it's not so fresh?" He said, "Alright, but can we at least agree to be cool again?" I looked at him, took a quick breath and said, "Yeah." We both smiled and hugged.

During our hug, the doorbell rung, and we both jumped. I thought my mom came back, Shaun was plotting to sneak out the back. I walked to the door quietly and looked through the peep hole. I looked back at Shaun like, really?? Then I opened the door. When I opened the door Shaun saw Jacoby standing there. I said, "What are you doing here??" Jacoby smiled and said, "Is that how you welcome your guests?" I said, "Jacoby, you are not my guest and you out of all people know you should not be here." He said, "Oh because yo mama not home?" I said, "You know good and well that ain't it, we both banned from being around each other since we dated."

He said, "Oh uh since you mentioned it, I came over to find out if I had another chance since you know, you single and all." My mouth dropped. Before I can say anything, Shaun jumped up and said, "Man what?!" Jacoby said, "Oh snap, I ain't know you was here Shaun! Aye man what's up?!…aye you know I'm clowning." Shaun said, "Yeah alright." Jacoby looked at me and whispered, "Ya'll back together?" Shaun said, "What's up??" Jacoby said, "Oh naw nothin, we cool, we cool." Jacoby clapped his hands once, got real excited, smiled and then he said, "Well since everybody here, let's have a party then!" I said, "No Jacoby, you have to go." As I pushed his chest for him to leave, he pointed and said, "But Shaun here…" I said, "He has to go too."

Jacoby stopped for a second and turned around like he was leaving. Then he said, "I'll leave…but you gotta catch me first." I said, "What??" At that second, he pushed the door opened and ran in my house. My mouth dropped again, I was so shocked. I said, "Jacoby no!" He was smiling and standing by the stairs and said, "Catch me." I said, "Jacoby, seriously??" He started dancing around saying, "Ooh, ooh, look I'm Speedy Gonzales…Camille Andale! Catch me." I was so annoyed, then Shaun burst out laughing.

I looked at him and said, "It's not funny." Then I started laughing. Jacoby said, "Okay if you don't wana catch me, let's play hide and seek." I said, "Jacoby no, you need to leave before my mama come back." He said, "One game, I promise." I said, "No." Then Reci came downstairs and saw them. Reci said, "What are you guys doing?" Jacoby said, "Aye Reci, we were just about to play hide and seek…" As they were talking, I quickly whispered, "No…no." He said, "You wana play?" Reci was ecstatic because that's her favorite game, she gasped and said, "Yes! Let's play!" I covered my eyes and said, “Oh my gosh.” I knew we had to play now because Reci would not let me live it down if we didn’t. I said, “One game Jacoby, one! Then you leave.” He said, “I promise.”

I turned to Shaun and said, “Shaun, I guess you can go, we can talk later you have my number now.” He said, “I’m not leaving.” I said, “What?? But you said if we talk about what you wanted, you would leave.” Shaun said, “Camille, Jacoby just showed up and tried to get back with you…I’m not leaving ya’ll here alone!” I took a breath and said, “Fine, let’s just play this game so ya’ll can get out of here.” As we were about to start the game, Crystal came out the room and saw both of them. She knew they were not supposed to be there, her mouth was wide open. I said, “I know Crystal and it’s stupid, but I have to play hide and seek so they can leave.”

Crystal said, “What?” I said, “I know, it sound dumb.” Crystal said, “Why don’t we play flashlight tag first??" My mouth dropped yet again, I said, "What?! I'm trying to get them out of the house before Mommie come back, and you worried about the game of choice?!" Jacoby said, "What's flashlight tag? That sounds interesting." Crystal smiled excitedly and said, "We run around with flashlights and tag each other with the light, but of course we have to do it in the dark." Jacoby said, "I wana play!" Crystal said, "I'll go get the flashlights!"

As she ran off, I said, "No! Crystal wait!" But she was already gone, I turned to Shaun and said, "Please leave and take him with you, I don't even wana play anymore." Shaun slowly said, "I kind of wana play flashlight tag." I said, "Shaun!" He said, "I'm sorry, it sounds fun!"

Crystal came back down with the flashlights. We all took one and she explained the rules. I turned off all the lights and closed the curtains for the windows, it was pitch black in the house. Everyone was giggling and laughing in the dark. We all had to flash our lights one time before the game began. Of course, they chose me to be it first. Whoever I tagged becomes it and does the same thing and so forth. The game started. At first, I was annoyed because no one listened to me, but then I started to have a lot of fun and forgot about everything.

We played upstairs, downstairs, in the rooms, the kitchen, everywhere. In the middle of the game, we

heard something fall. I said, "What's that??" Jacoby said, "I hit something, ouch, I got it." The game went on. We played flashlight tag for a long time. The game probably would not have ended if it wasn't for the loud noise of something breaking. We all gasped and stopped in our tracks. I turned the light on. We saw my mom's favorite vase in pieces and Jacoby was on his knees next to it holding his side in pain.

I ran over to the spot and said, "What happened?!" He was making faces showing he was in bad pain as he struggled to say, "I hit my side on the stand and the vase fell and broke, but I'll be okay." I said, "Not you, how the heck you broke the vase?!" Shaun said, "Dang Camille, that's cold, he hurt." I said, "I'm sorry, I'm glad you're okay…but I'm gone be sorry when my mom sees this!" Shaun said, "We'll take care of this." Jacoby and Shaun cleaned up the mess and took the pieces toward the kitchen area.

When they came back in the Livingroom, I said, "Okay, we played your game, now it's time to leave." Jacoby said, "No we didn't, that was Crystal's game. I still want to play hide and seek." I said, "You can't be serious." Shaun said, "Camille, you did agree to it." I looked at Shaun and said, "Whose side are you on anyway?" Shaun shrugged his shoulders and said,

“What’s fair is fair.” I said, “Okay fine, one quick game of hide and seek and ya’ll both leaving.” Jacoby said, “You can’t rush hide and seek…not it!” After he said that he ran and everyone else quickly said, “Not it!” And ran too. I said, “UGGGGGH!” With my head thrown back and my eyes closed. Then I said, “Fine!” I started to count while everyone hid.

After I counted it took only two minutes for me to find Shaun. I guess the rest of them thought I gave up and they walked out from their hiding places. They were not satisfied because they were not found, so we had to play again. Since I found Shaun, they said he had to be it. Shaun found me easy, and he found them too. They all took turns being it. After a while they realized, I was not trying to hide and allowed them to find me easy. So, they all agreed to only let me be the seeker and they added a new rule. The new rule was that I had to find all of them before the game can be considered complete. We started a new game of hide and seek, but this time they made it more challenging for me to find them. I guess Jacoby and Shaun really didn't wana go home.

I didn't find one person until after 5 minutes and like the first time, I found Shaun first. Afterwards he helped me to find everyone else, but he did it in a slick way so they wouldn't say I cheated and make me play again. Together we found Crystal and we persuaded her to help us find Jacoby and Reci. We found Jacoby after about a minute, and we started to look for Reci. We could not find Reci, so everyone agreed to help me find her after I spent 5 minutes looking for her.

About 30 minutes passed by and we still couldn't find her. Shaun said, "Where she at?? We looked everywhere!" I said, "Hide and Seek is Reci's favorite game and she is very good at it." Jacoby shrugged his shoulders and said, "Just say it's over…Yo Reci! ...Reci! Come out, game over you won!" Crystal laughed a little bit and said, "That ain't gone work, Reci is not gone go for that. She not coming out until somebody find her." Jacoby said, "For real?? Camille why you chose that game?" I said, "I told you no, but you wanted to play hide and seek so bad like a big kid."

He said, "I'm sorry, I'll help you find her." I said, "No, it's okay. Ya'll just go, I'll look for her." I opened the front door to let them out. As Shaun was walking out, we heard, "Help!" We turned around to see Jacoby's head stuck in the stair rail. I closed the door, and we ran to him. I said, "Jacoby, what happened?!" He said, "I was trying to see if Reci was on the stairs, and I got stuck!" I rolled my eyes and said, "Oh my gosh, Jacoby you can see through the stairs!' He said, "Now you tell me!" I said, "Are you doing this on purpose?!" He said, "Who would get their head stuck on purpose?!" I said, "Never mind, can ya'll please help me get him out?"

Everybody tried to pull him out, but every time we tried he would scream. We stopped because we got scared. I said, "We need something slippery." Crystal said, "Like what?" I said, "Oil." Shaun said, "Oh yeah, yeah get some oil!" Crystal said, "Okay." She ran to the kitchen. I looked at Jacoby and said, "This is your fault, I don't know what made you think this was a good idea." Jacoby said, "I realize that now, but this is not a time to argue with you while my head is stuck in your stair rail!" Shaun said, "That's what you get." Jacoby said, "What??" Shaun said, "You had no business coming over here trying to talk to my girl behind my back."

Jacoby said, "Yo girl?! Last I heard ya'll broke up." I said, "Alright, alright, ya'll stop it. Let's focus on the issue at hand please." They stopped arguing, shortly after Crystal came running around the corner with a bowl. She said, "I got it!" I said, "It's about time, you took forever." She ran up the stairs a little to where

Jacoby head was and said, "What do I do?" I said, "Just pour it on his neck." She poured all of it quick and Jacoby started screaming loud, he scared us. I said, "What?! What happened??" He said, "It's hot! ...ahhhhh! Help! Ya'll tryna kill me ahhhhh!" I said, "Shaun get me a wet rag quick!" He ran and got one, I put it on Jacoby neck and started to dab it. He eventually calmed down.

I said, "Crystal, why would you heat up oil?!" She said, "I didn't." Jacoby said, "Oh ya'll just keep the oil in the oven then??" I said, "It was that hot??" Jacoby said, "It was scorching hot!" I said, "Crystal, you had to heat it up. Why would you heat up oil??" She said, "That wasn't oil." Me, Jacoby and Shaun all said, "What?!" Crystal said, "I couldn't find the oil." I said, "So what did you pour on his neck?" She said, "Well, since I couldn't find the oil, I used butter and melted it so it would look like oil."

I looked at her with a blank expression while I batted my eyes repeatedly. Shaun said, "WOOOOW!" Jacoby shook his head and said, "What?!" Then I said, "Crystal, you could've just brought the butter how it was, it still could have worked…why would you pour hot butter on somebody's neck??" She said, "You told me to!" I said, "I didn't know it was melted butter!" Shaun said, "Hold on ya'll, let's try to take him out now since it's already on there." We said, "Okay."

Shaun said, "On the count of 3…1,2,3 pull!" We started to pull, and Jacoby started to scream, he screamed louder and louder and started to say, "Stop! Stop!" Then we all heard, "Camille, what the h*ll?!" We all jumped, gasped and turned toward the door just to see my mom standing there looking pissed and confused. Everything was quiet, then we heard Jacoby say, "Uh oh."

Latoya said, "Uh oh is right, Camille why do you have boys in the house?! Especially Shaun and

Jacoby!" I said, "I can explain." She threw her purse on the couch, crossed her arms and said, "Oh you better." Then she noticed Jacoby head. She started to walk towards the stairs as she said, "Is his head stuck in the stair rail?!" We all moved back, when she got to him, he looked at her, smiled and said, "Hi Ms. Lockhart." She said, "Camille, what were ya'll doing?!" I smiled nervously and said, "Playing hide and seek." She stopped to looked at me for a second and said, "That makes absolutely no sense, but we'll talk about that later."

She started to tend to Jacoby and asked a lot of questions. Eventually she decided to call the fire department to get him out. During the time we waited for them to come, her and Jacoby talked about a lot. He apologized about the things that happened before when we were dating, and about other things they never talked about because of the tension between our parents. They understood each other more and Latoya forgave him. Just like that, she didn't have an issue with him being around me anymore.

After a while the fire department showed up. They tried to get him out like we did, but of course it didn't work. So, they had no choice but to cut him out. When they took out the cutting tools and started cutting, I put my hand over my face while I took a breath. As they started to cut, I slid my hand down and saw my mom looking at me. I knew she was mad because they were cutting the stair rail and we would need it fixed. I tried not to look at her too long. We all watched.

After about 10 minutes he was free, and we were relieved. The fire department left. Jacoby said, "Whew! Feels good to stand up right." He was smiling and started to walk to the front door. Latoya said, "Where is Reci??" Crystal said, "She got lost during hide and seek." Latoya said, "What?!" Jacoby said, "Well, that's my queue, I'm out!" Latoya said, "Wait a minute!" He stopped walking. Latoya said, "Nobody is leaving until my child is found…" I said, "Yeah Jacoby, especially since it's yo fault." He said, "My fault?!" Shaun said, "Yeah, it's yo fault!" I said, "You wasn't gone leave until we played hide and seek!" We all argued for a minute until Latoya stopped us and said, "Less arguing more finding!" We started to look for her but still couldn't find her.

Shaun walked past a wall and heard something move, so he back tracked. There was a little compartment at the bottom of it. He said, "Camille!" I came around the corner and said, "What?" He pointed to it and said, "What's that?" I nonchalantly said, "A door I guess," as I shrugged my shoulders. He said, "What's in it?" I said, "I don't know, I don't think much can fit in there." He said, "Can I open it?" I said, "Yeah." I started to walk away. Shaun opened it and then he said, "I found her!" I turned around so quick. Everybody came running.

We looked and she was sound asleep. This girl really take hide and seek seriously. She was there the whole time, and that wall is in the Livingroom. Latoya picked her up and made sure she was okay. Reci woke up halfway squinting her eyes and said, “Mommie, you found me.” Then she went back to sleep. Latoya went upstairs to put her to bed, then she came back down to us. When she got down there, she only saw me and Shaun. She said, “Ya’ll let Jacoby leave?” I said, “No, he went to the kitchen as soon as you went upstairs.”

She went in there and about 10 seconds later she ran out the kitchen towards the stairs. All we heard was, “This boy!” She went to her room and came back out with a belt. We were confused. When she ran past us and back to the kitchen, we looked at each other and ran to the kitchen too. When we got in there, we saw the bottom half of Jacoby sticking out from underneath the sink counter. He was on his knees with his butt in the air. We were even more confused. I said, “What the heck??" He didn't know it yet, but Latoya was standing behind him with the belt.

When he heard me, he said, "Oh good, thank God! Camille, please help me. I got hungry while we was waiting so I came to look for a snack and you won't believe this but…I got my head stuck underneath this drain!" Shaun burst out laughing so hard, I laughed too and said, "Oh my gosh!" He said, "Shh, I hear ya'll laughing but help me before yo mom come down, I don't want her to know I got stuck again." Latoya said, "Too late Jacoby." He screamed short and loud, "Ahh!" Then he jumped and that made him trip while being on his knees. I'm not sure how that works but it was funny.

He said, "Uh…how much of that did you hear?" She said, "All of it." He said, "Uh oh, I'm sorry." She said, "Are you really stuck??" He said, "Yep, tight." She said, "Good." Right after that she started to hit butt with the belt. He was squirming and screaming, "Mama! Ahhhh Mama!" Latoya was laughing and so were we. She wasn't hitting him really hard because she was playing around, but he was getting hit hard enough for it to be a beaten. After she stopped hitting him, he moved so much his body fell flat. He laid there for a minute to catch his breath, then he wiggled out from underneath the sink.

We were all shocked. I said, "I thought you was stuck." He said, "I was but I guess I moved so much, I set myself free." Latoya said, "Stop sticking yo head in places they don't belong, that's a hard lesson." Jacoby rubbed his butt and said, "And painful." Shaun said, "That's what you get, nobody told you to come over here." Latoya said, "About that, how did this all happen anyway?" We all explained what happened and gave our view on it. Latoya talked to all of us. She let them know they can't come over while she's not home, and she let me know not let anyone in the house when she's not home.

She got on their cases for persuading me to let them in and she really got on my case for falling for it. She did tell them that she doesn't mind them being around me or talking to me on phone anymore now that we all seemed to resolve our issues. As they were leaving, she told them, "But since ya'll did come inside knowing that ya'll shouldn't, ya'll are banned from coming here for two weeks." They both said, "Aw man!" Latoya smiled sarcastically and said, "Ya'll have a good night." As she closed the door, they said, "Good night." Then they left.

I got in so much trouble. I had a very stern talking to and then she took my phone. On top of that, I wasn't allowed to answer the door for those two weeks. Someone else in the house would have to answer the door if someone came. If I didn't follow these rules, she threatened to have a babysitter, or my grandma come sit with us if she had to go anywhere. I assured her I would follow them. After a long while of being drilled, she sent me to my room to go to bed. I didn't give an attitude about the restrictions, I was just happy that it wasn't me who got the beaten this time.

Chapter 2

Don't Run Now

During the two weeks of my restrictions, I still went to school. I had to explain to my cousins why I didn't pick up or respond to their text messages. They got mad because we all needed to talk, especially because we had an awards show coming up. Carmen and Alisha ended up calling Shaun and Jacoby and fussed them out about what happened. At this point none of us were on good terms with each other. Shaun and Jacoby were confused but then got mad because they got fussed out. Me and my cousins could only speak at school or if they came over, in which they couldn't come over during this time.

Close to the end of the two weeks, my cousins finally came over to my house. When they got there, we went to my room. Carmen said, "What are you wearing to the show?" I looked at her and said, "I don't know." They all sucked their teeth and threw their hands up. I said, "What?" Cashae said, "Camille the show is this weekend, and you don't know what you wearing yet??" I said, "How am I supposed to know?" Alisha said, "We called you…oh I forgot you didn't have your phone." She was being sarcastic.

I looked at her like, really? Carmen said, "If you had your phone, you would've been at the fitting with us." I said, "Fitting? What fitting??" Alicia said, "The fitting for our gowns for the show." I said, "When was this??" Alisha said, "About a week ago." I said, "Why ya'll didn't say anything when ya'll saw me at school?" Cashae said, "Girl, once we found out why you didn't have your phone, it was no point in telling you. It would seem like we were rubbing it in your face." I took a breath and sucked my teeth.

Lashae said, "Camille, how did you even get in a situation like this? You know how they are, and you let them in the house?" I said, "I don't know, first Shaun was telling me he wasn't leaving before he tell me what he wanted, I thought it was an emergency. Then Jacoby come in saying he not leaving until we play hide and seek…" They all laughed so loud. I had to stop explaining. I looked at them for a few seconds while they laughed uncontrollably, then I said, "It's not funny." They kept laughing.

Carmen was holding her stomach still laughing and said, "I'm sorry Camille, something wrong with that boy." Cashae said, "Seriously, he got his head stuck twice and he wanted to play hide and seek before he left?" Lashae said, "Jacoby know what he be doing, he was just being a jerk because Shaun intercepted his move on Camille." I said, "Okay, can we just forget about that for a second? I still can't wrap my head around it." They laughed a little bit more. Then Alisha said, "You really don't know what you wearing?" I said, "No." Lashae said, "We were supposed to match in some type of way, that's why we needed to go at the same time."

I said, "Can ya'll go again?" Carmen said, "Our gowns are already picked out." Alicia said, "I think they might have yours picked out already, you just wasn't there to try it on or give your input." Cashae said, "So you might just have to wear what they give you." I took another breath and closed my eyes. I opened my eyes again and said, "I don't even care at this point, I already don't wana go." Surprisingly they all said, "Me either." Just then my door opened, it was my mom. She said, "Camille you have to go to your fitting so get ready." I said, "I thought they had a gown for me already."

She came in the room a little bit more and said, "They do, but you need to try it on because we do not need any wardrobe malfunctions this weekend." Lashae said, "Oh, at least you can still get fitted Camille. It should be similar to ours." Latoya said, "Oh that reminds me, ya'll gotta go too." Their mouths dropped. Latoya said, "There may be a situation with the gowns ya'll chose and they might have to change them, so ya'll need to go too." They gasped. Carmen said, "We spent all day being mannequins for nothing??" Latoya said, "Be ready in 30 minutes." They were so mad.

We were ready in time and went to our fitting. Once we got there, Carmen had questions but didn't want to flat out asked them, because it would come off disrespectful. So, she tried her best to eat her words and you can see it all on her face. The lady came in and greeted everyone, she apologized to have them come back and then she said, "Any questions before we get started?" I looked at Carmen side eyed because I just knew she was gone say something.

Carmen sat there at first but then she said, "I was just wondering why we had to come back here after we spent the day here last week. We thought everything was taken care of." The lady said, "Right, I'm so sorry. We have the gowns, but your stylist had questions about the shimmer color on some of the gowns. So we needed all of you back here in case anything changed, so there would be no surprises on the big day." Cashae lowly said, "So it was the stylist." They were pissed. Carmen said, "I'm sorry, one more question." The lady said, "Of course." Carmen said, "Are we gonna have to be mannequins this time?"

The lady laughed a little and said, "Oh no dear, all of your measurements are taken." Carmen said,

"Whew! Okay then I'm cool." The lady said, "Right this way ladies." We went to the back. I saw their gowns because they pulled them out for them and the stylist while I was right there. They were so pretty and shimmery. Someone was taking my measurements while they all discussed their gowns. We found out that the stylist was questioning the shimmer color on Carmen gown. Carmen did everything in her power to not change the gown. She did not want to do another fitting. She told them she was okay with the color, and it looked fine to her.

Her shimmer was a lighter goldish color, and the other dresses had a little more color to them. They were just going to switch them, then the lady said, "Please bring Camille's gown out!" We all looked quick because we had no idea how mine looked. When they brought it out, it was absolutely beautiful. My gown had a white sparkly shimmer effect. Our mouths were to the floor, I said, "Wow that is gorgeous!" My cousins said, "Whoa that's nice!" The stylist said, "Maybe we wouldn't have to change Carmen dress because Camille's dress is a lighter color too."

Carmen said, "That would be great if we didn't!" The stylist said, "Can we have all of you try on the gowns together?" We all went inside the dressing rooms, they were side by side and there were 7 of them. Once we were dressed, they told us to come out at the same time and walk to the middle of the floor. The stylist said, "You ladies ready?!" We laughed and said, "Yes!" He said, "Okay on the count of 3 you come out! ....1...2...3!" When he counted to 3, we all came out of our dressing rooms and walked to the middle of the floor. Once we got to the middle of the floor we stopped because we were standing next to each other. Our moms, the stylist and the lady were looking star struck.

It was crazy seeing them look that way, but we knew from the looks the gowns were pretty. The stylist smiled so big and got excited. He said, “OOH! Wait, wait! First, you ladies are absolutely stunning. Second, go back in the dressing rooms because we gotta get this on video!” We laughed and went back in the dressing rooms. He recorded us and said, “Omgee, I’m gonna put this video together for you ladies, it’s gonna be everything!” The lady said, “I love it! Moms what do you think?” They all said, “We love it!” The lady said, “Perfect! So these will be the gowns of choice for you ladies for the big day!” We smiled and said, “Thank you so much.”

We were happy with our selections, and we were also happy we didn’t have to spend the entire day there. Shortly after, we took the gowns off and we left to head back home. We had a jeweler coming to our house so that we can pick out the jewelry for that day also. Our stylist also came to our house, because we had another designer coming to us for our after party outfits. We were excited for the after party because it was a party and a lot of people we knew were going to be there. Plus being in trouble, this was the closet we were going to get to a party.

We picked out our jewelry and after party outfits. We didn't know what our parents were wearing because they didn't reveal their gowns or anything yet. Everything was like this the whole week. We had to do so much that we couldn't go to school that week, instead we had to be homeschooled. It was so much pressure and tension from getting ready, practicing for the red carpet, and practicing for any speeches in case we needed to speak.

Sometime during the week, we were pulled aside while our moms were busy and were told that we would be presenting an award. We were shocked. The person coaching us told us not to tell our moms, and a few minutes later we found out why. He told us our moms were nominated for the award. We were so excited because if they won this award, it would be a huge milestone for them. They didn't even know they were nominated, to even be nominated for it is an honor.

So of course, we were on board with it. We managed to keep this a secret for the rest of the week. The week was busy, but it went by fairly. But on Friday I guess the stress of the week weighed in on me and I had a break down. Latoya was on edge because she needed me to be in right head space and the show was the next day. I kept telling her I didn't want to go every now and again, but this started to get her in a different head space. We had our assistants there that day, thank God. They took over the situation.

One of them started talking to my mom bringing her back in a good head space, while the other one assured her that she would take care of me and make sure I'm okay. They had us in separate parts of the house. It took a few minutes for the assistant to talk me down, the breakdown I had was horrible. I was crying and everything.

After she got me water and distracted me with things outside of the show and the celebrity world, I calmed down a lot. The team had a few more things to do with me but she kept them away from me. She would whisper to her team not to mention any of it to me and not to bother me with it right now. Instead, she finished whatever it was the way she felt I would have wanted it done. Soon, I was laughing and talking with her about regular everyday things. Someone came in and said, “Camille, we need you for your shoe fitting.” The assistant said, “No, she’s…” I stopped her as I got up out of the chair.

My eyes were still red from crying, and I had a water bottle in my hand. I said, “It’s okay, thank you, I’ll do it.” She said, “You sure? Because I know your size…” I said, “Yes, thank you.” I left out of that room and followed the guy for the shoes. I happened to walk pass where Latoya was as I followed him to the shoes. After passing by her a little bit, I walked back to her. When I got to her, I gave her a hug, since she was sitting down, I was kind of hugging her neck. She smiled as she touched my arm and leaned her head in against mine. After we stopped, I started to walk away and she said, "You alright now?" I turned to her and said, "Yes." She said, "Good." I went to try on my shoes.

After my shoe fitting and selections, I was told we had to do a photoshoot that night. I could feel myself getting overwhelmed again, I was already tired. The people were trying to get me to follow them so that they can prep me for the photoshoot. They thought I was behind them, but when they turned around, I was still where we did the shoe fitting. Latoya happened to look back and saw my face, so she got up and walked over to me. When she got to me, she said, "What's wrong?" I said, "I'm sorry…" I started crying again, then I said, “I’m trying, but I don’t know what’s wrong.”

She grabbed me and hugged me. Her hand was on the back of my head and her other arm was around my back, my head was rested on her chest. As she rested her head on top of my head she said, “I know baby, it’s a lot, and it’s okay to feel like you do.” I just cried more, which is what I needed. She was still holding me, then she said, “What happened? You said you was alright.” As I tried to catch my breath, I managed to tell her, “They said they want a photoshoot tonight.” Latoya didn’t even know about a photoshoot.

Just then her assistant walked up to us and said, “What’s happening?” Latoya looked at her still hugging me and said, “Can we schedule the shoot for tomorrow? She’s tired, she’s had enough, I don’t want to burn her out.” The assistant said, “Of course!” They wrapped up everything and called it a night. That night Latoya made sure I destressed and went to bed at a decent time so I wouldn't be tired.

The next morning, I felt so much better, and that was great because our photoshoot was scheduled early. Everything was going to be fast paced today up until the event. We all had to meet at the photography studio. When we got there, Carmen said, "Why was the shoot changed to this morning, I thought it was supposed to be last night?" Cashae said, "Camille had a breakdown." Carmen said, "Really?" She looked at me and said, "You okay??" I said, "Yeah I'm fine today." Alisha said, "Cashae, how you knew that?" Cashae said, "My mama duhh." She was playing around but she did find out from her mom. Alisha laughed a little.

Right after that we started our photoshoot. The photoshoot was surprisingly fun and quick. Once we were done, our parents did their photoshoots. After the photoshoots, we all had to go to hair and makeup. This part took the most time. We also snapped a few selfies with our moms and each other while we were getting ready. Once we were finally done with hair and makeup we had to move on to wardrobe, because it was closer to the time we were supposed to show up for the show. Our stylists dressed us and made sure everything looked flawless. They made sure they took pictures of us all together and as groups, they also took pictures of us with our moms individually as well. Once we were done, it was time to head to the show.

Everybody was pulling up to the red carpet. We were in a different car than our parents, our car was in front of theirs. When we got to the carpet, the driver opened the door. As we got out people were screaming and yelling our names, we waved and said hi back. Once we all were out of the car we looked to the left and saw our dads lined up waiting for us. We were shocked but happy. We each took their hand after hugging them and they escorted us down the red carpet. Everyone watching thought it was so cute. Our moms planned that without us knowing. They were watching from the car behind us smiling when they saw our expressions.

While we were talking to reporters, we heard the crowd go wild they were so loud. We looked up and saw that our moms just made it on to the red carpet. We smiled. The reporter we were talking to said, “Oh wow is that your moms?” We said, “Yes.” They came up toward us, our dads greeted them and then our moms greeted us. Flashes were everywhere, people do not see all of us together like this, so it was an iconic moment. You can hear the crowd saying, “It’s their moms and dads!” and “They’re all together!” After a few interviews, we all were escorted into the venue to take our seats.

The show started, it was actually a good show. Although the show was interesting and entertaining, the one thing me and my cousins could not stop thinking about was the afterparty. Soon the time came for us to present the award. We told our moms we had to go to the bathroom, which is what we were told to tell them. They wondered where we went. Then the announcer started to introduce the category and name the nominees. Our moms group was the first to pop up and all of their mouths dropped, they were so surprised.

After naming all of the nominees, the host said, "And to present the award, please welcome to the stage Angelic!" We walked out in our gowns, the crowd was so loud clapping and cheering us on, we had the biggest smiles on our faces. The cameras went on our moms, they were about to cry holding their chests and everything. When we got to the microphone, we all looked at them and said, "Hi Mommie!" Then we looked at each other and laughed, so did the crowd and our moms. Our moms started to shed a few tears at this moment as they shook their heads at us.

We acknowledged the crowd and then Carmen said, "And the award goes to…" I opened the envelope, we all gasped, smiled and said, "Dynasty Chosen!" Everyone was clapping, cheering and screaming. We were so excited on stage, we were screaming and cried because this was huge. Our moms were getting up from their seats crying, while everyone was hugging them, they couldn't believe it. When they got on stage, they hugged us and saw us crying which made them cry more. We stepped back and let them speak to everyone.

Other people in the crowd cried happy tears for them too, especially after seeing us cry. During their speech, Latoya slightly looked back as she said, "Our babies back here crying, got us up here crying extra." The crowd laughed. Beonca said, "It's such an honor to be nominated, to have our babies present this award, and for us to win this award it's priceless. We will cherish this forever." Latonya said, "We're crying more because this is such a surprise, we had no idea they were presenting anything." She turned to us slightly and said, “How did ya’ll do this?” The crowd laughed and so did we.

They closed their speech and we all walked off the stage. They were escorted back to their seats, but we were taken in a different direction. When they got back to their seats and didn’t see us behind them, they asked the person where we were. They were told we needed to go to our makeup artist for a touch up. Our moms just went with it because we did just cry. There was a commercial break and during this break people were going to the bathroom and getting touched up and everything.

We were backstage and somehow my dad ended up back there. When he walked through the hall, he happened to see us talking to some boys. He came up and said, “Aye, break this up!” The boys walked away fast. I looked at him and said, “Dad, they just wana talk a little bit.” He said, “No, ya’ll can’t talk to no boys and I don’t want ya’ll around them. I’m sure the rest of ya’ll dads will feel the same way." Carmen said, "But we wasn't doing anything, we were just enjoying their company."

That made Andre go off the deep end a little bit, he said, "What?! The only company ya'll better be enjoying is each other's…backstage by ya'll selves, who agreed to this??" I said, "Dad chill." He said, "Chill?? …alright I'll chill, but if I see ya'll with them some boys again, I'ma tell ya'll mamas." We said, "Aw man!" He started to walk away and said, "See how far ya'll get with that." Cashae said, "Camille, would he tell them for real?" I said, "I don't think he will, unless he gets really mad and he's not mad." Just then the director came and said, "Okay ladies, commercial break is over, it's show time!"

Out where my mom them were, they started to get worried. Andre just got back to his seat and heard them asking each other where we were, and that we should've been back by now. Andre said, "Oh I just saw them backstage, they good." Latoya said, "Why you didn't bring them out here with you?" He said, "It look like they were in the middle of changing." Latoya said, "They didn't have a wardrobe change." Andre shrugged his shoulders and made a face like, I don't know.

The host came back on stage and was talking, making jokes and what not. Then they started playing back footage submitted of the celebrities before they came to the show. They showed us when our stylist recorded us walking out the dressing room and it was so fierce, everyone loved it. Our moms were like, "They're missing it." They showed our pictures with our moms too. After the clips and pictures of random celebrities, the host said, "Alright we have a special treat for you tonight! Please help me welcome to the stage our very own Angelic!"

Our moms said, "What?" and "Did they say Angelic?" The crowd clapped. The room got dark, and the screen started to play. It showed clips of our moms performing at different places. It showed at a normal speed and then it sped up the clips as the voice over the video said, "Tonight we are you." The lights on the stage came on and everyone started laughing, our moms laughed the hardest. They saw us in our different poses on stage mimicking them, some of us were sitting down and some were standing up.

Once the crowd went quiet, Cashae looked down at the crowd. She originally had her head up towards the ceiling, that was her position. When she looked at the crowd she said, "You ready?" Then the beat dropped, and we all got up and started to do the routine and eventually started to sing. Our moms were so proud they stood up and so did a lot of other people. They really enjoyed the performance. It was entertaining. At the end we threw in a joke. After we finished everyone cheered, and when the crowd died down a little, I looked at Cashae with my arms crossed giving attitude and said, "Where them kids at??" Cashae said, "That's a good question." We all ran off stage yelling our own names.

They thought it was hilarious. We did that because this happened before when they were rehearsing on stage for a show, and someone caught it on camera. The video itself was funny because they ran off stage and the people there thought it was part of their performance, until they realized that we really went missing. But we were just exploring being kids. It went viral, so everyone at the show got the joke. We had fun performing, the show was becoming a success and they had us involved a lot. We sat back out with our moms after the performance.

Latoya said, "Now I understand your breakdown, you were practicing all of this in secret?" I said, "Yes." After the show was over, everyone mingled a bit and talked to everyone. During this time, I told Latoya I had to go to the bathroom. Me and cousins all went to the bathroom. When we came out, we were waiting for Carmen because we didn't see her. After about 2 minutes, I said, "I'm going back in there to look for her." Right before I went in the bathroom, this boy grabbed my arm and said, "Camille! They got yo cousin!"

I said, "What?! Who?" He said, "Some boys, they taking her to that hotel behind the building." Alisha said, "Let's go!" We ran outside and followed him. When we got in the parking lot, Carmen came running out the building we just came from, yelling, "Hey! Wait!" We looked at her confused. When she caught up with us she said, "Some boy said somebody had my cousin." We looked at the guy and said, "You told us some boy had Carmen." Carmen said, "What?? I had issues with my gown, ya'll left me in the bathroom."

He said, "Oh wow! That's what they told me, I saw her, and I ask somebody who that was, and they said Carmen. I was kind of far…don't ya'll have another cousin our here?" Alisha said, "Natasha?" I said, "Alisha." She said, "What? If it's a girl there, it's best to help her." I said, "Let's go get our dad's." The boy said, "It's no time, we have to go now! I'll go with ya'll, I'll help ya'll!" Alisha said, "Camille, let's just go." So we all followed the boy, running to the hotel. When we got to the front and went in, another guy saw us and started to run back toward the venue. We didn't see him.

Once we were inside, we said, "Now what?" It didn't look like anyone was in that hotel. It looked abandoned. The boy said, "I heard them say the 3rd floor." We all got in the elevator. Meanwhile, the guy who saw us was friends with Shaun and Jacoby. He ran all the way back to the venue to them and said, "Aye man, ya'll gotta come quick!" Shaun said, "What happened?!" He said, "I saw Camille and her cousins going into the hotel in the back, I think they being set up! We gotta move fast." Shaun, Jacoby and their homeboys started running as fast as they could. Our dad's saw them run past them, that made my dad suspicious. He started to look for us.

Back at the hotel, the elevator stopped on the 3rd floor. As soon as it opened, we were pulled off the elevator abruptly. The guy who was with us saw the guys and hid against the wall inside the elevator so they wouldn't see him. We were screaming and being pulled in different rooms. By the time Shaun, Jacoby and their homeboys got inside the hotel Jacoby said, "Man, now what??" Then they heard screams. Shaun said, "You heard that??" Jacoby said, "Yeah." Shaun said, "H*ll nah, we searching this whole building until we find them!"

They ran to the elevator and as it opened, they were ready to run in, but instead the boy ran off the elevator and bumped into them. Shaun grabbed him quick and jacked him up then he said, "Where they at?!" The boy said, "I was just running for help, they on the 3rd floor!" They took him with them. When they got up there, they started kicking every door in and was fighting the guys that were in the rooms. Those guys were outnumbered. We were fighting the guys the entire time, it was just enough to hold them off until Shaun them got there. We were still fighting them while Shaun and his boys were fighting them. Then Shaun let his boys take over while they got us out of there. We went back in the elevator and down to the lobby.

We thanked them so much. Even though we all were not on good terms, they still came to our aid. They were so mad and questioned the boy down who made us go back there. But we found out that he was tricked too, the guy who told him the information was in on it. They knew he would tell us. Then Shaun said, "Don't worry about it, let's get ya'll back. I think ya'll moms were looking for ya'll." Although some of his boys were still upstairs, there were a lot of them with us. At this point our dads came outside to look for us, because Andre told them what happened earlier and suspected we were with some boys.

We all walked out the hotel and back towards the venue. We were just getting some relief from what just happened, just to look up and see our dads at the end of the only walkway we can go down. Andre looked up and saw us with all these boys coming from the hotel. His eyes got so big, I said, "Oh no." We walked a little faster trying to separate from the boys. Shaun grabbed at my arm and I moved my arm for him to let me go and said, "No Shaun, that's our dads." All of the boys stopped walking quick.

My dad yelled, "Ya'll with all them boys?! Didn't I say no boys??...I'm tellin!" We started running to them trying to stop my dad from telling our moms. I yelled, "Dad wait!" My cousins were yelling, "No!" and "Let us explain!" But by the time we got to where they were, he was already inside the venue. We were so scared to the point we were shaking, because our moms did not play with us when it comes to stuff like that. On top of that during an important event. We tried to explain ourselves to the rest of their dads, but they were just as upset.

We had to admit, walking from a hotel with a group of guys did look bad. We stood in the parking lot waiting for another 5 minutes. Then we saw my dad come out and point in our direction, after that we saw our moms coming out the building walking kind of fast. They held their composures until they got in the parking lot, that's when we knew he told because their faces went from smiles to livid. I said, "Oh crap." Cashae said, "What do we do?" I said, "I'm not trying to get embarrassed out here, we might as well meet them at the car." I took off running. As soon as I did Latoya was on my a**.

Both of us was out there running in heels. After I ran my cousins were too scared to stay there, so they ran too. Our goal was to get to our moms cars. Although we were escorted there, everyone's cars were parked in a private lot on that side of the venue. We all made it to their cars, next thing you know all you see is us being chased through the parking lot and around the cars. We were crying from being so scared of what they wanted to do to us, and we didn't know what Andre said to them. We would scream every now and again when we almost got caught.

After a while our moms stopped. Latoya looked at me, unlocked the door and said, "I'm not doing this with you, get yo a** in the car." I said, "Mommie, please it wasn't what he said." She said, "You know good and well you f*cked up, otherwise you wouldn't be out here running. Get in the car now!" I opened the door and got in the car. When she got in the car, all our dads saw was her back handing me, then her jacking me up for a second, she let me go after a few seconds, and pointed at me while she was telling me off.

She stopped herself because she didn't want anyone seeing that out there. When Cashae was running from Beonca, she got a shoe thrown at her. It's a good thing she ducked on time, because she would've been wearing that shoe. Carmen mama threw her purse at her, which actually hit Carmen. Alisha and Alicia were running in two different directions trying to throw their mom off. But Trinity being Trinity, somehow, she managed to trip one twin which caused her to fall and grab the other twin before she hit the ground. So she had both of them against the car, until she made them get in the car.

Our dads were watching all of this. They were mad enough to feel like we deserved to get in trouble, but they were also shocked and a little scared for us because of the way we were trying to get away from our mamas. We drove off, all of us were terrified on the ride home. My mom got a call on the way there, it was our stylist. He wanted to know where we were because they were waiting for us at the afterparty. I heard Latoya say, “I’m sorry, we’re not gonna make it, the girls got into some trouble so we’re on our way home.” I was looking sad because I knew she was talking about the afterparty.

Then she said, “Okay, let us drop them off and I’ll call my sisters.” She started to drive a different way, next thing you know we pulled up to my grandma’s house. Latoya looked at me and said, “Let’s go.” I got out the car, she walked me to the door and rung the doorbell. When my grandma answered the door Latoya said, “Hey Ma.” My grandma said, “Hey baby.” Latoya said, “Ma, can you please watch Camille for a few hours. I’ll be back to pick her up tonight.” My grandma said, “Of course.” Latoya said, “Thanks Ma, I gotta run…” Then she looked at me, pointed and said, “I’ll deal with you when I get back.” Then she left.

My grandma looked at me and said, “Oh wow, Camille what did you do??” I said, “Grandma it wasn’t my fault." We went inside. After about an hour Cashae called me and said, "Camille where you at?" I said, "My grandma house." She said, "Me too…you know they went to the afterparty without us?" I said, "That's where my mama went?!.... ugh!" Cashae said, "Yep, we should've just listened to you and got our dads." I said, "Exactly! Now we can't go to the afterparty for something we didn't do…and I'ma get in trouble when my mama pick me tonight!" Cashae said, "Yeah me too." I said, "Where the rest of them at?" She said, "At they grandmas houses too." We talked almost the whole time we were at our grandmas house.

We were mad too because that was a waste of time, money, and outfits. We spent a lot of time choosing our outfits for the afterparty and made plans to hang out with some people who was waiting for us there. I was mad because no one asked us anything or let us explain. They only went with what my dad told them, whatever he told them. The night was so perfect and then that happened. Around 11pm my mom came back to my grandma's house to pick me up. I was low key still scared.

When we got home, she said, "What the h*ll happened tonight??" I explained it to her, and it didn't seem logical to her, she sent me to take a shower. While I took a shower, she spoke to her sisters who also spoke to their kids and they all gave the same explanation. Although it was bizarre, they couldn't help but believe us because the stories we told them were identical and significantly detailed. When I got out the shower, my mom talked to me about it and decided she would need to speak with Shaun to see if his story matches up. My dad didn't say who we were with because he didn't know any of them.

When I first explained it, I told her who we were with or at least the people I knew. She was still mad. We didn't know until they told us, but they were mad we didn't go to the afterparty also. They told us we disappointed a lot of people including them. We were going through it, we were so mad because it wasn't our fault. We cried out of frustration and was sent to bed.

The next morning, my mom had already spoken to Shaun and his story matched our story from when he became involved. Shaun told her he tracked down the guy that led us over there. He also told her that they called the police and the boys who were at the hotel went to jail that night. After hearing all of this information, she called her sisters and they felt bad because we missed the afterparty. Latoya came to me and told me everything she was told, then she said, "Now I'm upset because we couldn't find out sooner. I felt that missing the afterparty was punishment enough for ya'll. That's why we didn't beat ya'll when we came back home."

I said, "Yeah, that was hard on us considering we knew it wasn't our fault." She said, "Well, I'm sorry that happened to ya'll and charges were pressed. But let this be a lesson, next time don't follow a random person somewhere not knowing what's going on…" She touched my leg and said, "Ya'll should've just got ya'll daddies." She got up to walk away. I sat there looking crazy. I took a quick deep breath and quietly said, "That's what I said." I was still mad Alisha didn't listen to me when I suggested that, but it was done and over with. We went about our day. We missed what was probably the best afterparty ever, but at least we didn't get in further trouble over it.

Chapter 3

Mama Need a Break

A couple of days later, we were all together at my house. We were all chillin at first until Cashae brung up the afterparty. She said, "I heard the afterparty was lit." Carmen rubbed her hands down her face and said, "Ugggh, why would you bring that up Shae? I'm still mad about it." Cashae said, "H*ll I'm still mad about it, that's why I brought it up. That sh*t wasn't fair how we got punished and missed it. I'ma keep talking about it until I'm not mad no more." I had my hand on my temple, rolled my eyes a little and took a deep breath.

Alicia said, "I'm mad we had all of our stuff picked out and we couldn't wear it, I feel like we got robbed." They kept talking about it, then noticed that me and Alisha didn't say anything yet. Cashae said, "Camille, I'm surprised you not saying anything, you was pissed when I spoke to you. You seemed the most upset about it." I said, "I'm not trying to relive it, I'm still trying to get over it." Alisha looked at me, then she looked at the rest of them and said, "We shouldn't have gotten in trouble, they should've listened to us."

I said, "Like ya'll should've listened to me??" Alisha said, "What?" Carmen knew where this was headed and said, "Alright ya'll different subject." Alisha caught an attitude and said, "No, I wana know what Camille talking about because it seem directed at me." I was ignoring her while resting my face on my hand, Lashae said, "Alisha leave it alone." Alisha looked at me and said, "No, she can talk to me. Camille say what you what's on yo mind." Carmen said, "No…"

I interrupted and said, "You know what I'm talking about." She said, "No I don't, tell me." I said,

"Don't play stupid." Alisha said, "Play stupid about what?? Nobody playing Camille, what you gotta say??" I started talking with my hands pointing at her and said, "If you would've listened to me in the first place, we wouldn't have missed the afterparty. I told ya'll let's get our daddies, but you was all like no let's just go." My cousins said, "Oh." They got quiet because they agreed.

Alisha said, "That wasn't my fault, if one of ya'll was in trouble we would've went right away." I said, "But we were all there and what that boy said made no sense. My mom even told me we should've got our daddies…I felt so dumb." Alisha said, "What would've been dumb is if we didn't go and something happened to someone." I said, "You made us look stupid and fast." She said, "Ya'll are stupid if ya'll thinking like that." Everyone said, "Aye, aye…" Except for me, I said, "You the one that's stupid and it showed."

Alisha got mad and threw a pillow at me and said, "Watch yo mouth!" I stood up and picked it up to throw it back, but my cousins jumped between us. I said, "You watch yo mouth!" Alisha said, "Camille, I wish you would fight me." I said, "Be careful what you wish for." She was shocked and laughed a little as her mouth dropped. Carmen said, "Stop it! Ya'll not fighting each other." Cashae said, "For real ya'll chill." We sat down and managed to calm down for 5 minutes. Carmen was talking about other stuff and about another party we should go to, which wasn't for a couple of months.

Alisha said, "We should go…oh wait let me not suggest that before Camille blame me again…who should we go get first, our moms?" When she said that I side eyed her, she pissed me off. I still had the pillow she threw at me. I picked it up quick and hit her with it and we started fighting. We were fighting for real but not how we would fight someone in the street. Carmen,

Cashae, Lashae and Alicia were scrambling to make us stop but every time they got us apart, we would reconnect. Alicia ran out the room while the rest of them kept trying to keep us apart.

She ran to our moms and said, "Camille and Alisha fighting! We can't pull them apart!" Our moms ran upstairs to my room and saw us fighting. They also saw Carmen and Cashae mixed in, because they were trying to break us up. Latoya and Trinity immediately walked in the middle of us snatching both of us up, they man handled us. They started to beat us on the spot while they fussed us out. Trinity said, "Ya'll know f**king better!" Latoya said, "What the h*ll ya'll fighting for?!" Carmen explained what happened. They yelled at both of us.

Latoya said, "Point is, ya'll should have never did it in the first place, regardless of what anybody said. The sh*t was dangerous to begin with and that was stupid on all ya'll parts!" Trinity said, "And they not stupid for thinking like that either Alisha! You the oldest, yo a** should've been the one to stop them from going!" They were so mad at us they made us separate. My mom and Trinity took me and Alisha downstairs with them so they could watch us. We were sitting across the table from each other in the dining room, just giving each other the eye.

All our moms were in the kitchen near the dining room. Carmen, Cashae, Lashae and Alicia were in the Livingroom. Lashae said, "I can't believe they fought each other, like real deal fought." Carmen said, "Me either, I knew it wasn't a good idea for you to bring that up Shae." Cashae said, "I regret it, I forgot how mad it made her." We sat in the dining room for a good 30 minutes. I looked at Alisha and she looked back at me like, what?? I rolled my eyes and looked away from her. She was still mad that I actually fought her.

Next thing you know, a small balled up piece of paper flew and hit me in the chest. I looked up at her, she tried to hold her smile. I flicked it back. She hit me with it twice after that. I quietly said, "Stop!" While mockingly smiling, she said, "You stop." I turned my body to the left and rested my head on my hand. She kept flicking paper. Since I was not responding to it, she threw a fork and it hit me on top of my head. As soon as that happened, our moms heard the fork hit the table and looked. Then they saw me stand up, take the metal container that we kept flour in, and throw it on Alisha.

She was covered in flour, she stood up and threw another fork, so I threw the container at her and just like that we started fighting again. It happened fast, our moms rushed over there saying, "'Stop it!" Our cousins heard it and ran from the Livingroom to the dining room and saw us fighting. Our moms pulled us apart, then I grabbed the chair like I was gonna throw it and so did Alisha. Trinity said, "Put them sh*ts down now!" We wouldn't let go, Carmen said, "Oh my gosh! Ya'll stop it!" She jumped in the middle to grab the chair I had, Cashae and Lashae grabbed the chair Alisha had.

Once we were pulled apart, Latoya said, "Ya'll gone stop this fighting today!" They got belts this time and wore us out. We snapped back into reality and didn't want to fight each other no more. They even sat us by each other after that and we didn't even give each other one dirty look. By this time our moms were mentally and physically exhausted, they had enough. Almost an hour later the doorbell rung. We were all still sitting in the same spots. When Latoya opened the door she said, "Ya'll couldn't get here no faster?"

We heard a man say, "We came as soon as ya'll called." We looked up and saw all of our dads walk in. I was thinking like, great, they called them over here to talk about it again. But I was wrong. Once they came in and greeted everyone, Latoya looked at us and said, “Get ya a**es up and go.” We looked at her confused. Trinity said, “What ya’ll looking like that for?? Get up and go, ya’ll going with ya’ll daddies.” We all said, “What?” We got up and started saying, “But we…” and “Why we…” But they cut us off and said, “Nope, bye, bye, go, ya’ll they problem now.” So we got shooed out the door.

Once we left, our moms took a breath of relief. Our dad’s laughed a little at how bad our moms wanted us out the house, because they didn’t think it was that bad. Until we got in the driveway. I turned to Alisha and said, “See! It’s you again, we would’ve stayed if you didn’t throw stuff at me. You keep getting me in trouble, now you got all of us kicked out and they didn’t even do nothin!” Alisha said, “Nobody told you to throw it back!” I said, “Oh so I’m supposed to sit there and just let you hit me with stuff??” Carmen told our dads, “Don’t let them get close, they gone fight each other again!" My dad grabbed me, and her dad grabbed her. Her dad said, "Fight?!" My dad said, "What ya'll fighting each other for?!" Our moms heard the commotion and came outside.

When they got out there, they saw both of us being restrained. They walked up to us, Latoya said, "What did I just say?! Do you need yo a** beat again?!" I said, "No." She said, "Well you better act like it, because I have no problem doing that. You understand me?!" I said, "Yes." She said, "Get yo a** in the car!" I went to get in my dad's car. Trinity told Alisha, "The same thing goes for you! Cut the crap, you understand me?!" Alisha said, "Yes." Trinity said, "Take yo a** on!" Alisha got in her dad's car. At this point our dads started to freak out a little bit, they didn't know what they got themselves into. They were on the verge of a mini breakdown from what they felt was going to be a stressful situation.

During the car ride, I noticed we were going a different way and was driving a little further. I didn't say anything, I just figured he had something to do. At this point, I was just happy to be from around Alisha. We eventually pulled up to this condo building, once we parked, he said, "Come on." I got out the car. I thought maybe he was stopping to see a friend or something. We got in the elevator and went to the top floor. We walked to a door, he pulled out a key and unlocked the door. I said, "What are you doing with a key??" He opened the door and moved so I can walk in. I walked in and stopped by the front door.

I looked up and saw my cousins and their daddies in the Livingroom of the condo, and it wasn't a condo it was a penthouse. I covered my eyes and tried to walk out as I said, "Oh uh un." But Andre stopped me and said, "Gone head in there." I turned back around and walked slowly to the Livingroom. I was hesitant because I didn't want to deal with Alisha no more that night. When I got to the Livingroom I was still standing up. I looked at Andre and said, "What's going on?" Andre said, "Well, since we all have ya'll for a week, we decided that it would be easier if we did it together. So, we got this penthouse."

Me and Carmen shook our heads and took a breath. Cashae laughed to herself a little bit and said, "Not a good idea." Cashae's dad said, "Ya'll go check out the room." We all went to the room. The room was huge, it was really nice. One thing we all noticed after a few minutes was that, there was a bed for each of us positioned around the room comfortably. We still had a lot of room to spare, but that wasn't the problem. Our dads came in the room to check on us. Carmen's dad was rubbing his hands together and said, "Hey, hey, hey…how ya'll like it?" We all said, "It's nice."

I looked at Andre and said, "Why are all the beds in one room?" He said, "Because we know how ya'll like to be together, normally when we separate ya'll, ya'll always end up back in the same room." Carmen said, "She fine Uncle Dre, she just still mad that's all, it's cool we love it. Thank ya'll for doing this." We all said, "Yeah thank ya'll." They said, "Ya'll welcome." Andre said, "Alright, well ya'll get comfortable and we'll order food and stuff. Ya'll can let us know what ya'll want when we come back in here." We said, "Okay."

They left out the room. We started to choose our beds and put our stuff down. Carmen saw Alisha about to get the bed closest to me, so she hurried up and stood next to Alisha and put her bag down while she looked at her. Then she started laughing, Alisha smiled. Carmen said, "Uh un, nope. I'm getting this bed." I looked up at them because I knew what Carmen was doing. Alisha said, "Then where is my bed??" The rest of them pointed and said, "Over there." Then they all laughed at the same time. It was funny because they gave her the bed furthest away from me.

Her mouth dropped. I tried not to laugh but it was too funny not to, so I laughed a little bit still trying to hold back. I even turned my back but somehow Alisha saw me. She went to her bed, kind of threw her stuff on it and said, "Camille wana be petty, it's not that serious." I said, "Yeah because you been starting with me." Cashae said, "UM!" Carmen said, "Ya'll don't start!" Lashae said, "For real!" We got quiet.

I was getting my stuff so I can take a shower. Then I heard Cashae say, "Oh my gosh girl! Go to the bathroom." Then Lashae said, "That's stuck in yo hair, you have to wash it out." I looked up and saw Alisha trying to rake the flour out of her hair from when I threw it on her. She had a lot in her hair, we saw it more when she took her hair down. Carmen said, "You getting it on the floor Alisha, you gone make a mess." Alisha started to walk towards the door, I turned my back to get some more of my stuff to take a shower. I assumed she was going to the bathroom.

As I turned around, Cashae said, “Alisha!” Right after she said that Alisha shook her hair out as she rubbed it so it can come out more. Only this time she did it so that it can get on me. She was so close to me facing me while she did it. I was holding my stuff. I closed my eyes and my lips were tucked in a little bit. My cousins mouths were wide open, and they were all stuck because they were in shock. I opened my eyes and took a breath as I looked at her. They all thought I was going to go off.

But I thought about it, I was about to take a bath anyway. Instead of saying anything I tried to walk past her. As I started to walk, she blocked me and shook her hair out again. This time a lot more came out and it got all over my clean clothes, my bed and me. I threw my clothes on the bed, flung Alisha by her hair and we were fighting again. Carmen ran across her bed to get to us while Cashae, Alicia and Lashae ran to us. They were yelling, “Stop!” This time I was madder, so we were fighting harder than we were before. When Cashae tried to break it up, she ended up rolling around with us.

Carmen laughed because it looked funny but then she got in the middle of us and was being flung around too. Our dads were watching the game, so they couldn't really hear us. That is until we bumped the door. It made them jump and they ran to our room. Andre tried to open the door, but it was a struggle because we were behind it. We moved while still fighting. All they saw was all of us falling on my bed, Carmen flying over my bed hitting the floor and Cashae jumping on top of us trying to stop us.

All of our dads rushed in the room and said, "Aye!" They started grabbing their daughters, when they grabbed Cashae she said, "Stop them! They fighting again!" Carmen said, "We tryna break it up!" My dad grabbed me, and Alisha's dad grabbed her, we were still trying to get to each other. Andre said, "Calm down!" While Alisha's dad said, "Cut it out!" While they held us Andre said, "What happened??" Carmen quickly said, "I ain't gone even lie, I'm tired of this Alisha keep starting with Camille." She was so aggravated she was talking with her hands. The rest of them agreed and said, "Yeah."

Alisha's dad said, "Alicia, that's true?" Alicia said, "Yes." Alisha said, "She threw the flour on me first!" I said, "At the house?! We got in trouble for that, plus you started with me first then!" Andre said, "Alright, alright, ya'll gone separate if ya'll don't stop." Alisha's dad said, "Ya'll supposed to be getting along. Alisha leave her alone because if yo mama knew what you was doing, you know she would beat yo a**." Andre said, "Camille you too, if something happen let us know." Cashae said, "She was about to take a shower." Cashae's dad said, "That's a good idea, how about all ya'll go shower and cool down." They all said, "Okay."

They let us go. I walked out to go to the bathroom. There were 4 bathrooms, so some of them took a shower at the same time I did. After about an hour we all were done with our showers. Alisha and Lashae were the last two to take a shower. When they walked in the room, we were all kind of quiet. We were just trying to come down from what happened. Once they put their stuff down, we were all on and crowded around my bed. We were having small talk about random things. Then Carmen said, "Alisha stop acting like that dang let it go." We looked at her, Cashae said, "What?" Carmen said, "She rolling her eyes and stuff." They all sucked their teeth.

Alisha said, "I just don't wana get in trouble again." I said, "Well if we do it's yo fault." Then we started going back and forth again. Carmen was resting her head in her hand and said, "Ugh…" About a minute later Carmen was looking confused and said, "Shh…" But we kept going, Lashae saw her and said, "What?"

Carmen said, “Ya’ll hear that??” Cashae said, “Yeah, who is that talking??” Lashae said, “Ya’ll be quiet!” We kept arguing, we thought they were just trying to shut us up. Then Carmen put her hand over my mouth and said, “Shut up!”

Alisha kept talking until Alicia put her hand over her mouth. I took Carmen hand off my mouth and said, “What??” Carmen said, “Listen, you hear that??” We all got quiet, then we heard a lady’s voice say, “What ya’ll got going on in here?” Another lady said, “Where they at??” Carmen looked at us and said, “Who that sound like?” Me and Alisha eyes got so big and at the same time we all said, “Our mamas!” All of us got so scared. Right after we said that the door flew open and low and behold it was Latoya and Trinity. They came in so forceful that our cousins jumped up and ran out the way.

We jumped up too, but they came straight to us and started to beat the crap out of us, they had belts and all. While we got hit, my mom said, “Ya’ll still fightin?!” Trinity said, “What did we tell ya’ll?!” We were screaming crying. While Carmen them watched, they got madder because they felt like I was getting a beaten for defending myself. They wanted to say something, but they knew it wasn’t the right time. After about 10 minutes they stopped, and Latoya turned to Carmen and said, “How this happened??” Carmen explained the whole thing and then said, “Alisha started it.”

Alicia said, “Yeah ma she did start it, they wouldn’t have fought if she didn’t do that.” Cashae said, “Ever since they first fought, Alisha started it. Camille was only defending herself.” They were mad and was over me getting in trouble for being picked on. After we calmed down, they asked us what happened. I was able to tell Latoya what happened during the times we fought. Once it came out that Alisha started it or instigated it, her mom jumped on her again.

After she got a second beaten, they made us apologize to each other and make up. It wasn't forced because we didn't want to feud, we just didn't know how to stop it. Once everything seemed back in order Latoya said, "We leavin ya'll here, and this better be the end of it, ya'll understand me?" Me and Alisha said, "Yes ma'am." Trinity said, "If we gotta come back out here, we takin ya'll home and ya'll gone get a lot worse than what ya'll just got, ya'll hear me?" We said, "Yes ma'am." They went to talk to our dads for a little bit and then left. We were all left looking in each other's faces. Our dads noticed that after another hour, everything was super quiet.

They even turned the tv down to make sure. They were on edge about coming in the room again, but they got up and came to the room to check on us. When they got in there, they saw my cousins on my bed except Carmen, she was sitting on the floor with me leaning on my bed. We were looking at some trading cards we found that had celebrities on them. We were laughing about the misinformation on some of them. We were so into what we were doing that we didn't notice our dads at the door. They were surprised to see Alisha laying right by me talking and laughing with me like we never fought at all. Then Andre said, "Ya'll alright?" We all looked at them at the same time, shocked that they were right there and said, "Yes."

He said, "Good…how about we go catch a movie?" We all said, "Yeah!" We jumped up and got ready to go. After this, our week went by very smooth, and we had a lot of fun. On the last day we were with them, they picked out our clothes for a dinner date with them. We didn't know. We came back from shopping and saw the clothes on our beds with notes on them, which turned out to be dinner invitations. After looking at the clothes I said, "Well, at least they know how to dress us." My cousins laughed and said, "Yeah."

We got dressed and they met us in the Livingroom. They took us to a nice upscale restaurant and treated us like princesses all night. We went out for desert afterwards and when we got back to the penthouse, they gave us gifts. When we opened the boxes, we screamed. We were so happy, they got us matching bracelets with symbols of loving each other infinitely. We were like, "Aww." They helped us put them on and then me and my cousins gave each other a group hug. Our dads were so happy to see that. Eventually we went to sleep.

The next morning, we packed up and they took us back home. They spoke to our moms of course about our week. Andre and Alisha's dad spoke to our moms about us and the situation we had. They gave them the update that we got along again and did not fight after that. Our moms were satisfied with that. During their conversation, I found out that our moms called to check on us. While they checked on us, they asked about me and Alisha. My dad told them that we fought again but it was under control.

Apparently, they didn't know our moms were going to stop by until they got there. They wanted to pop up on us to catch us in the act. I thought our dads had told on us that whole time. After our dads left, we showed our moms our bracelets, they loved them. I eventually called my cousins and told them how our moms ended up at the penthouse. They were all like, "Oooh." They said they were wondering about that but didn't want to ask. The important thing was that we were on good terms again and no longer fought. We both finally let it go.

Chapter 4

Party Host

A few weeks later I planned to hang out with my cousins and some of our friends, we were excited about that and looked forward to it all week. On Friday, I was literally headed towards the door. When I got to the door and touched the doorknob to open it, Latoya came around the corner and said, “Cee Cee, where you goin?” I said, “Oh, me and Carmen them wanted to hang out for a lil bit remember?” She looked like she was thinking as she lightly took a breath, rolling her head and looking up.

Then I said, “Ma, I meant to ask you, can I stay at Cashae house this weekend?” Latoya said, “Oh dang it, I forgot about that.” I said, “What happened?” She said, “Camille I’m sorry, but you can’t hang out this weekend.” I was shocked, I said, “But Ma! We been planning this for like 3 weeks, I didn't get in trouble since the last time or anything." She said, "I know but I need you to help me with Reci's party." I looked so confused and said, "Party?? It's not her birthday." Latoya said, "No, but it's a feel better party." My mouth dropped, I sat there for a few seconds trying to digest what I just heard.

Then I said, "Feel better for what?? What's wrong with her?" Latoya said, "We'll while you guys were with your dads, Reci was here with me, and she was sad that she couldn't go with ya'll. I felt bad, because she was moping around the house but was a good sport about it. So, I want to throw her a party so she would feel better and to help her forget about it." I said, "That was a punishment for us!" She said, "Yes, but her 5 year old mind didn't see it that way. Plus ya'll ended up going to all these places and came back with gifts, so yeah, you're staying here and helping." I took a deep breath.

She said, "Go get ready, her guests should be here soon." I said, "Get ready? Guests?? Mommie, I thought it would just be us." She said, "No, it's a party. Go, your clothes are on your bed, there's a party theme." I laughed a little bit and said, "Seriously?" She said, "Yes, now hurry up." As I walked away, I lowly said to myself, "Where were these feel better parties when I was little?" I got to my room and saw the clothes on my bed, they were colorful and fun. I shook my head and put them on.

I went to my mom so she can make sure I had on everything I was supposed to have on. She gave me some balloons and said, "Go put these in the guest room over there." I went to the upstairs guestroom closest to Reci's room. When I walked in there, I saw a lot of tents for little girls with personalized pillows and gifts bags. The room was decked out, I mean it looked really good. But it worried me a bit to see all this stuff. I went back to Latoya and said, "Ma, the room looks really nice." She said, "Thank you, I had a party planner do it." I said, "Wow you went all out…why are

there tents in there??" Latoya said, "They're for her guests." I said, "Yeah, but why tents?" She said, "That's part of the sleepover theme." I gasped so loud and said, "Sleepover?!" Latoya firmly said, "Yes, that's why I need you here this weekend."

I said, "Who are the guests??" She said, "Her friends from school and her cousins." My eyes got so big, then I said, "So Ma, you about to have a bunch of 5 year old's sleeping over at the same time, for a party…" Just then the doorbell rung, she said, "Yep, they're here, go get the door." I covered my face with my hands and took a breath and said, "Oh gosh." She said, "Go, and you better not break character." I took another breath and went to answer the door. I had to make it sound fun and exciting for the guests when I welcomed them in.

My job was to also open the door when the guests arrived. I had to keep them entertained downstairs until everyone came, because Reci was going to make her grand entrance. One of the first guests to arrive was a little girl from Reci's school. I opened the door and greeted her and her mom, she was very excited to the point where she was smiling big and bouncing a bit. She waited for me to stop talking and hyperactively said, "Hi, I'm Taylor, hi!" I smiled and said, "Hi Taylor, I'm Camille."

Her mom smiled, Taylor was still smiling and did not stop looking at me, she said, "Do you know Reci??" I said, "I do, in fact, I'm her sister." Taylor was amazed and said, "Whoa." I laughed and said, "Come in." The moms were told to wait with their daughters until Reci came out, so we had servers to serve them with drinks and snacks while they waited. There were 7 girls that came already. As I was thinking about how I'm going to get through this sleepover, the doorbell rung again. In my head I was thinking, dang more people. I opened the door in character, just to see my cousins with their little sisters.

I paused for a second because I wanted to laugh but I couldn't break character, so I finished my welcome greeting. After letting the little ones in, I looked at my cousins and we all laughed. We laughed because we all had on similar outfits. I whispered to them, "Why are ya'll dressed like that?" Carmen said, "The same reason you dressed like that." I said, "What?? So ya'll helping too??" Cashae looked down at her clothes and then back up at me and said, "Yep, found out in the middle of getting ready for our hangout this weekend." I said, "Me too!"

Then I noticed that everyone was there, so I told them to come in. We spoke with my mom to find out what we were supposed to do next. She went over a script, which we learned within two minutes. We went downstairs and got everyone's attention. We did the script which turned out to be fun, we were laughing and enjoying ourselves. The guests loved it. At the end of it, we introduced Reci as the girl of the hour. The lights were dimmed, and I don't know what my mama did, but a freakin spotlight was on Reci and it followed her downstairs.

Me and my cousins were just stuck, we couldn't believe it. Not to mention when she first appeared, confetti popped out. The whole effect and entrance was so nice. When she stepped off the last stair, the lights came on and some dance theme music started playing. We told her friends to get up. They ran to her, and they all started holding hands and dancing around. I have to admit it was cute and Reci looked happy. We were just smiling.

After their dance break, Reci started to hug everybody. She hugged us too. Before the parents were dismissed, Reci made a little speech thanking everybody for coming to her party. About 5 minutes later, the parents left. The first activity was a dance party. There were a number of songs arranged and choreography to some of the songs to entertain the girls. Following the dance party, the girls sat down to have refreshments and snacks. Then it was game time. During game time we had different types of games planned, some games were physical, and some games were board games. The girls were having a blast.

When it was time for a board game, Crystal sat down to explain it to the girls. She sat next to Taylor. We watched as she explained the rules. The girls started to play the game right after and was having a good time. We all drifted off a little bit and started talking to each other. Then out of nowhere Crystal screamed. We all jumped and looked at her. I said, “What’s wrong?!” She stood up with her mouth wide open and said, “This lil girl drew on me!” She turned her head towards us, and we saw the right side of her face, it was all marked up with red marker so was her right arm and hand. Our mouths dropped.

Cashae said, “How did that happen??” Crystal pointed to Taylor and said, “By sitting next to this lil girl!” Taylor looked at us and we didn’t see a marker or anything. Carmen said, “Crystal, she don’t have a marker and there are no markers in this game. How the heck…” Crystal said, “Trust me, she whipped it out! She faster than you would think.” I said, “Crystal go clean yourself up, we’ll watch them.” Crystal walked away upset. Alisha said, “Taylor come here please.” Taylor jumped up with a smile, when she got to Alisha she quickly said, “Hm?!” Alisha said, “Do you have a red marker?” Taylor looked confused and said, “What’s that??”

Alisha said, “Oh my gosh, I don’t think she had it. Maybe Crystal did that to get out of helping.” I squinted my eyes at Taylor a bit. Then I said, “Taylor come here please." She came to me, and I said, "Put your arms out." She put her arms out so fast and she spread her legs out too, it was almost like she knew what I was gonna do, like she was used to it. My cousins were shocked but laughed. Taylor was smiling the whole time. I patted her down and said, "Turn around." She did and I patted her down again.

Then she turned to me and said, "I'm having so much fun!" I said, "Yeah okay, go ahead and finish the game." She said, "Okay!" She had her hands together looking innocent and sat back down to play. After she sat down, Carmen said, "Did you feel anything?" I said, "No, but that's weird. If she don't have a marker and Crystal don't, who drew on Crystal?" Alisha said, "We never asked Crystal if she had a marker." I said, "Hmm." Soon it was time to move on to the next activity. Crystal was not back downstairs yet, so we had to be in charge of the next game. The next game was a treasure hunt.

The game started and there were really good prizes during the game and for the winners. The game went on for about 30 minutes. We had a whistle that we had to blow for the girls to meet at the designated spot when they finished. Carmen counted down, "Three, two, one…" I blew the whistle, and the girls came running. They were laughing and holding the things that they found. I greeted the girls and said, "Wow! You girls found a lot of cool things! Let's put them down and…" I paused after looking at one of the little girls faces and then I said, "What happened to your face?" I said it quick, my cousins looked and gasped.

The little girl was smiling but she had two big red circles around her eyes like she was a racoon or something. I bent down and said, "It's marker." I looked up at my cousins and Carmen lowly said, "Oh d*mn." I stood back up and said, "Who did that to your face?" The girl just smiled while she looked to the left with her eyes. She kept doing that, I even looked over to the direction she kept side eyeing. I asked her a couple of times and she finally said, "Did what?" I took a breath and said, "I didn't sign up for this."

Just then Latoya came out of the kitchen and said, "Okay dinner time girls!" They all said, "Yaye!" Latoya said, "Camille and her cousins will help you girls put your treasure away and then you'll come in the kitchen." Latoya walked out. I said, "Okay let's put everything away." The little girl raised her hand and said, "Can I use the bathroom?" I said, "Okay, let's go…Carmen ya'll help them." As I walked her to the bathroom, she pulled on my shirt and said, "I don't have to use the bathroom." I took a breath and said, "Why did you say you had to use it?" She said, "Taylor did it." I said, "What?"

She said, "My face, Taylor did it." My mouth was wide open while I gasped. I said, "What? How?" The little girl said, "During the treasure hunt, she told me to close my eyes and she would give me a surprise.

When I opened my eyes, my treasure was gone, and I felt her doing something to my face." My mouth dropped again, then I said, "So she does have a marker." The little girl said, "What color marker is on my face?" I said, "Red." The little girl said, "Yep, Taylor has a marker."

I never saw the marker, so I said, "How do you know?" The little girl said, "Taylor has a thing for red markers." I said, "But I didn't see it." The little girl said, "Oh you'll see it soon, trust me." I looked kind of scared and said, "Come on let's get you cleaned up." I took her hand and walked her to the bathroom. After washing her face, I walked her to the kitchen, my cousins were surprised to see I was able to get the marker off. I asked Latoya, "Ma, can you watch them for a second while we clean the Livingroom?" She said, "Yeah, go ahead." We all went in the Livingroom and started to clean.

Then I said, "Aye ya'll…I think Crystal was telling the truth, Taylor do have a marker." They were shocked. Alicia said, "How do you know?" I told them what the little girl told me. They were amazed she managed to pull that off and telling me in private. Now it was obvious that she was afraid to tell on Taylor in her face. I said, "It's so weird, they say for sure she has a marker, but we checked, and she had it nowhere on her. But she had it again during the treasure hunt."

Carmen said, "Well we gotta keep an eye out because if that lil runt draw on me, I'm putting her in a head lock." We laughed, then I said, "She did say we'll see the red marker soon." Just then Latoya said, "Camille, are ya'll done?! We have to get ready for the movie!" We looked at each other, I said, "Yes ma!" Then I looked at my cousins again and said, "Uh oh, this is gonna be a challenge." Cashae said, "Why?" I said, "Movie, lights off, girls close together, Taylor and her slick a** marker." They all said, "Ooh! Dang." We all went back to the kitchen and Latoya told us to get the movie room ready.

While we got it ready for the girls, we started plotting on how we could do it in order to catch Taylor in the act. I said, “Let’s sit them two chairs apart.” Cashae said, “Yeah and make sure no markers come in here.” We started fixing everything, then Carmen said, “We should leave the lights on a little bit.” Alisha said, “But it’s a movie.” Carmen said, “No, we can dim the lights but not turn them off, that way we can still see, like this…” She dimmed the lights and we said, “Oh yeah, that would work.” We left the lights like that. As we were finishing up, Latoya and the girls walked in.

I said, “No wait, Ma they gotta go back to the door.” She said, “For what?” I whispered to her, “We gotta frisk’em.” She sucked her teeth and said, “Camille, cut it out.” I said, “Okay Ma, at least let us frisk Taylor.” She looked at me and said, “Camille!” I jumped and said, “Okay.” The girls came all the way in, when they got to the seats Latoya stopped and said, "What ya'll did to the seats?" Carmen said, "Auntie Toya, we was going for a more comfortable feel, you know let the girls stretch their legs a lil bit." Latoya said, "They're 5 years old, how long do ya'll think they legs are??"

Cashae said, "We might as well leave it as it is right? I mean since it's like this already and they're here." Alicia said, "Yeah that's true, ya'll come on in and take a seat!" Latoya said, "Wait…" The girls stopped walking, then Latoya said, "I don't know why ya'll acting so weird, but ya'll gone help me fix this. Camille, Alisha ya'll help me fix the chairs the way they were supposed to be fixed." We took a light breath and looked at each other, then Latoya said, "Carmen, Cashae, and Alicia, ya'll go get the snacks." They looked at each other and went to get the snacks.

After we were done fixing the chairs and passing out snacks, Latoya noticed the lights. She said,

"These lights should be off." We all said, "Nooo!" She paused and looked at us, even the girls turned around because we scared them. Latoya said, "This is a movie they're watching, the room should be dark." She turned the lights off, looked at us curiously and said, "What's wrong with ya'll??" We got quiet. When she walked away Carmen whispered to me, "Bet somebody come out of here with red marker on them." I said, "Somebody if not all." The movie started, we all waited and tried to watch Taylor as best as we could in the dark.

Me and my cousins fell asleep during the movie. We literally fell asleep on our posts assigned to us by Latoya. Once the movie was over Latoya stood over me and Carmen, we were on the floor closest to the door. Then she cleared her throat. When she did that, we jumped and woke up quick because it scared us. When we opened our eyes and looked at her, we stood up as she said, "Sleeping on the job I see." Carmen said,

"Sorry Auntie, movies about princesses make me fall asleep." I said, "Yeah." While we yarned, Latoya looked confused and said, "The movie was about a pony." Me and Carmen looked at each other with our eyes big and said, "Oh…" at the same time.

Latoya said, "Help the girls and get ready to set up the bedroom." We said, "Okay." Alisha came to us and whispered, "Hey, we can check to see if any of them have that marker on them." We said, "Oh yeah!" As the girls were walking out to follow my mom, we looked at all their faces, arms and hands. Alicia said, "None of them had anything on them." I said, "Well I guess that's a good thing." They agreed and said, "Yeah." I said, "Wait a minute…where's Cashae??" Alisha walked around the room looking and then we heard her laugh and say, "She still sleepin!" We laughed.

I said, "Oh my gosh." I walked over to where she was and said, "Shae come on you gotta help us clean the…AHHH!" When I screamed my cousins jumped and said, "What?!" I even scared Cashae, she was looking at me crazy. When they got to me, I pointed to Cashae and said, "Look." They all looked at Cashae and screamed. At this point Cashae was freaked out and screamed too, then she said, "What?!" We all said, "Red marker!" She touched her face and said, "On my face?!" We said "Yeah!" Then we all burst out laughing.

Cashae said, "That's not funny, ya'll for real??" I said, "Yeah, go look in the mirror in the bathroom, but don't let my mama see you." Cashae got up and went to the closest bathroom. While she was gone, we started cleaning again. When Alisha went on the first row she jumped, holding her chest and said, "Whew! Oooh this child scared me!" We looked and Alicia said, "What child?" Alisha picked up something and held it up high and to our surprise, it was one of the little girls. She got left in there somehow.

I said, “Oh no, you got left behind??...Carmen can you take her to my mom please.” Carmen grabbed her hand and said, “Yeah…come on.” When they started walking, Carmen stopped and bent down as if she was trying to hear something the little girl was saying. Then Carmen stood back up and said, “Ya’ll heard her??” We said, “What?” Carmen looked at her and said, “What did you just say? Say it loud so they can hear you.” Then little girl looked at us and said, “Taylor did it, I saw her!”

We all gasped and stood there for a few seconds. Then I said, “Wait, Taylor did what??” The little girl said, “She wrote on that ladies face while she was sleeping.” I turned to Alisha, pointed and said, “That freakin red marker!” Alisha said, “If yo mama let us check them we probably would’ve found it.” Then the little girl said, “Yeah, she’s pretty good with that marker.” Carmen asked the little girl, “If you were up, how did you get left behind?” The little girl said, “I stayed." We said, "What??" She said, "I stayed so I can tell you Taylor did it, I knew you would ask." We were so shocked and said, "Oh."

Then the little girl looked at Carmen and said, "Can I go back to the party now?" Carmen said, "Yes, but one question…why did you stay behind to tell on Taylor?" The little girl smiled while she shook her head in a no motion and said, "You don't want Taylor to know you told on her, she'll get you." We all looked like, dang. Carmen petted the little girl's head and said, "Let's get you back to the party." From that point on, we decided to keep a close eye on Taylor. We didn't tell my mom because we couldn't prove it. Judging by how the girls told on Taylor, we knew they wouldn't fess up if we said something. So we decided to catch her in a way she can't deny it.

When we were finished cleaning, we went upstairs to get the room they were sleeping in ready. On our way there, Cashae came out the bathroom. She looked at us and said, "That was hard as h*ll to get off, that's permanent marker." I said, "Then she definitely brought a marker from home, because all the markers we put out are watercolor markers." Alisha said, "Well at least it's bedtime, when they wake up, they can go home." When we got to the room, there wasn't much to do because Latoya had everything set up already. We figured she wanted us in there to help the girls find their tents. Me and my cousins were just talking about Taylor and that marker while we waited for my mom to come up there.

About 10 minutes later, my mom came in there. When the girls saw the room, they were ecstatic. They ran in the room smiling and screaming. We started covering our ears, I said, "Oh my gosh." Carmen said, "My goodness." Cashae was staring at the girls with her arms crossed because she was still mad at Taylor. Latoya said, "Okay, settle down, settle down…" The girls got quiet, Latoya continued, "Everyone has their own tents, you also have some goodies as a thank you gift for coming to Careecia's party. Camille and her cousins will help you find your tent." The girls all screamed, "Yaye!" We started telling them which tent had their names on it. They were excited, getting settled in and playing in their tents.

After they got settled in, it was time for them to brush their teeth. We didn't have to worry much about them at that time, because Latoya had us stay in the room and watch the girls while she took them two by two in the bathroom to brush their teeth. After teeth brushing time, it was bonding time. The girls were able to play in each other's hair and give each other facials. That was actually fun to watch and monitor. After bonding time, we all painted their nails and toes. We did a lot of hands on girls stuff and the girls loved it. During these activities, I noticed how much Taylor and Reci were together or somehow always ended up together. This was weird because our sisters didn't have marker on them, but Taylor managed to stay close by them especially close to Reci.

After the activities were done, it was story time. Latoya read them a couple of stories and then it was bedtime. The girls were tired and started to crawl in their tents. Latoya told me and my cousins we can go and do our own thing at that time. I was the last one out. While Latoya was tending to another girl across the room, Taylor stopped me and was crying. I kind of felt bad for her and said, “Taylor, what’s wrong? Why are you crying?” She rubbed her eye still crying with her lip poked out and said, “I want to go home.” I was low key happy. I was ready to tell my mom to call her mom so we can get this red marker drawing sneak out of our house. But instead my big sister instincts kicked in thanks to having Reci as my sister.

I said, “Why, the night is almost over, and you can go home then, do you miss your mommy?” She said, “No, it’s not that.” I said, “Then what is it?” She said, "I can't sleep without my bear, and I left him home by mistake." My mouth dropped, I said, "Is that it?" She said, "Yes." I said, "Okay, follow me." I took her to my room, when she came in the doorway my cousins all jumped and gasped. Carmen pointed as she jumped on the bed like she was running and said, "Camille, something is behind you!" I laughed a little bit and said, "Really Carmen? She about to go back in there." I went in my closet and took out my favorite bear.

I walked to her and said, "This is my favorite bear, I had it since I was a kid. I never let anyone borrow him, but I think I can make an exception for you." She instantly smiled, gave me a tight neck hug and said, "Thank you Camille! Now I don't have to go home, you're the best!" I smiled. She let go and I said, "You're welcome, make sure you take care of him." She said, "I will!" I watched as she ran back to the guestroom. After she was in there, Carmen said, "It's hard to be mad at her when you feel sorry for her…lil turd." We laughed and in agreement said, "Yeah."

Me and my cousins spent the rest of the night enjoying each other's company and just having a fun teen night. We were exhausted so we didn't go to bed too late. Before we knew it, it was morning time but most importantly the girls were leaving. We couldn't be happier. We got up to help my mom get the girls ready for their moms. They ate, brush their teeth, got dressed, they even played more games. I asked Taylor, "Hey, where is my bear?" She smiled and said, "In my tent, thank you again. I slept like an angel." I smiled and said, "Aw that's so sweet, you're welcome."

I went to the room and looked in her tent. I couldn't find it at first but then I noticed a lump under the cover. I pulled the cover back and couldn't believe what I saw. I picked up my

bear with my mouth wide open, it had marker written on every inch of the bear. This was proof enough, although I wish it was a different type of proof it was exactly what I needed. I screamed so loud. My mom came running. When she got in there, I had tears in my eyes, she said, "What happened?!" I explained to her what had been going on during the entire sleepover. She was shocked.

Then I said, "And now I know it's her, look!" Latoya grabbed the bear and said, "Is that your favorite bear??" I said, "Yes…" I tried to dart to door while I said, "I'ma throw that lil girl!" Latoya grabbed me and stopped me. Then she said, "How you know she did that?" I said, "She told me she couldn't sleep because she left her bear at home, so I let her borrow mine for the night so she would stop crying." Latoya said, "Okay, I'll talk to her mom when she gets here."

We went downstairs and I told my cousins what happened. They were so shocked but happy we finally got evidence. In the meantime, we made sure they had their goodies and their goodie bags. Soon the girls started to leave one by one, I wanted Taylor to leave first but she was still sitting there. Taylor ended up being the second to last girl to leave. When her mom came Latoya talked to her about it and showed her the bear. She told her everything I told her regarding the red marker incidents at the party. Taylors mom said, "Really Taylor?! You brought the red marker?! I told you not to bring that marker with you, I took it from you. What do you have a pack of them or something?!"

Her mom was embarrassed and apologized so much, she made Taylor apologize to us. Then she offered to pay for the bear, but we declined. Her mom looked at me and said, "Camille I'm so sorry, she doesn't even sleep with a bear at home." All of our faces dropped, I said, "What?!" She said, "Yeah Taylor hates stuffed animals, I don't know why she did that..." I was speechless and so was everyone else in the room.

Her mom turned to her said, "But I'm going to tell your dad Taylor, no more red markers!" They left soon after. Once they were gone, I turned to Latoya and said, "Ma, don't let that lil girl come back over. You shouldn't even let her be friends with Reci." My cousins said, "Yeah, she bad." Latoya said, "I think that's Reci's best friend or something." I took a breath shaking my head in a yes motion and said, "Great, just what we need."

We finished cleaning what we could clean, and Latoya had a cleaning service come over to do the rest. She did this so that me and my cousins could still hang out like we wanted to at the start of the weekend, which turned out to be cool. We were free to go and happy to get out the house after being tormented by Taylor. One thing's for sure, we never wanted to encounter Taylor again. I just had high hopes that Latoya would take into consideration everything that happened and not allow her back. But if she's Reci's best friend, only time will tell.

Chapter 5

We're Innocent

One Friday sometime after Reci's party, I was at my friend's house. I was planning on spending the night, we was having fun and everything. She was telling me about some stuff that went on with her and some boys, it was interesting. Right when she got to the good part my phone rung. I instantly had a bad feeling about it. I looked down at my phone and saw that my mama was calling. I signaled my friend with my finger, saying hold on.

I picked up and said, "Hello?" I said it like I was already scared. Latoya said, "Hello? ...Camille were you in school today?" I said, "Yes." She said, "Are you sure?" I said, "Yes." She said, "Okay." We hung up after that. My friend started talking again, after like ten minutes my mama called back. I picked up and said, “Hello?” She said, “Camille, somebody spotted yo cousins over by 16th court during school hours and now everybody saying you was with them…” I said, “Ma, I wasn’t over there with…” She cut me off and said, “So why they say you was?” I said, “I don’t know, maybe they don’t know what they talking about.” She said, “And maybe you need to come home.” I said, “No, for what? I…” She said, “Be ready when I get there…” I said, “Ma…” But she had already hung up.

I kept looking down as I called Cashae phone. When she picked up, I said, “Hello?” My voice was kind of shaky. She said, “Hello?” I said, “Cashae, who told my mama I was with ya’ll on 16th today?” At this point I was lightly crying. She said, “I don’t know who said that, but it ain’t true and I’m getting in trouble for it. I was in school…you still at yo friend house?” I said, “Yeah,” as I rubbed my nose a little bit. Cashae said, “So why you cry…oh, yo mama making you come home ain’t it?” I said, “Yeah, but this time it wasn’t me…" Cashae said, "Yeah, my mama got me on lockdown for the whole weekend. I'm not even supposed to be on the phone. I don't know who said it but, if you was over here it'll probably be easier to find out."

I said, "But still she don't have to…" Just then my phone rung, I said, "Hold on." It was my mama, I clicked over and said, "Hello?" She said, "Camille, you do know that I'm coming to get you to figure everything out right?" I said, "Yes." She said, "Alright I'll be there in five minutes, you do understand right?" I said, "Yes." She said, "So it shouldn't be no problems…" I said, "No." She said, "Alright." I clicked back over after she was finished talking to me and said, "Hello?" Cashae said, "Yeah…" I said, "That was my mama." She said, "What she said?" I said, "The same thing you said about me being there to figure stuff out." She said, "Oh, I knew it." I said, "I'ma call you later before she get here." Cashae said, "Alright."

When we hung up, I apologized to my friend about me not spending the night. She was disappointed but she understood. My mama came shortly after that. I said bye to my friend and got in the car. We didn't talk much on our way back, but my mama did explain the situation to me. It was crazy. The way my mom told it, somebody lied. It seemed like a teacher lied and ironically somebody else said they saw us that same day. I didn't know what was going on. When we got home my mama said, "We'll talk about it in the morning, go to bed." I said, "Alright." I went to my room so confused.

Before I went to bed, I called Cashae to tell her I was home. But that's all I could say, before I said anything else she said, "Alright…I think my mama coming, I gotta go." I said, "Alright." She said, "I'll talk to you tomorrow." We hung up. I sat up for a few more minutes to think, but I only made myself more confused. So, I went to sleep. The next day when I woke up, my mama took me to Cashae house. When I got there, I saw Cashae sitting on the couch. She signaled me to go to her room. Me and Cashae hurried to her room. When we got up there Cashae said, "What's about to happen?" I looked at her so lost and said, "Huh? …something about to happen?" She said, "You're here, the twins on their way and we just got accused of skipping last night…" I had a confused look on my face.

Then we heard the door close, so Cashae got up and looked through the crack of her room door. She took a breath as she closed the door back and said, "And now Carmen here…when do Carmen ever be here?" I said, "Okay now you scaring me, what's going on?" Just then Carmen walked in, closed the door, and said, "Okay, am I in trouble? Cause if I am let me know now." Cashae said, "Why you say that?" Carmen said, "The only time they have us together like this, is when we did something real stupid that we thought they didn't know about, but it turns out they did, and they want to let us know at the same time to see our reactions, so they can know if we lyin or not." She was talking real fast.

Me and Cashae looked at each other and smiled as she finished talking. Cashae said, "Calm down we ain't…" Just then Cashae door opened again. It was Lashae! Now we really knew something was wrong. Lashae never show up anywhere we at when we in trouble if she not already with us, even if she was in it. All of us just got quiet while our eyes got big. Lashae came in, closed the door and said, "Why do I feel like I'm in trouble?" All of us turned towards each other and started talking at the same time. Lashae was looking confused, then she said, "What's going on?" I looked at her and said, "You heard about somebody saying we skipped school?"

She rolled her eyes and said, "Oh that…that wasn't me." I said, "It wasn't us either." Lashae sat down, I said, "Okay, I agree with Carmen when she say they got us all together to see our reactions, so they can know if we lyin or not…I say we all act confused no matter what they say. Act like ya'll don't know nothin, the littlest difference on one of our faces can cause us the whole thing. Don't overdo it, just act like ya'll thinking and don't really interact with each other." All of them shook their heads as if they thought it might work.

Then Cashae said, "What if it don't work?" I said, "Trust me…it'll help if ya'll had feedback from time to time, like I don't remember that and so on…" They all agreed. About 20 minutes later Alisha and Alicia came, but they didn't get a chance to come in the room. My auntie kept them downstairs while my other auntie came to get us from upstairs. When we got downstairs, we sat down. The twins looked like they were spooked. I wondered if they mama whooped them or something. I wanted to get their attention so I can tell them to act confused, but when I looked their way Beonca guided me by my shoulders to the other couch.

I kept staring at them as she did that because they wouldn't look up for nothin. I guess Trinity noticed it, because when it got quiet, she said, "Camille!" I jumped a little bit and looked at her. I was looking pissed off. She said, "Something wrong?" I looked back at the twins with only my eyes. She said, "Look at me!" I rolled my eyes and looked back at her, she just looked at me for a minute then she said, "You okay?" I said, "Yes." I managed to glance at Cashae as she shook her head no while she rested her face in her hand.

Then I saw Lashae mouth, "No, stop." I guess my aunties and my mama was watching where I was looking, because Lashae almost got caught. She was shaking her head no and mouthing it as she used her hand to say stop. She looked behind me and quickly put her head down. Then Latoya said, "What was that

Lashae?" Lashae looked up quicker than she did when she looked down and said, "Huh?" Beonca said, "You said something?" Lashae said, "No." Cashae started smirking. I knew somebody was finna get in trouble before we left that house.

Then Latoya said, "Anybody wana go first?" We all just looked at each other. Then she said, "Okay, so the story is that ya'll skipped school yesterday…" All of us had straight faces listening, she continued, "The names that popped up when I was told were Camille, Lashae, and Cashae." My face went from straight to confused as I looked at Lashae, then to pissed when I looked at Cashae. Then I said, "We wasn't even together." My cousins looked at me with big eyes, while my mama and my aunties looked at me like, oh really??

I cleared it up quick and said, "No, I'm saying we was in class…" Trinity said, "You sure you wana speak for everybody?" I glanced at Lashae, then Trinity said, “Stop lookin at her!” I looked back at Trinity, she said, “Did you skip?” I said, “No.” She turned to Lashae and said, “Did you skip?” Lashae said, “When?” Our mouths dropped a bit. She realized what she said right after she said it, her facial expression showed just how scared she was. She just sat there with her mouth and eyes wide open staring into space.

At this point we couldn’t hold back no more, this moment was too funny. The rest of us snickered at the same time. Me and Cashae tried to turn our heads while the rest of them covered their faces. Then Lashae looked around and Beonca said, “Something funny?” We stopped. Beonca closed her eyes and opened them again when she looked back at Lashae. Then she said, “Go ahead, what happened now? You said when??” Lashae said, “No, I was tryna make sure…I mean I was tryna see what day ya’ll was talking about because I was in school.”

Beonca said, "Well how ya'll was seen on 16th then, people do know how ya'll look." All of us said, "I don't remember that!" Except the twins, we looked at each other. We wasn't supposed to say it at the same time. Beonca them looked at us but didn't pay it any mind. Then Latoya said, "How many of ya'll skipped Friday?" Me and Lashae said, "None of us," and at that same time Carmen and Cashae said, "Not me." We took a quick look at each other and switched words, this time me and Lashae said, "Not me," while Carmen and Cashae said, "None of us."

My mama them looked so confused. Me and Lashae had smirks on our faces while Carmen and Cashae was down hard laughing in silence, trying not to be loud. The twins started smirking. My mama them got mad. Latonya told Carmen, "Shut yo d*mn mouth!" We all looked at Latonya then at Carmen. She was sitting right next to me. Then Carmen just looked down at her lap with a smirk on her face.

Her mama wasn't playing, she looked like she was gone murder Carmen. That scared us so bad, she made us stop laughing. It got real quiet, but that only made it funnier. I almost laughed and Carmen heard it. Everybody else heard me but thought it was Carmen, because right after I made a sound Carmen busted out laughing thinking I was going to laugh full out, but I didn't. Carmen let out a big burst of laughter when she did that. Latonya darted at her, but Latoya saw when I laughed and pulled Latonya back. Latonya said, "Laugh again!" Latoya said, "Naw, it was Camille."

I looked at my mama and she was looking at me so pissed off, so I stopped and just looked down with a straight face. I leaned to one side of the couch and Carmen leaned on the other side of the couch at the same time. Lashae was smiling shaking her head. Then Latonya said to Lashae, "So what's yo story?" Lashae said, "Well, I went to school as usual, I went straight to class because I came right after the bell rung…"

Latonya said, "Did you see yo cousins?" Lashae said, "No…so I went to all my classes, and I never left."

Trinity said, "Alisha?" Alisha looked and said, "Ma, I was with Alicia and Camille all day…" Then Alicia said, "Not all day." Alisha looked at her as I looked up. Alisha said, "Well, during lunch Camille told me she'll be back, but she didn't come back before the bell rung…" Latoya said, "Where did she go?" Alisha said, "I guess to the bathroom or…" Then Alicia quietly said, "She ain't tell you that…" I looked at Alicia like she was crazy.

Alisha rolled her eyes and said, "Anyway, we went to class." Then Latonya said, "Go head Camille." I was looking at Alicia, Latonya was looking down with her arms folded as she told me to go. She looked up because I didn't respond and said, "Camille?" I looked at her then looked down as I said, "I was in school like the rest of them, and I went to my classes that I was supposed to go to…" Latoya cut me off and said,

"What happened at lunch Camille?" As I looked up, I glanced at Alisha, looked at Latoya, then looked back at both twins quick. I was scared to talk, because I didn't know the next thing that might've came out of Alicia mouth.

Latoya said, "Camille?" I looked back at her and said, "I had to go to my classroom, my bag was in there." I looked at Lashae from the corner of my eye, she was looking kind of scared. Then Beonca said, "Okay, Cashae and Carmen we haven't heard from ya'll yet." I don't think Carmen was gone say anything, but nobody could tell because Cashae opened her mouth. Cashae said, "Well, I was in class all day and I didn't see nobody, wait no…I did see Camille like 2nd, 3rd, I saw her three times. The first time was 2nd hour somewhere by her classroom. Then I saw her about to go in her 4th hour, but she didn't see me. I saw her and Lashae after lunch, but I had to go back to class, because the time on my pass was about to be up…"

When she said that Beonca looked confused as she pointed to Lashae.

Latonya caught on and pointed to Lashae. Then Latoya said, “So if you had a pass, then you must’ve seen them in between classes?” Cashae said, “Yes.” Latoya looked at us and said, “So what ya’ll was doing out of class?” Beonca said, “Why, Lashae I thought you, didn’t you say you didn’t see none of them, the whole day?” Latonya said, “I was just thinking the same thing, something not adding up.” We froze, all of us got scared.

Me and Lashae was scared to talk, the rest of them was scared for us. So they let Carmen talk, she basically said the same thing. That she went to class and what-not. But when she said, “I was in school the whole day in class,” Latonya didn’t really believe her and said, “You bet not be lyin either, cause if I find out I’ma…” Just then Cashae said, “No, auntie she was in school all day. Her classes close to mine, and I saw her in them when I was in the hallway…with my pass." Latonya said, "Okay," as she turned her head back to Lashae. Latoya said, "Lashae, why were you and Camille outside of class?" I turned my head away from everybody and almost started crying instantly.

I just knew they wasn't gone let it go. As Lashae started talking, my body got warm. She said, "Well I, we…" I started shaking as she started stuttering. My mama looked at me and said, "Camille, you got something you wana tell me?" I shook my head halfway saying no. Trinity looked at Beonca and mouthed, "She crying?" Beonca nodded yes. Latoya said, "Camille," as I turned my head towards everybody again, they saw that I was crying. They were confused, that's when they really got scared. Latoya said, "You say no, but why you crying?" Lashae said, "Because! ..." She took the attention off of me and said, "Well me and Camille…we got kicked out of class yesterday…"

Latoya said, “Both of ya’ll? At the same time?” Lashae said, “We have the same 4th hour and 6th hour.” My mama them looked surprised, all them said, “Oh.” Lashae said, “Because the teacher not too fund of us and said we was talking during a test, but that was 6th hour. I remember seeing Cashae with a pass.” Latoya said, “What about 4th hour?” I said, “We ran out.” Everybody looked at me, Lashae was shocked. Latoya said, “What?” I said, “We ain’t wana be in there, so before the last bell we ran through the crowd, and I guess that’s when Cashae saw me. I didn’t look back.” I looked at my mama and said, “But we never left the school.”

The way my mama looked at me, I can tell she felt that it was a lot more to why I was crying and a lot more to the story. She said, “Okay, ya’ll go upstairs, Camille and Lashae stay here, I wana talk to ya’ll.” My cousins looked back like they knew we were in trouble. Me and Lashae just sat there looking down, while the rest of them went upstairs. After they were in the room, Latoya looked at me and said, "What the h*ll you mean ya'll ain't feel like being there?! Who gave you the right to decide that?!" I just closed my eyes and started crying more, she said, "Don't cry now, cause you know better!" Then she looked at Lashae and said, "And I guess you followed her?!" Lashae put her head down, Latoya said, "Pick yo d*mn head up!" Lashae took a minute, but she looked back up at Latoya.

Latoya said, "Something wrong?!" Lashae said, "No," as she started crying. Her voice was cracking. She started wiping her eyes continuously because her tears was coming down so fast. Latoya said, "Well I suggest you act like it!" She paused and then she said, "Now I'm only gone ask one time…where the h*ll were ya'll two on Friday?!" I put my head in my shirt while leaning on my legs still crying. I think we were more embarrassed than scared, because we started crying like we was at home with Latoya by ourselves.

None of us said anything. My mama said, “Oh, so nobody wana talk?” I was waiting for Lashae to say something, but she wouldn’t. So Latoya said, “Alright, take ya’ll a**es outside! We gone find out…” I looked up and said, “But ma…!”

She shook her head no as she was telling me and Lashae to come on as I said, “We ain’t do nothin…!” She said, “Uh-un.” I said, “You ain’t give me a chance to talk!” She paused and looked at me like I was crazy. Then she said, “Yo a**…outside…now! ....make me come get you.” I got up with an attitude and walked out, Lashae walked out after me. Latoya was pissed. Her and my aunties stood there for a minute just taking it all in, then Latoya said, “I’ll be back.” Beonca them just looked at her walk out. When she got outside, I was under a tree on the phone crying. Lashae was standing on the sidewalk looking at the ground trying to stop crying.

Latoya got by the car and said, “Let’s go.” Lashae heard her, I didn’t. Lashae got in the car, I didn’t even see my mama. Then she said, “Get yo a** off that phone and get in the car!” I hung up and walked to the car. Good thing I was talking to Cashae. My mama drove off. My cousins stayed in the room the whole time. They was talking at first, but when Alicia agreed that she felt bad for us Cashae jumped up and said, “You the one who gave them away! If it wasn’t for you opening yo mouth, maybe they’d be up here with us!” Alicia said, “I wasn’t finna get caught…I was already in trouble!” Cashae cut her off and said, “You shouldn’t have said nothin, you know how they are, they catch on Alicia!”

The entire time Cashae was talking, Alicia kept repeating, “I was already in trouble!” So when Cashae repeated, “They catch on Alicia!” Alicia just sat there, when Cashae saw a tear run down her face she said, “What’s wrong with her?” Alisha said, “She get like that sometimes, just leave her alone." Cashae said, "I'm sorry Alicia…" Then Carmen said, "Cashae you added on to it, when you said you saw them between classes." Cashae almost cut her off and said, "Uh! ...I was talking without thinking." Alisha said, "Is that why Camille called you cursing you out?" Carmen chuckled. Then Cashae sarcastically said, "She was crying not cursing." A little while later Latoya came back.

When she came in the house, Beonca said, "Where the girls?" As Latoya forcefully put her purse on the couch, she said, "They are in some deep sh*t. I left them home. I don't wana see them right now because I might end up killin'em." Beonca said, "What happened??" Latoya said, "I went to the school…" Latonya said, "Ooh, that's where you was?" Latoya said, "Yeah when I asked for the records from Friday, they pulled them up. It's real crazy because Camille went to 1st hour, but after that they have no record of her being there at all." Beonca shook her head like, naw. Latonya said, “So she lied?” Latoya said, “Well, they did say that she was in I.S. during 4th hour, because she got kicked out of that class the day before for something stupid she did.” Trinity said, “What about 6th hour, she say she went there?”

Latoya took a deep breath, rolled her eyes and said, “She did go, but before attendance was taken apparently Camille and Lashae mouthed off to the teacher. They were told to go to attendance, but they never showed up.” Trinity said, “Okay, well maybe they did do some stuff…but this whole thing was about them leaving school, and if Camille and Lashae was in school acting out, then they couldn’t have been on 16th. Maybe they tellin the truth…” Latoya stopped to think, then she called my phone and said, “Camille, ya’ll two come down here to Beonca house, and try to hurry up.”

Latonya said, “You gone make them walk?” Latoya said, “They was still actin up.” All of them was like, “Oh, okay.” They agreed and left it alone. I told

Lashae and we got there in the next fifteen minutes. Before we walked in, my mama them was talking. Beonca said, “So they told you that?” Latoya said, “After the school told me about the classes, they just told me what the school couldn’t…they wasn’t in here crying for nothing.” That’s when we knocked on the door and Trinity opened it.

You could tell something was wrong with us, from the way we was looking. Latoya said, “Sit down,” without even looking at us. Me and Lashae sat down. Then Latoya said, “Are ya’ll sure ya’ll never left the school on Friday?” I said, “I didn’t leave.” She said, “What about you Lashae?” Lashae said, “I never left.” Latoya said, “So I’ll take ya’ll word for it…go upstairs.” We got up and went to Cashae room with everybody else. When the door opened Cashae them was shocked to see us. Cashae closed the door and said, “I thought ya’ll left.” I said, “We came back.”

At this time Beonca went to her room for something. Then Carmen said, "Where ya'll went?" I said, "My mama gone take us to the school, so they can pull up our records and we got in trouble." Alisha said, "Why?" I said, "All of ya'll knew me and Lashae was in trouble, and all ya'll knew not to say nothing…except for Alicia…" When I said that Beonca was about to pass by Cashae room. But as soon as she slightly passed the room, Cashae jumped up and said, "See Alicia! …I knew it was yo fault!" Beonca stopped with a confused looked on her face.

My mama them didn't see her. Then Cashae said, "Camille would've never got caught if you would've played along with the rest of us!" Then Beonca opened the door and was looking at Cashae. Cashae's back was turned to the door. We paused just looking at Beonca. Cashae was pointing in Alicia face saying, "But you just had to be the one to give everybody away. I knew we should've called you upstairs when Camille was telling us what to do!" My eyes got big, Beonca looked at me like, oh really?? All of us looked at each other. Then Cashae said, "But I guess you ain't got common sense like the rest of us." As she started to turn back around, she said, "Because if you did, you wouldaoooop…" When saw Beonca she closed her mouth and swallowed her words.

Her eyes got so big, and I could've sworn she stopped breathing. Beonca gave her a look, Cashae looked around. Beonca said, "So yo a** lied?! Why you lied to me?!" My mama looked up as Beonca came in the room. Cashae jumped, she was so scared. Latoya them ran upstairs, when they got up there, they said, "What happened?!" Beonca said, "They lied! ...Go ahead tell her what you just said!!" She was telling her to tell my mama. Cashae looked at me for approval, I put my head down and looked the other way. She knew she couldn't say different because her mama heard her say it. She looked back at Beonca.

Then Beonca said, "Apparently, before everybody got here, they agreed to do something that Camille told them to do!" Latoya said, "Like what?!" Beonca said, "Oh I don't know like…cover up for her according to Cashae…I caught her up here yelling at Alicia for not sticking with them, because she wasn't in the room to hear the plan!" Tears ran down Cashae face, then Alicia quietly said, "Oh now the shoe on the other foot." Alisha nudged her and said, "Shh," while the rest of us sucked our teeth. Beonca said, "And until <u>we</u> go to the school, I don't know what to believe. But I guess they knew more than what they told us!" All of us had our heads turned, we couldn't look at them.

My head was leaning on the bed. Then Latoya said, "Camille like always…but why ya'll risk getting in trouble for her? I don't understand that." I whispered, "Another day, another problem." I could see that all the pressure was gone be on me. Latoya said, "Camille, why you told them to do that?" I said, "I didn't tell them to cover up for me." She said, "So what did you tell them?" I said, "Ma…" She looked at me, I took a deep breath and said, "I told them to look confused so ya'll wouldn't suspect anything."

I was shaking my head looking down, my cousins looked at me so shocked. Then my mama said, "And why did you…" I said, "Because somebody was accusing us of something we didn't do, and if we would've just sat there while ya'll asked us about it, ya'll would've just knew we was guilty. So we needed a defense, I'm sorry." Then Alicia said, "We don't even be in the streets to be seen…"

She looked at my mama them as we rolled our eyes from them to her. Then she said, "If we did skip…but we didn't." I squinted my eyes at her while my cousins made a face at her. That made my mama them think a little bit more. Then Latoya said, "So you saying ya'll never left school?" I said, "Yes ma, we didn't leave." She said, "Okay." As my mama them walked out, Beonca looked at Cashae and said, "I'll deal with yo a** later."

Cashae watched her as she closed the door. She stood with her back towards us. We was quiet. Then Carmen said, "Cashae?" Cashae turned around and said, "Camille I'm sorry!" I said, "Don't worry about it, I couldn't get in no more trouble than I was already in." She said, "But I am so sorry." I said, "It's okay." Alisha said, "So what we gone do now?" I said, "Enjoy our freedom, because this probably the last time we gone chill like this for a long time. I know as soon as I get back home it's straight lockdown for me."

Lashae said, "And it's the weekend…" I said, "I know." We sat in Cashae room bored that whole day. We did talk, but every time we was about to have a fun moment, the thoughts of punishment didn't let us. Soon we all left. Lashae stayed at my house, but we had to go in separate rooms. It wasn't really a punishment, we just couldn't have a social life with each other. We still had tv, phone, and everything else, but that's boring without each other.

Cashae couldn't be on the phone until her mom went to the school. Which she did on Monday, along with Trinity and Latonya. They found out that we really didn't leave school. So, we got off the hook and we started chilling with each other again. It was all good. Well, except that my mama called me between every class to make sure I was going. All of them checked in with the school occasionally to see what went on with us. We really couldn't get away with much no more at this point, because they had everybody in the school watching us.

They didn't ask them to, but sense they were calling often the people decided to watch us. They did this so they can tell everything we did, if we did something. It was crazy, but at least we got our freedom back. After a while my mama stopped calling me, and everything gradually went back to normal. They trusted us again and that's all we wanted.

Till this day, we still had no idea who those girls on 16th street was. Nobody was worried about it anymore. I figured if nobody tried to lie on us, then maybe it's somebody trying to set us up or get us back for something. Oh well, it didn't work anyway. Maybe they'll keep trying, who knows?? But we cool and everything in our life is normal as it was before.

Chapter 6

Unsupervised Staycation

One weekend sometime after being accused of skipping school, my mama sent me to my daddy, because she had to go out somewhere. I didn't really wana to be there, but she didn't want me to be unsupervised. When she was about to leave, I ran behind her and said, "Ma, I'm ready to go." She turned around, paused, looked at me and said, "Don't start."

Then she looked up at my daddy who was standing in the Livingroom the whole time and said, "If she act up…" Andre looked up at her as I looked at him as she continued, "If she do ANYTHING, please call me…" I looked at her, she continued, "Cause she already know I ain't with it."

Andre said, “Alright, I’ma take you up on that.” She opened the door, I grabbed her and said, “Mommy! Don’t leave me, I wana go with you.” She said, “Camille, cut it out. I’ll be back for you Sunday.” I said, “But Ma…!” She said, “Bye!” Then she left. After she left, I stood there looking at Andre. He picked up the phone and called somebody.

After a few seconds he said, “Hey! What’s up, aye put Rashonda on the phone.” Then he said, “How you doing? …You wana come over here? Camille bored.” She said, “She over there?!” I said, “How you gone say I’m bored?! You don’t know that!” He said, “Look at yo face, you can tell!” I said, “No you can’t!” He said, “So why you standing there?!” I started mumbling in the background.

Rashonda laughed and said, “She there for today or she staying?” Andre said, “Her mama dropped her off for the weekend, since she don’t know how to act by herself…” I butted in and said, “Yes I do!” He looked at me, shook his head and said, “Ya’ll please come cause she bothering me.” Rashonda laughed and said, “Alright.” When they hung up the phone, I said, “I’m bothering you?” He didn’t say anything, so I said, “Why you ignoring me?” He said, “Gone Cee-Cee why you bothering me?” I said, “Cause I’m bored.” He said, “Yo cousins coming later…I hope they hurry up.” I gasped and sarcastically said, “Okay! …I’ma leave you alone.” I went to my room.

An hour passed and Andre said to himself, “It’s quiet, I wonder what she doing up there.” He got up to come to my room. But when he got to the stairs somebody knocked on the door, so he went to go answer it. When he opened it, it was my cousins. He said, “I am so happy ya’ll here.” Rashonda said, “Where Camille at?” He said, “She upstairs, I was just about to check on her because she been up there for a while.” So all of them came to my room.

When Dre opened the door, I was on the phone with Cashae. After I saw them, I said, "I'ma call you back." Andre said, "What you was doing up here?" I said, "Nothing." He said, "You was too quiet to be doing nothing." I looked at him for a second, then I looked at my cousins, smiled, and said, "Hey ya'll!" My cousins said, "What's up!" Andre walked out. My cousins came in and sat down.

Latisha said, "Why yo mama dropped you off over here?" I said, "I don't know, she going out somewhere that she didn't tell me about. But that's alright cause she ain't coming back until Sunday, and I ain't finna sit here bored all weekend." Rashonda said, "See! Here you go Camille!" I said, "What?" She said, "You bout to do something that you know you ain't supposed to do, and not get in trouble for it unless yo mama find out." I said, "No I'm not…"

Just then somebody knocked on the door, I said, "It's open!" The door slowly opened, and Cashae walked in. When I saw her, I got so excited. I jumped up, hugged her and said, “You came! ...girl I am so bored, what ya’ll doing today?” My cousins paused and stared at me. I said, “What? I’m not gone do nothin to get in trouble.” Cashae said, “Hey ya’ll!” They said, “Hey Shae!” Then Cashae turned to me and said, “We supposed to go out tonight, but I don’t know if Carmen coming cause she ain’t answer her phone. But all of us definitely skipping town tomorrow.”

I said, “What?!” She said, “Yeah, we not staying here for the weekend.” I was looking devastated and said, “Where ya’ll going?” She looked at me and with her finger and arm extended, pointing back and forth from me to her, she said, “We going a little bit up the road tomorrow.” I looked at her confused and said, “Who all going?” She said, “Me, Alisha, Alicia, Carmen, Lashae, Crystal, and Camieka.” I was shocked.

I laughed a little bit and said, “Crystal going?!” Cashae said, “Yeah! …girl our mamas went to.” She was referring to the place my mama went to. I said, "When ya'll coming back?" Cashae said, "Sunday.' I said, "Oh." She sat down. I texted her, it read: Okay, but I gotta be back early on Sunday, cause my mama coming back to get me. She texted back, it read: Okay cool, but why you texting? I texted back: My daddy called them over here for me and I don't want them to know that I'm going.

She texted back: Okay, we'll talk. After about an hour Cashae got a phone call, when she hung up she said, "Camille, come outside with me." So I went outside with her. When we got out there, it was some of our homeboys in the car. We came up to the car and they said, "What's up?!" We was like, "Hey! …What's up ya'll?!" We got to talking. Then we started clowning and jumped in the car on them. Andre went to my cousins and said, "Where is Camille?" They said, "She went outside." He came out the door and saw us in the car playing around.

We barely saw him, then he said, “I’m calling!” I jumped up and ran towards him as he walked in the house. I yelled, “No!” My cousins was coming downstairs and Cashae was on her way in the house to see what happened. He picked up the house phone to call my mama, but I grabbed it while he was still holding it. I said, “No! Please?? No!” Cashae came in looking confused. Andre said, “Nope, let it go.” I said, “No please don’t call my mama!”

He said, “Why?” I quickly said, “Cause I’ma get in trouble!” He said, “Alright now, this the last time…” I said, “But this was my first time.” He looked at me for a minute, picked up the phone again and said, “You know what?” I said, “No!” But this time, he held me away from the phone and dialed the number. I started screaming, “No!!” When he said, “Hello?” I shut up and my eyes got big. Cashae looked at me and back at him. She got scared cause her mama was with my mama, and if he told on me, he was gone tell on her.

Then he said, "Yeah, aye talk to yo daughter." My heart and face just dropped as if I was saying, you actually telling on me? Then he said, "She bout to start acting up." He paused and said, "She got some boys at the house." A second later he was handing me the phone. I just stood there straight faced, until he said, "You better get the phone, that's yo mama." So I grabbed it and said, "Hello?" Latoya said, "You got a f*cking problem?!" I said, "No." She said, "What the h*ll you doing having boys over there?!"

I said, "I didn't…" She said, "You pushing me Camille! Don't make me kick yo a** when I get back there!! Let yo daddy call me one more time, I'ma come get you and beat yo a**!! You understand me?!" I said, "Yes." She said, "Now try me…give Andre the phone." I gave the phone back to him. I kept staring at him as he was talking. When he hung up, I said, "You got me in trouble." He said, "Yeah okay." Then we all went back upstairs.

While I was on the phone, all them heard my mama yelling at me. So Cashae said, "Camille, you in trouble?" I said, "If he call again I will be." She said, "Dang." Soon after that she left, before she left, she said, "Call me." Around 5:00 that evening, I called Cashae, she said, "Hello?" I said, "I thought Crystal went to grandma house?" Cashae said, "She did." I said, "But how ya'll got her to where ya'll at?" Cashae said, "Yo grandma think she at her auntie house." I said, "Oh."

She said, "So, we leaving in the morning around 5am, what time we coming to get you?" I said, "Dang! I don't know, I'm always the one with my butt on the line…you can come at 4." She said, "You sure?" I said, "Yeah, I just gotta make sure I tell my daddy them something that's gone make them think I'ma be in my room all day tomorrow." She said, "Alright, I'll check with you later." We hung up. Just then Rashonda came up behind me and said, "What are you up to Camille?"

Without turning around I gasped and said, "Nothin, wh…what you talkin bout?" She shook her head in a no motion and said, "Well, whatever it is, I really do hope you think it over and do the right thing." I turned to her smiling and said, "Rashonda I'm up to nothing." As I walked passed her, she turned me back around by my shoulder and said, "Camille listen…I never thought I'd tell you this but, you're like a role model to me. Since you still let me know you was here for me even after all those years, you gave me something to look up to. You know, here I am like wow this girl is really something special. She's strong and gets done what she needs to get done, and even though you still are all that…I guess what they say about celebrities is true…if you wana keep admiring them, it's better to know nothin about them…than to know them at all."

Then she stared at me for a second and walked out. I was so shocked, I just stood there staring into space. Soon after, I went downstairs where Andre was. He was sitting on the couch. When he saw me, he said, "What Camille?" I said, "Nothing, I just thought I should come and let you know that tomorrow is officially your day, I won't aggravate you. You can relax and I'll stay out of your way." He said, "Aw you don't have to, but I'll take it." He said that last part quick. We laughed and then I went to my room.

I thought about what Rashonda said, but I was so bored. Later on, I was kind of throwing a fit to my daddy cause I was bored. I was saying stuff like, "I wana go with my cousins," and "I wana go home." So Andre said, "You want me to call yo mama?" I just looked at him and he said, "Alright, I'ma just call yo mama." I sat there looking sad. Andre called and when my mom answered, Andre said, "Toya, yo baby over here bout to cry." She said, "Why??" He said, "Oh she bored, she wana go home, she wana go with her cousins." Latoya said, "Tell her to call me."

After he hung up, he said, "Yo mama said call her." So I went upstairs. I saw my cousins in my room, so I went to another room. I called my mama and she said, "What's wrong?" I said, "Mommy I'm bored, I been in the house all weekend so far doing nothing." She said, "I thought yo cousins was there?" I said, "They are but they bored too, he kept us in the house this whole time." She said, "Okay, well Camille it's only for a weekend…"

Just then Rashonda was passing by and stopped when she heard me talking. My back was facing the door, then I said, "But he don't wana be bothered with me." My mama said, "Camille stop that…" At this point, Rashonda looked down in concern then walked to my room to my other cousins.

I started crying and saying, "I'm ready to go…mama?" She said, "Camille just…" I said, "Mommie, I'm ready to go." It was a long pause, I said, "Mommie?" She took a deep breath just as I started crying harder, then she said, “Alright Camille.” Shortly after that we hung up. Eventually I went to my room. My cousins were just sitting there, I knew they had been talking. When I sat down, Ashley said, “Camille, you okay?” I looked at her and said, “Yeah, I’m just bored.”

Latisha said, “You seem mad.” I said, “I’m not mad, I’m just…” Rashonda cut me off and said, “Camille, we know you think yo daddy don’t wana be bothered with you.” I said, “What? ...oh, no, it’s just that…” Ashley said, “We understand.” I looked at her, then looked around and said, “Understand what? That’s not the problem, sure he wasn’t there all the time when I was little. But it don’t matter if he be here for me or if I go without him, either way I’ll be okay. I just don’t wana make him not a factor with me. It’s bad enough I have to come here, don’t get me wrong I love hanging out with ya’ll, but on top of me having to come here, he ignores me…the only time he talk to me is when my mama drop me off, even then all he say is hi. After that he go his way, I go mine, and then it's like I was better off staying home by myself cause that's how I feel here, like I'm by myself."

Rashonda said, "But he used to have you all the time, how you think you always ended up at grandma house?" I said, "Grandma used to get me." Ashley said, "What you mean?" I said, "I mean, my mama used to leave me with my grandma when she wasn't home. When grandma found out I was still here when my mama was out of town, she started picking me up like every other time I was there, to spend time with me and so I can spend time with ya'll…my daddy never got me. Even when I was over there sometimes, he would just give me a kiss and go bout his business…I guess that's just the type of person he is."

Rashonda said, "Camille…" I said, "No…don't worry bout it, I'm used to it, it's okay." Rashonda said, "No it's not, you should tell him then maybe…" I said,

"He'll ignore me like any other time??…I'm just ready to go home." Ashley said, "Camille, you know he care." I said, "I know he do, I'm just bored." Later on that night, Rashonda came in my room and said, "Camille, can I talk to you?" I said, "Yeah, what's up?" She said, "Well, I know you wana go home and I know you bored, but do you really rather run into trouble than to deal with it?"

I said, "What you mean?" She said, "You thinking about going with Cashae them up the road tomorrow." I looked at her with a blank stare. She said, "See! And I know Crystal going and she hardly get in trouble. But you thinking you have a chance of not getting in trouble just because she never get caught. It can still backfire it's not like it's just you and her…it's all ya'll, that's a big possibility of ya'll getting caught…I mean I know it sound tempting to you now, but what about later when everybody in trouble?? Why not be the one that don't get in trouble this time?"

I said, “When Crystal in trouble my mama take it out on me too.” She said, “Well she can’t take it out on you too much cause you here, you in the clear, but if you leave…” I said, “If I leave, I’ll be back before my mama get here…” She said, “How you so sure?” I said, “She coming back Sunday for me, and anyway when my cousins in trouble I don’t have nothing to do…not saying I’m trying to but, that’s why we usually get in trouble together. If it’s something we wana do but we know we gone get in trouble for it, we think twice about it. But if like 3 out of all of us do it, we all just do it because we rather get in trouble together than separately, because the ones that didn’t get in trouble gone get in trouble eventually…and that will never work.”

Rashonda was shocked and said, “Well, could you at least think about staying here until yo mama get back? I know how yo mama can get…I be feeling bad for you.” I laughed a little bit and said, “I can handle it…but yeah, I'll think about it." She was relieved. We chilled until like 1:00am, then she went to another room and went to sleep. I went to sleep too. At like 3:00am that morning, Cashae called my phone. When I picked up, I sounded tired.

Cashae said, "Hello??" I said, "Yeah." She said, "Girl, you sleep?! Come on, we ready to go." I said, "But…" Still trying to open my eyes, then Cashae said, "But what?" I said, "Nothing." She said, "Come on." I said, "I'm coming." We hung up. I sat up to put my shoes on. As I grabbed my bag I paused and thought about what Rashonda had said. When I started to feel bad about what I was about to do, my phone rung and scared me. So I jumped up fast and left out the front door. I got in the car with Cashae and the rest of my cousins. They drove an Escalade so all of us fit comfortably.

Once we got down the street, I said, "Why ya'll came so early??" Cashae said, "We had a change of plans, we wana get there early…but let's get on you…" I said, "Huh?" Cashae said, "How the h*ll you just walked out of the front door?!" They started laughing. I said, "I don't know I'm tired, I was half sleep…my daddy be sleep anyway." Then I looked over at Crystal and said, "Hi Crystal…" With a smirk on my face being funny.

She slowly looked at me quietly, then I said, "Surprised." She smirked and turned to look out the window. We got to Ft. Lauderdale in like half an hour. We went to our close friend house, we got there at 3:50am. As soon as we put our stuff down, we went to sleep. Around 9:00am somebody knocked on my daddy door. By the time he finally got to the door and opened it, Rashonda came out the room and stood leaning on the rail. My daddy opened the door wider. When Rashonda saw my mama, she just stood there.

Andre said, "What's going on?" Latoya said, "I'm coming to get Camille early, since she so traumatized." Rashonda walked to my room to get me, but she didn't see me. After a few seconds she realized that I probably left. Her eyes got so big. She went back in the hall and said, "Camille going home auntie?" My mama looked up and said, "Oh! I didn't know ya'll was still here??...Camille need to stay then." Rashonda said, "I think she changed her mind." Latoya said, "She up?" Rashonda shook her head, no.

My mama waved her hand like, oh well and said, "Uh…oh well, don't tell her I came…I'll see ya'll later." They laughed a little bit. My mama left and Rashonda was relieved that it worked. After my mama left, Rashonda called me. I picked up and said, "Hello?" Rashonda said, "Hey, Camille yo mama came for you this morning." I said, "She what?!...why??" She said, "Yeah, she came to get you early. She said since you was so traumatized." I said, "Oh my gosh, she know I'm not there?!"

Rashonda said, "No, I let her see me and said you was sleep, she said you need to stay cause we was here." I said, "Okay good." She said, "Why did you leave?" I said, "I don't know, sometimes I just do crazy stuff if I'm bored too long." She said, "Well, you need to hurry up and come back before yo mama do." I said, "She supposed to come back tomorrow." She said, "Yeah, like she came back today??" I said, "Well, I'll be there." She said, "Alright." We hung up.

Around 2:00pm me and my cousins was just chillin, then my mama called my phone. I said, "Ya'll shh be quiet…" I picked it up and said, "Hello?" My mama said, "You alright?" I said, "Yes." She said, "They told you I came this morning?" I quickly said, "Yeah, what you was doing back on this side?" She said, "I came to get you." I said, "But what were you gonna do after?" She said, "I would've stayed home." I said, "No, ma enjoy yourself don't worry about me." She said, "But didn't you wana leave?" I said, "Ma, I'm with my cousins now, that was before when I was just with him."

When I said that my cousins started smiling, cause I was talking about my auntie them kids not the kids on my daddy side. My mama said, "Alright, I'll be there tomorrow then, love you." I said, "Alright, love you too Ma." We hung up. After I got off the phone, Alisha said, "Camille you so slick." I laughed. Cashae said, "What time you tryna be back tomorrow?" I said, "Before nine."

Meanwhile back at the house, my cousins was covering for me. Like if my daddy called me or was looking for me, they would say stuff like, "She in the bathroom," or "She went to the other side of the house to get something." They was doing real good until night fall and he realized he ain't see me all day. So while my cousins was out in the front, he got up to go check my room. When he got close to my door, my cousins walked in the house. Rashonda quickly said, "She not in there!" He turned around quick and slowly headed back downstairs while he stared at them without breaking eye contact. Then he said, "Really? ...So where she at?"

Ashley said, "She on the other side of the house." He had his back turned to them in the Livingroom looking at some papers on the table and said, "I checked." My cousins looked at each other, Rashonda said, "She in the bathroom!" He said, "They empty." My cousins eyes got so big. Then Latisha said, "Oh, well then she outside." He slowly turned to them and said, "But ya'll just came from out there." Everything got quiet, my cousins looked around at each other. A split second later, they broke for the door full speed.

When they was almost completely out the door, Andre yelled, "STOP!!" They all paused kind of ducking knowing they got caught. Then he said, "Get back in here." They backed up slow. Andre looked at them, he calmly but firmly said, “I got the feeling Camille not here.” My cousins looked as if they all was holding they breath. Then Andre said, “Which one of ya’ll gone spill?” They just stood there not knowing what to do.

So Andre said, “Okay I’ll tell ya’ll what, I’ll call Camille and ask her. If she don’t answer, all ya’ll gone tell me. Then I’ma call everybody mama including Camille’s and we all gone deal with it.” At this point, my cousins was really holding they breath. They watched as he called my phone. I didn’t see when he called cause we was having fun doing our own thing. When my daddy hung up the phone, they got so scared. He said, “Well, I guess we gone do this the hard way.”

Ashley blurted out, “We don’t know where she at!” The only one who knew was Rashonda. Andre said, “I’m supposed to believe that? After ya’ll lied this whole time??” Latisha said, “She not lyin we don’t know where she at, we just woke up and she was gone.”

Rashonda and Ashley looked at her irritated. Rashonda rolled her eyes as she took a deep breath and turned back towards Andre. Andre said, "Oh! So ya'll knew she was gone since this morning??" Rashonda said, "Please don't call her mama!!" Andre said, "Naw, her mama gone know bout this, trust me…and ya'll just can't let her get in trouble by herself could ya'll? I don't know why ya'll do it."

Ashley said, "We didn't mean…" Andre said, "Where is Camille?" Ashley looked confused as she lifted her hands a bit and said, "We don't know." He said, "Okay, go upstairs…we gone find out and if ya'll lyin again then so help ya'll God!" They all went in the same room and sat there. They was scared and looking sad. Latisha said, "What if it get back to her mama??" Ashley said, "Well, they ain't gone know nothin more, cause we don't know where she at."

Rashonda was looking the most worried and she was still quiet. Ashley said, "What's wrong?" Rashonda said, "I know where she at." They stared at her in shock, then Latisha said, "Why you didn't say nothing?" Rashonda said, "What was I supposed to say?!...Oh Camille in Ft. Lauderdale for the weekend?" Then she gasped and covered her mouth. Ashley and Latisha both said, "Ft. Lauderdale?!" Rashonda said, "Shh!!" Latisha said, "Regardless of anything, you can't tell her daddy that you know where she at, cause you already told him you didn't know." Ashley said, "Then all of us gone be in more trouble."

After like an hour, Andre called out, "Aye! Rashonda, ya'll come here!!" They heard him and got up. When they opened the door, they looked down in the Livingroom and saw they mamas standing around. They ain't know what to do. When they got down to the Livingroom, Andre said, "Ya'll have a seat." My cousins sat on the couch across from they mamas. Then Andre said, "Tell them why I called them here." Rashonda said, "They don't know??" Andre said, "No, since ya'll wana lie, then ya'll gone tell them…EVERYTHING!"

Latisha mama said, "What happened?" Ashley said, "Okay, when we woke up Camille was gone, she left the house, we didn't know she was leaving, and she didn't tell us nothing. But we covered for her anyway, because we knew that she wasn't supposed to leave the house." Ashley mama said, "So why did ya'll get involved? Ya'll just as guilty." Andre said, "Exactly."

Rashonda mama said, "Where did she go?" They looked at each other cause they couldn't say they didn't know, because now they did. Andre said, "They say they don't know." He pointed at Rashonda as somebody knocked on the door and said, "But I know Camille always talking to this one right here the most, so I doubt if she don't know nothing." Then he opened the door.

As everybody looked at the door, my cousins took deep breaths tryna hold back tears. My mama walked in looking upset already, everything got extra quiet. She closed the door and said, "Hi," to everybody. They said, "Hi." Andre said, "Don't get quiet now, tell her mama where she at!" They was looking so scared, they didn't know what to do cause Latoya was intimidating them. Latoya said, "When did she leave?" Ashley and Latisha looked at Rashonda, she was looking down and said, "Sometime this morning."

My mama said, "Do you know what time?" Rashonda looked at my mama, glanced at her mama, then looked back at my mama with tears in her eyes and slightly shivering lips. My mama reached her hand out to Rashonda and said, "Come here, let me talk to you." Rashonda got up, Latoya took her hand and walked towards a room downstairs. Before they turned the corner, they saw Rashonda wiping her eyes. Andre said, "See! She know something, she bout to cry already…Toya gone break her."

Latoya took Rashonda in the back room. As soon as they sat down, Rashonda burst out in tears. Latoya just watched at first, then she said, "Rashonda, calm down and tell me what's going on." Rashonda said, "I just don't wana get in trouble or get Camille in trouble." Latoya said, "Oh no baby, Camille already in trouble just as soon as I find her a**…that's her fault, not yours."

Rashonda said, "Well, she must've left around 5 this morning. That's what I heard her whispering on the phone…I tried to stop her, but she said she was bored and she would think about it. I thought she would stay and be good this one time, but when I got up, she wasn't in her room, and I knew she left!" Latoya said, "Where did she go??" Rashonda said, "Ft. Lauderdale, she said she'll be back before you got here. She wasn't even here when you came the first time."

Latoya was shocked when Rashonda said Ft. Lauderdale, she looked surprised, and her mouth dropped. Latoya said, “When was she planning on coming back??” Rashonda said, “Tomorrow morning.” Latoya said, Okay, thanks.” They came back in the Livingroom and everybody saw that Rashonda had been crying. She sat down as Latoya stood by the front door. Latoya got her phone out and everybody knew what time it was.

She tried to hold her facial expressions back, but you can see that she was pissed off. She called my phone. I picked up not knowing she found out and said, “Hello?” She said, “Camille, where the h*ll yo a** at?!” I said, “Mommy what you talkin bout??” Latoya said, “What the f*ck yo a** doing in Ft. Lauderdale?!” Everybody was shocked. I said, “Mommy I…” Latoya said, “Mommy I nothing!

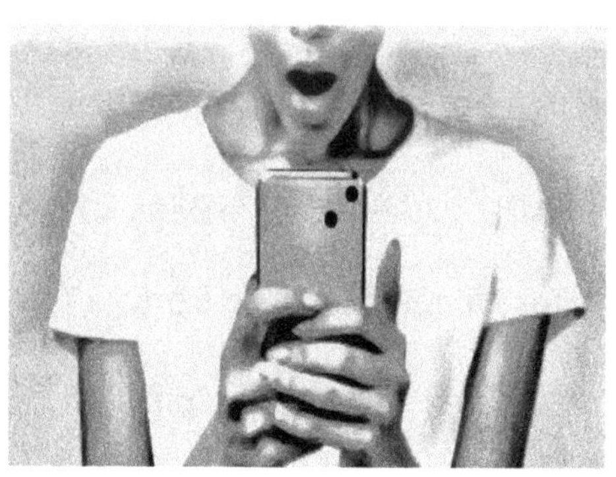

I'm beat yo a** Camille, don't f*cking play with me!! …Bring yo a** on now!!!!"

I said, "Ma but…" She said, "But?? …You know what?! Where you at?!" I said, "Ma I'm comin." She said, "No you not, what's the address??" I gave her the address. She was writing it down, then she said, "What part?" I was lightly crying and said, "Ft. Lauderdale." She said, "Alright, I'm on my way, be yo a** in place." I started crying harder and said, "Ma, you don't have to come I'm already on my way!"

She said, "Yo a** better be there when I get there!" She hung up on me. She turned to Andre them and said, "I'll see ya'll later." Then she looked at my cousins and said, "Pray for ya cousin, cause Lord knows when I get to her ain't gone be nothin nice." They all said, "See you later." Andre thought about how mad Latoya was, he got concerned and said, "Take it easy." Latoya threw up her hand in aggravation and left. My cousins sat there looking worried.

Meanwhile, I straightened myself up before anybody else saw me, and acted like everything was normal. I couldn't get ahold of any of my cousins I was with to let them know what happened, because we were in different parts of the house. So about 20 minutes later, Crystal them was running through the house just playing. She was playing with this boy that liked her. Somebody said, "Somebody at the door."

Nobody really could hear it because it was so loud in the house. One of the boys opened the door. As soon as the door opened Latoya said, "Is…" Before she could finish, she saw Crystal run past behind a boy while they played against the wall. Latoya face dropped. She couldn't believe it! She yelled, "Crystal?!" Crystal looked up still playing. When she saw my mama, she gasped, and her eyes got big.

Latoya said, "WHAT THE H*LL <u>YOU</u> DOIN HERE?!!" Crystal was so shocked she didn't know what to say. She looked back at the boy who was right behind her, then she looked back at my mama. Latoya said, "Where yo sister?!" Crystal pointed towards the room with her mouth still wide open. Latoya said, "Go get yo sh*t and let's go!!" As she said that, Alisha and Cashae walked from the back and said, "Crystal! Girl where ya'll had went?!" Latoya said, "Ya'll here too?!!"

Alisha and Cashae mouths dropped, and they froze. Just then Lashae, Camieka, and Alicia came running out the room. They bumped into everybody, laughing, almost falling and said, "We was looking for ya'll h*es!!" Before they could see my mama, Carmen ran out and bumped into the end of the line which made everybody move. She was just'a laughing, then all them looked up at my mom at the same time.

They were in shock, but instead of standing there like the rest of them, they all ran back to the rooms they came from. Carmen ran in the room I was in and said, "Girl yo mama out there." I said, "For real??...Oh sh*t." Then somebody tried to come in, but Carmen was tussling with the door until somebody said, "Open the door, it's me!" Carmen let the doorknob go and Lashae walked in. She was nervous but she calmly said, "Camille, yo mama here, d*mn all of us in trouble."

I said, "What she said?" Lashae said, "Iono we ran, Crystal, Alisha, and Cashae still out there." I took a deep breath and got up. I went out there and when Latoya saw me, she said, "Camille, go get yo sh*t and let's go!" I went in the room to get my stuff. When I came back out, Latoya said, "Lashae! Ya'll get ya stuff and let's go!!" She saw the car we came in, so all of them got they stuff, and she watched them put it in the car. Then we left. Me and Crystal was getting cursed out all the way back home.

She made us ride with her and made my cousins drive in front of her all the way home. When we got home, she made all my cousins come inside and sit down in the Livingroom. Then she said, "What the h*ll ya'll was thinking?!" She let us all have it, then she said, "Camille, Crystal, ya'll know better!! All ya'll do! ...Go to ya'll rooms until I deal with ya'll!!" Me and Crystal got up and went to our rooms. Then she turned to my cousins and said, "As for ya'll…it's enough rooms in this house, so until ya'll mamas get here I want ya'll in one of'em!"

As they got up, they were almost walking in a group going the same way. Latoya noticed that and yelled, "Separate!" They jumped and separated instantly. They all went to a room by themselves. Camieka went in my mama's room, Carmen went in a guestroom downstairs, Lashae went to another guestroom which was also downstairs, Alisha went to Reci room and Alicia went to a guestroom upstairs. The house was so quiet.

Carmen was laying on her back on the bed looking at the ceiling. Alisha was sitting on the floor in a corner staring into space. I was laying under the cover holding it tight cause I was scared as h*ll. Crystal was sitting on the side of her bed scared. Alicia was laying on her stomach hanging halfway off the bed, and Camieka was sitting on the floor on the right side of my mama bed in the corner, rocking back and forth in a daze.

All of us was bored and a little worried. We ended up staying in the rooms all day, because my aunties wasn't supposed to get back until like 11:00 that night. My mama was gone wait until morning, but she knew my aunites was gone be mad enough to go upside my cousins heads if they knew the same night they got back, because they was tired. So she called everybody's parents, except Lashae's…she planned to deal with Lashae herself.

Chapter 7

Reality Check

When my aunties got to my house late that night, they was talking about the trip and how much fun they had. In the middle of an outburst of laughter, my mama said, “Okay, now let’s talk about something more serious.” Beonca said, “Like what?” Latoya said, “Like me havin all ya’ll kids here.” They all looked confused. Latonya said, “What you talking about??”

Latoya said, “I got a phone call from Andre saying Camille was missing all day she left. So I went to check it out. Her cousin told me she went to Ft. Lauderdale.” Beonca said, “Why??” Latoya said, “I don’t know, but I called, she was there, so I went, and guess who I see running through the house along with some boy companions? …All of our kids from Alisha all the way down to Camieka." She looked at Trinity and Beonca when she said Alisha and Mieka name.

They all gasped. Latonya said, "I thought ya'll dropped Mieka and Crystal off to they grandmas houses before we left." Latoya and Beonca said, "We did." Trinity said, "So how they managed to…" Latoya said, "I don't know how they got past our mamas, but they did something believable." Trinity said, "You should ask them, did you talk to yo mama today?" Latoya said, "No, but I should…Camille?!"

About a minute later, I came out the room and paused at the site of all my aunties. Then I stared at them. Latoya said, "Come down here." When I got to the bottom of the stairs, Latoya said, "How did ya'll end up together?" I said, "Huh?" Then Trinity said, "How did ya'll get Crystal and Mieka out the house to go with ya'll?" I said, "I don't know." Latoya said, "I know you had something to do with it…so what happened?!" I said, "I…Ma! I don't know, I didn't have nothing to do with it!" Latonya said, "But you was there."

My mouth dropped. I gasped with my arms out in shock and said, "Yeah, but this time I have nothing to do with it! All I did was ride with them, I was shocked to see Mieka and Crystal too!" Beonca said, "So you mean to tell us, none of them told you nothing before all that happened?" I said, "No." Beonca said, "Camille na, that don't even sound right." I said, "It don't but it's true, whenever I'm at my daddy house, they don't tell me nothing!" Latoya said, "So how you end up with them??" I looked at her, then at the rest of them from the corner of my eye quick and confused. Then I said, "Cashae came over there and told me!" It got quiet.

Trinity said, "Okay Camille, don't sit here and lie knowing you know the truth." I took a breath and said, "I'm not lyin…" Beonca cut me off and said, "So she came to you, and you still didn't know nothing about Mieka and Crystal?" I said, "She told me they was coming, but I didn't know how she got them to come." Latoya said, "So you knew they was coming?" I said, "At the last minute."

Latoya said, "That's hard to believe…Camille didn't have nothing to do with it?? …I have to talk to the rest of them." She got up and knocked on the room door Carmen was in, then Lashae and yelled, "Carmen! Lashae! Let's go!!" She went upstairs knocking and yelling, "Cashae! Alisha! Crystal! Mieka! Let's go!!!" Soon all of them came walking slowly out the rooms, because all of us was sleep before she called us out the rooms. They all made it to the Livingroom and stood there.

Latoya said, "Crystal and Camieka…which one of them got ya'll out of ya'll grandmas houses to go to Ft. Lauderdale??" They was looking scared in the face, Trinity said, "Ya'll ain't gotta be scared, they ain't gone do sh*t to ya'll!" They was still looking around, then

Beonca looked at Camieka and said, "Who did it?" Mieka pointed and said, "Cashae." I looked at Cashae, while the rest of them looked at each other. Beonca turned her attention to Cashae looking surprised.

Latoya said, "Cashae?? …wow I would never have expected that." Beonca was still zoned in on Cashae looking so mad. I don't even think she blinked. Beonca finally said, "So what did you do?" Cashae looked at her and said, "I just picked her up and said she'll be back." Everybody kind of glanced at Cashae so it wouldn't be noticeable because she lied. But we let it go, because if she got caught it was just gone come back on her and that was a lot for one person to deal with.

Beonca squinted and said, "That don't sound right." She kind of quietly said that to herself. Latoya looked at me and said, "If I find out you had anything to do with this, that's yo a**." I just looked away from her looking sad. Just then Beonca said, "Yo grandma said, you told her Mieka was going to her auntie house." Everybody stopped and looked at Beonca, because nobody knew she was on the phone. Cashae said, "No I didn't." Beonca said, "Ma she said she didn't, what you said she said?" Cashae was shocked. You can hear her grandma talking loud on the phone.

Beonca said, "Hold on, hold on Ma…" She put the phone on speaker and said, "Okay, na tell her what she said?" So her mama said, "You told me, I'm going to my auntie's house. I'm taking Camieka so she can get more clothes she'll be back, did you not tell me that?" Cashae said, "I never said I didn't tell you that." Cashae said it kind of low, her grandma knew she said something but didn't know what she said. Her grandma said, "Huh? What did you tell your mom you didn't say?"

Cashae said, "My mama didn't say all that, I just…" Her grandma said, "Excuse me?" Cashae got quiet, then her grandma said, "Cashae?" Cashae said,

"Ma'am?" She said, "What did you tell me? Tell your mom what you told me." Cashae said, "Grandma, I told you she was going to my auntie house…" She said, "And didn't you tell me she was going to get some clothes?" Cashae said, "Yes ma'am." She said, "And did you not say she would be back?" Cashae said, "Yes ma'am." Her grandma said, "Okay, so why are you sitting there lyin to your mother?" Cashae mumbled, "I wasn't lyin, she got some more clothes so she can go to Ft. Lauderdale." All of us heard her and bust out laughing so loud.

Our mamas looked at us so shocked. Beonca mama was on the phone saying something, but we couldn't hear over our laughter. While we were laughing, Cashae said, "Sh*t oh well, I would've brought her back, but we got caught before they got back." When we heard her say that we laughed even harder. Beonca told her mom, "Ima call you back."

When she got off the phone, Latoya said, “Camille, bring yo a** here!”

I came and she said, “What’s so f*cking funny?!” Still laughing, I said, “Ma you ain’t hear Cashae? …” She said, “That ain’t no reason for you to laugh!” I sucked my teeth and said, “Ma she saying…” Latoya said, “I don’t care what she saying! …” I had the giggles, so I was still laughing, she said, “Oh so you still laughing?! …go get yo sh*t!!” I instantly stopped laughing and was looking shocked.

I said, “For what?!” She said, “Get yo sh*t so you can go somewhere else before I have to kick yo a**!” As I walked to the stairs, I said, “How I get in trouble for laughing?” Latoya said, “Shut yo a** up!!” I went to my room and got some clothes. After a while, Latoya called me. By the time I got downstairs, Cashae was getting into it with Beonca. I guess she must’ve got hit, because Beonca was sitting in a different chair closer by the door and Cashae was standing on the wall looking pissed off.

I stood next to her while she zoned in on Beonca with tears in her eyes. Then Latoya said, "Lexi on her way for you." I instantly got tears in my eyes and said, "I don't wana go to her house!" Latoya said, "And I didn't want you to go to Ft. Lauderdale, but you did, so you going!" I dropped my arms lazily throwing a minor fit, breathing hard and crying medium-like. Trinity said, "D*mn, what's so bad about her house?" She was just asking expecting to not get an answer, but I answered anyway and said, "She don't let me do nothing!"

Latonya said, "That's because you always in trouble whenever you go over there." Just then Cashae had a little outburst and said, "I know she bet not touch me again." I managed to look over at Cashae, she was holding her face and looking at Beonca puffing up. Unfortunately, Beonca put together what Cashae said, and said, "What?!" Cashae eyes got a little bigger, then

Cashae ran out the door. She ran so fast nobody saw it coming. Beonca got up and said, "I'm bout to kill this girl." As she walked out, I heard her yell, "Cashae!" Then she walked towards her direction.

After that happened, my mom saw me inching towards the door and said, "Stay yo a** right there! I wish you would try that sh*t!!" At that point, I just bawled up on the floor crying with my back against the wall. I was crying so hard. My mama got up to go in the kitchen for a minute. While she was in there, I saw Alexi car pull up, so I went outside. I only went outside to hide, but when I was walking down the sidewalk, Alexi let the window down and said, "Camille!"

I turned around and she said, "Come here." She let the window up and got out the car. Just then my mama came out the kitchen. When she saw that I wasn't sitting there, she was about to lose it. She asked my aunties, "Where is Camille?!" As Latonya got up, she said, "I think she went outside…Carmen bring ya a**.” Latoya said, “What?!” She hurried to the door and stopped at the entrance. Then she said, “Cam…!”

She stopped because she saw me by Alexi car. Then she said, “You been out here?!” Alexi said, “Yeah!” She said, “Oh okay.” While everybody was about to leave, Latoya started explaining what happened. Towards the ending of her explaining to Alexi I started crying lightly, because I didn’t wana go and it was nothing I can do about it. Even when I get to her house, I wouldn’t be able to sneak away.

Latoya said, “So, don’t let her do <u>nothing</u>.” When she said that, I burst out with, “Ma, don’t tell her that!” Alexi looked shocked and said, “What?! You wasn’t gone do nothing anyway!” That’s when I started going crazy. I screamed as I started moving down the sidewalk trying to get away from them. I screamed, “No! I don’t wana go!! …No!” Both of them budged at me at the same time. When they did that, I screamed like somebody was murdering me.

That's when they stopped, all of my aunties and cousins turned around looking at me like I was crazy. I looked at my phone and started pressing buttons. Latoya said, "Camille, bring yo a** here and stop making all that d*mn noise!!" I had the phone to my ear and said, "No!!" Still crying. By then Andre answered the phone and heard me crying, all he could say was, "Hello?!!" Then he shut up and listened to my background. Latoya said, "Camille you got one more time before I…" I said, "Nooo!!" Which pissed her off.

She started walking towards me real quick and her face expression was pissed. I got sooo scared and screamed as I backed up, "No!!!!" Andre said, "Camille! What's going on?!!!" I said, "Leave me alone!!" I had my hand up trying to signal her to stop. As she walked up on me, she said, "Who the f*ck you talking to??!" I said, "No!!" Then I ran a little bit and she said, "Move one more time, I'ma beat yo a**!!!!" I said, "No! I'm sorry! Noo!!" When she got to me, she pointed to the car and said, “Get yo a** over there and get in the f**king car.”

I softly said, “No…” She said, “I’ma say it one more time, get yo a** in the…” I said, “No…” Then she back handed me, I fell to the ground as I let out a painful scream. Then the phone hung up. My aunties looked concerned, and you can tell Latoya didn’t wana hit me, because she eased up although she still hit me hard. I laid on the ground crying. Latoya picked me up by the front of my shirt and had me jacked up as she dragged me all the way back to the car. When she got to the car, she threw me against the car. I didn’t know what she was gone do next because she got a phone call.

She answered it and as soon as she picked up, I heard yelling, then I heard her say, “Andre don’t…!!” My eyes got big, I ran to the other side of the car and opened the back door. She looked at me and said, “So now you wana get in the car? Camille don’t f*ck with me!!" I jumped in the car because I was scared. My aunties was shaking they heads. As Alexi pulled out, my mama was walking in the house.

Trinity said, "What happened?" Latoya said, "She had Andre on the phone that whole time." Trinity shook her head, took a breath, rolled her eyes a little bit and said, "See ya'll later." Latoya said, "Okay." She went back in the house, and everybody left. My mama had done hung up on him. Soon after everybody left Andre called her back, she picked up and they went at it hard. He said, "What the h*ll going on?! Camille screaming going crazy and sh*t!" Latoya said, "Ain't sh*t going on! She lucky her a** still conscious right now!!"

Andre said, "What the f*ck you did to my daughter?!" Latoya gasped and said, "Oh, so now she yo daughter?! Where were you when she had time to do all this stuff?! If you care so much!! You should've been paying attention and watching <u>yo</u> daughter!!" He said, “What the h*ll you think I was doing?!” She said, “From what she was telling me, you was ignoring her!!” He took a breath and said, “She had her cousins, I was in the Livingroom, why would she need my attention?!”

Latoya said, “That’s why she go over there…to spend time with you!! Andre, I promise, you…!” He said, “She ain’t no baby! She should be able to go upstairs by herself or with company for a while!!” She said, “Long enough for her to devise a plan big enough to go away for the whole weekend?!” He said, “Where is Camille?” She said, “She gone.” He said, “What you mean?!” Latoya said, “I couldn’t take her, if she would’ve stayed here, she would’ve been in the hospital!”

Andre got real heated and said, “You hit her?!” That’s why she called me screaming?!” Latoya sucked her teeth. He said, “What the h*ll you did to my child?!!” Latoya hung up. Meanwhile my cousins on my dad side was listening to everything, from the time I called my daddy screaming, to the time when Latoya hung up on him. By this time their parents left, they slowly walked up to Andre.

Rashonda nervously said, "Uncle Dre…what happened to Camille?" Andre said, "Her mama sent her away." He was still pissed off. Rashonda was looking sad. Afterwhile, Andre couldn't take much more of it. He got up and started mumbling, "Hanging up on me, got her screaming, probably beating on my child…sending her away." He grabbed his keys and walked out the house slamming the door. At that point Rashonda turned around and ran for the phone.

Ashley said, "What's going on??" Rashonda said, "I think he finna go to Camille house cause he mad at her mama." Then she dialed a number and finally said, "Grandma, if Uncle Dre go to jail, then that's on him!" She said, "Well wait minute baby, what happened?" She said, "Him and Auntie got into it bout

Camille, and now he on his way over there because he mad!" My grandma said, "Now why would he…I told him bout going after them girls like that, cause it's just gone get him in trouble. When did he leave??"

Rashonda said, "He just left, but none of us know where they stay at!!" She said, "Okay, well stay calm and I'll call him and see what's going on." Rashonda said, "Okay." Then they hung up. Ashley said, "What she said?" Rashonda said, "She gone call him then call us back." Ashley said, "Okay…I'm worried I can't sit around and just wait, I need to know if Camille alright…did you try to call her phone?" Rashonda said, "No, usually when she in trouble she don't have it…but this is an emergency." So she picked up the phone and called back to back like 3 times, and left me an urgent message.

She then left two text messages saying: CAMILLE PICK UP!! The other message said: I NEED TO TALK TO YOU! IT'S IMPORTANT!!!

Alexi had my phone and got a little curious about the text messages, so she called my mama. My mama picked up and Alexi said, "Hey, Toya is everything okay?" Latoya said, "Yeah." Alexi said, "Okay, who is Rashonda?"

Latoya said, "Camille cousin on her daddy side." Alexi said, "Well, she been blowing Camille up urgent, sending her messages saying pick up now I need to talk to you, and she left a voicemail, but I didn't…" Latoya said, "Check it." So Alexi hung up, called my mama off my phone, and checked the message.

It said, "Camille, I wish you would pick up the phone, yo daddy lost it and now he on his way to yo mama house to do Lord knows what…I know you not there, but you need to know in case something go down! Hurry up, we worried!!" After that message my mama said, "Uh! ...who…?!" Just then somebody started banging on the door, Alexi heard it through the phone. Latoya said, "Hold on, wait a minute…" She got up and look through the peep hole and said, “That’s him.” Alexi said, “Oh my goodness.” Latoya said, “Yeeeah, he look like he out of it, but he ain’t stupid.”

Just then he hit the door so hard, it sounded like he kicked it and he said, “Open this d*mn door!!” That pissed her off, she snapped and said, “You better stop hittin my mutha f*cking door like that!!” Then he hit it again and said, “I’ma knock this b*tch down if you don’t open this door!” Alexi said, “Oh no…” Latoya said, “Don’t f*ck with me Dre, I would beat yo a**!!” Just then Alexi said, “Toya!” Latoya paused to say, “Huh?” Alexi said, “Call yo sisters, I’m on my way!”

Latoya said, “Alright.” Alexi said, “Don’t open that door Toya!” She said, “Oh he ain’t getting in here!” Alexi said, “Alright.” Then they hung up. Alexi came to me and said, “Camille, let’s go <u>now</u>.” So I got up not suspecting nothing. It was 2 in the morning, and I was sleep when she came to me. Nobody told me nothing. A little while later we pulled up on the side of the house, closer to Beonca house because it was so many cars at my house.

I was looking down at first, but when I looked up, my eyes glistened like it was no tomorrow. My face was confused, then a feeling of worry came over me as I sat up in the passenger seat to get a better view. I softly said to myself while I looked, “What happened?” As Alexi parked the car, I saw my mama standing in the doorway zoned in at something. Then I saw her mouth move. Once her mouth moved, the crowd of my aunties, uncle, and cousins moved.

I stepped out the car stunned. As I closed the door, still not taking my eyes off of them, I saw Andre walking towards my mama yelling and pointing at her. Then I started speed walking up to the scene. Once I got close enough, I was right in the middle of them still looking confused. Everybody got quiet and looked at me as that happened. Alexi walked up a few seconds after me. Latoya whispered to Alexi, "Why did you bring her? I thought she was gone stay at the house."

Alexi said, "I'm sorry, she was sleep, I didn't wana leave her by herself." Latoya said, "I didn't want her to see this." Just then Andre said, "Camille! You alright?!" I just looked at him. My eyes were swollen because I had been crying so hard and so long. Then I looked at Latoya and said, "Mommy, what happened?" At that time, he grabbed me by the arm pulling me towards him quick. When he did that, Latoya stopped talking and said, "Don't pull on her like that!" All the attention went on us.

He kept pulling me, so Latoya came from off the porch to get me back from him. Andre said, "Back up…Toya back up!" My mama grabbed my wrist and said, "You better let my baby go." She started walking back towards the house holding my hand. As she walked, he loosened his grip until he finally let me go. She led me in the house with my own arm, she stopped at the door blocking the entrance. She was facing Andre again, I was standing behind her.

When Andre started talking again, Latoya kind of looked over her shoulder and said, "Go upstairs." So I went upstairs to my room not knowing what to do, because I wasn't supposed to be home." While all them was outside getting into it, I was sleepy so I fell asleep waiting on instructions on what to do next. No police had to come that night thank God. Soon everybody had done cleared it. Before Alexi left, she came to Latoya and said, "Camille staying here?"

Latoya said, "Oh…I forgot she was up there." She came to check on me and saw that I was sleep, so she told Alexi, "No, I'ma just keep her here, she sleep." Alexi said, "Alright, I'll bring her stuff tomorrow." Latoya said, "Alright." Then she left. Shortly after that, Latoya went to bed. The next day when everybody was up in the house, everybody kind of stayed in their room because of what happened the night before. I really wanted to stay out of the way because I knew it was tension. Crystal never did anything like this before, so she was just scared to move.

My mama ain't say nothing to us since before we all got into it. So we didn't know what to do. After a while, I figured that maybe she might let it go. But like 20 minutes later, I heard voices, so I turned my tv down. I heard Latoya fussing. She said, "You starting to act just like yo sister was acting before she started showing her a**!! …Either you cut the crap, or I'ma beat it out yo a**!!" Then I can hear Crystal's light voice trying to talk, she said, "Mommy I…" Latoya said, "Shut yo a** up! Why the h*ll you starting to act out?! …I should go cross yo sh*t right now! …"

Crystal got loud and said, "It's not even that serious!" My mama instantly hit her. I covered my mouth in surprise when I heard Crytsal yell that to my mama. But when I heard her get hit, I got so scared. Then I heard Latoya say, "Who the h*ll you think you talking to?!" I heard Crystal crying loud still trying to explain. This time Crystal shut her mouth. My mama said, "Don't try me Crystal, I will f*ck yo a** up!! …and you ain't going nowhere no time soon! Since you wana act like Camille, you gone get treated like Camille!!"

At that point, I ran in my bathroom and locked the door. Crystal was crying even harder because she knew what was up. Then I heard Latoya yell, "Camille?!" I turned on the shower so fast. Latoya came in my room and knocked on my bathroom door. I lied and said, "I'm in the shower!" She said, "Hurry up!" I stayed in there for like 15 minutes. When I came out, my mama was coming in my room again. She must've heard me coming out. When I saw her, she paused, then she said, "Okay first off, I'm tired of yelling right now, but I'ma ask this…why must you always be in something??"

I said, “Ma, I don’t mean to be bad or get into stuff, I just be bored.” She said, “Right now Crystal is doing the same sh*t you did when you was her age, and I refuse to go through it twice. She don’t need to be getting into nothing and you don’t either. So while you watching yourself watch yo sister, and the stuff I don’t catch you stop her from doing.” I just looked at her.

She continued, “I’m trying so hard to let ya’ll keep ya’ll freedom and ya’ll social life, but I am so tempted to put ya’ll in home school and limit and monitor where ya’ll go.” My mouth dropped. She said, “Ya’ll pushing me Camille and the only reason I haven’t gone over the edge is because I can’t, ya’ll my kids and I won’t allow ya’ll to push me to that point.”

I opened my mouth to say something, but she cut me off and said, “Don’t say nothing, and as of now ya’ll on punishment or you can call it lock down. Go tell yo friends, tell whoever you wana hang out with give’em a heads up, cause ya’ll ain’t going nowhere no time soon and I mean that sh*t…don't start trying to feel sorry for yourself cause it's too late to cry now, but you think about that…and if ya'll wana still do what ya'll be doing after this time …then it's really something wrong with ya'll, cause ain't no loop holes, lea ways, or getting by this round, ya'll on straight lock down…AND I WANT YA'LL TO FORGET IT." Then she walked out my room, I was scared to even move.

It's weird, out of all the times I ever got yelled at or got in trouble, this time I was scared the most. I always thought that my mama yelling scared me the most, but this time she was calm and consistent. I guess it was because she seemed like she really had enough this time. Like she would've went over the edge if we wasn't her kids, as if we really drive her that crazy.

Almost make you feel like she would give up on us if she could. That made me think a lot, I kind of felt bad. I went to Crystal room. She must've got hit in the face because she was holding it. I came in and closed the door, Crystal was pissed off. I calmly said, "Crystal what's wrong with you?" She angrily said, "Forget this Camille, I'm ready to have fun I'm tired of…" I said, "Crystal, shut up." She paused and looked at me confused.

I said, "What the h*ll happened to you? You don't act like this…I heard what you said to mommy, you ain't have no business saying that…" She said, "You talking bout me! Look at you! You do a lot of stuff to mommy, not verbally but physically and that's worst! This ain't nothin compared to what you do!!" I said, "Don't focus on what I do! I try to stay out of stuff, you try to get into stuff!! You need to go back to being yourself and stop trying to follow what I did wrong!"

She said, "But ya'll had all ya'll fun and you get away with it!" I said, "I ain't have nobody to tell me something was wrong to do while I was my peers, although I should've known better! And I don't get away with sh*t!! Mommy never wanted you to see me get in trouble because you would probably be scared!! All them times you was at grandma house and auntie house?! Why you think you was over there so much?! …She sent me to the hospital plenty of times, why you think you used to stay for the weekend when she dropped you off for a day?! She wanted me to recover physically before you came back! And you think I got away with it?! Everything I did even the littlest things she got me for! You would think I'm stupid cause I kept doing sh*t! But I learned and apparently, I'm still learning! You don't know the half Crystal! …And she bout ready to do you the same way! So either you cut it short, or you go through what I went through and learn the hard way!!!"

Crystal was looking down still kind of mad, but she knew she couldn't top what I said. She looked like she was thinking. Then I said, "Unless you gone straighten up, I guess we gone trade places cause I'm done with that sh*t." Then I walked out and went back to my room looking mad. After I went in my room, my mama stepped out of hers looking shocked but impressed. She smirked a lil bit and shook her head a bit in a yeah motion. She was amazed something like that came out of Camille's mouth.

She was so shocked by it, she didn't think about the few curse words I threw in. I would've got my face knocked off if she knew we spoke like that. Crystal thought about it long enough to feel bad, so she went on a silent streak. Monday, my mama dropped us off to school. Between me and my cousins we was pretty quiet. I guess all of us was in trouble some kind of way.

After school all of our parents was in the front and on time, we all got in our mamas cars without saying bye to each other. When I go home, I went in my room. Crystal get out of school a lil later than I do, so she wasn't home yet. My mama wasn't gone leave me home by myself, so Beonca dropped Crystal off since she was already at her school to get Camieka.

My mama was sitting in the Livingroom, I was standing by the rail upstairs leaning on it looking down at my mama. Then Crystal walked in the house. Me and my mama looked at her as she slowed down. She looked at me then she looked at my mama. She closed the front door and dropped her bag on the floor next to her. She said, "Ma." As she she slowly walked towards her, my mama was shocked and on edge.

When Crystal got closer, she said, "Mommy I'm sorry, I know this not me. I don't know what I was thinking, but I'm done with trying to do stuff I'm not supposed to do. Now I know Camille didn't get away with it and I won't either. I also understand that I have the choice that Camille may have been deprived of, so I'ma choose to take the easy way out and cut it short…Oh, and I'm sorry for mouthing off earlier, I didn't mean it." I took a light breath and smiled a little.

My mama said, “Wow, thank you for coming to grips before it was too late. I didn’t think you would come around, but I guess I was wrong.” Crystal said, “Yeah and besides, I don’t want you to put me in the hospital.” I laughed to myself as my mama looked up at me like, you told her?? I smiled and shrugged my shoulders as if I was saying, I had to. She smiled at me. Crystal hugged her and as my mama hugged her back, my mama looked at me and mouthed, “Thank you.”

I smiled big and shook my head as in you’re welcome. After that the tension in the house went to no tension at all. Yes, we was still on lock down, but we took it like soldiers cause we had to do the time for what we did wrong. The punishment lasted long, but it helped me and Crystal be better people and realize what we was getting into. It also showed my mama we changed and that we were still her little girls. Everything was better and normal again, at least for the time being.

Chapter 8

Careless

A long time after our punishment was over, we went to school feeling like ourselves for the first time again. We had a lot of time to recover from our punishment and being in trouble. We also had a lot of time to forget how intense the trouble was for us acting out. When we went to school this day, for some reason we were all in a really good mood.

We didn't know it yet but once we got in the classroom for the class we all shared, our playful side started to show. First, we were giggling randomly, any and everything made us laugh. We were supposed to be doing independent study, the class was very quiet. Carmen got bored, I saw her put her phone on Cashae's desk and heard her say press play. This girl stands up on her desk in the middle of class, oddly no one but the people next to her saw her.

When she was standing straight up, I guess that was Cashae's queue to press play on the phone, because the music started as soon as she did that. I mean it was LOUD. Carmen started to dance. She low key was seducing the boys in class without noticing it, it was a slower dance but not too slow.

Everybody looked at her as soon as they heard the music, even the teacher. Our teacher mouth dropped, she snatched her glasses off. She was in shock for a few seconds and Carmen kept dancing without a care in the world. We were surprised she did that, but we were laughing discreetly waiting to see what would happen next. The teacher finally stood up and said, "Carmen!" Carmen kept dancing. The teacher said, "Carmen!" Carmen didn't respond.

The teacher walked up to Carmen who was still dancing and said, "Carmen Rogers!" Carmen looked down at her with her eyes only and said, "Huh?" While she continued to dance! We laughed harder and hid our faces. Carmen was really wrecking this lady nerves. The teacher said, "Get off the desk please!" Cashae pressed the button on the phone to stop the music. She did it quick, so the teacher didn't see her.

The teacher was looking confused because she had no idea where the music came from and how it stopped. We were trying to hold back. Cashae had her head down in her arms on her desk silently crying laughing. Carmen stopped dancing and jumped off the desk. Carmen looked at the teacher and said, "You said something?" She said it like it was so normal. We were dying, it was so funny. The teacher said, "Are you serious??" Carmen said, "You heard the music?"

We all looked up at them, the teacher said, "Yes! I'm sure everyone down this hallway heard it, it was very loud." Carmen said, "See, I couldn't hear you. The music was playing, you gotta speak up next time."

The teacher stood there looking confused as she let out a quick loud breath. Carmen sat down and pretended to do her work like normal. The teacher walked away and sat back at her desk like nothing happened.

We couldn't hold it in no more and we all burst out laughing loud at the same time. The teacher stood up, looked at us and said, "Girls??" We stopped and got quiet. After she stopped looking at us, we all whispered to each other and laughed. We couldn't believe she got away with that. Another 10 minutes went by, but it felt like longer. Cashae said, "Uggggh, why is this class not over?!" She did not try to say that low, she was loud. Some of our classmates laughed and some even agreed, saying, "For real," and "Yeah I feel like I slept here last night."

The teacher said, "Excuse me!" The class got quiet. The teacher said, "Cashae, no more interruptions." Cashae said, "Okay, can you tell it to stop?" The teacher said, "Tell what to stop?" Cashae said, "You said no more interruptions." The teacher said, "Yes, I did." Cashae said, "But you not stopping it, can you please tell it to stop??" The teacher said, "Tell what to stop??" Cashae said, "Yo class, it's interrupting my sanity!"

When I tell you that whole classroom was filled with laughter, even Cashae had to laugh as she was leaned over backwards on her chair. We couldn't hide our laughter and didn't try to, we was almost on the floor laughing. We was so loud the teacher next door came to check on us, because his class thought there was a fight or something. After the teacher left, our teacher was so embarrassed. She said, "Cashae Knight!" Cashae was still laughing and said, "I'm sorry ma'am but yo class driving me crazy." The teacher went back to her desk. I looked at Cashae and shook my head. The teacher was pretty quiet for a minute.

Just as I thought she got away with it too, the teacher stood up and said, "Cashae?" Cashae looked at her, the teacher said, “Please come get this.” Cashae got up and when she got to the teacher, she grabbed the paper from her hand and looked at it. Cashae stopped as she looked at the paper confused and said, “You gave me a detention, because yo class boring??” The teacher said, “Cashae?” Cashae said, “You the one that need a detention, better yet you need to be expelled for this boring a** class.” We all laughed again.

The teacher said, “Cashae please have a seat.” Cashae said, “I’m changing my project too, I’ma write about you now.” We started laughing again, Cashae sat down. Then the teacher said, “Carmen?” Carmen was surprised and said, “Huh??” She said, “This is for you.” Carmen got up and took the paper, when she saw she had a detention too she said, “What I did??” The teacher said, “At first, I was going to let it go but since Cashae acted out afterwards, I had to give you one too. I don’t want anyone to think they can get away with acting out.”

Carmen walked back to her desk and said, "Acting out? I was dancing, you ain't see me act out yet." The teacher said, "Excuse me, is that a threat?" Carmen said, "No, it's the truth." The teacher was speechless, she sat back down at her desk. Carmen and Cashae was pissed off, they stopped doing their work for a while. Me, Alisha, Alicia, and Lashae was the only ones that didn't get in trouble. Carmen kept staring at me. She got mad when I would look back at her and laugh, because I knew she was doing that because she was in trouble.

Cashae interrupted her staring at me and said, "Hey ya'll look…" We all looked and saw her holding up a picture she drew of our teacher, we couldn't hold our laughter. She drew the lady so ugly. I don't know what type of shape that was, but I never saw anybody's body look like that. I'm not gone even get on the face and the two stitches she drew as the hair. She had the nerve to write a story about the lady and included a how to guide for having a fun class for dummies.

The teacher was annoyed at this point, she yelled, "Carmen! Cashae!" They both said, "Why you calling my name?!" The teacher said, "You two keep interrupting my class." Carmen said, "Everybody was laughing." The teacher went back to what she was doing. Carmen looked at me again, I looked at her and both of us laughed. She said, "It's not funny." I said, "Don't get mad at me because you in trouble." I kept laughing at her. She got mad, laughed and said, "It's funny huh?" I said, "Yep." She snatched my composition book off my desk.

Before I could say anything, she threw it at the teacher. I was standing up over Carmen because I was trying to get it back before she threw it. After she threw it, she sat down quick. She looked at me with her arms folded and a smirk on her face and said, "Now you in trouble too." My mouth was wide open. When the teacher looked up, she only saw me standing up looking at her shocked. She said, "Really?!" I said, "I didn't throw that." She looked in the composition book and saw my name, she said, "Camille Lockhart…this is your book and you're standing up. Come get your book and get this too."

She slapped a white paper on top of it. I walked to her desk and saw a detention. I looked at her and said, "I didn't throw that at you." She said, "Yeah, and you guys aren't acting up today either. Go have a seat." I took my book and the paper. As I walked back to my desk I said, "You ain't see acting out yet." She said, "Excuse me?" I said, "I believe you heard me…and that's a threat." Carmen was shocked I said that, you saw it all on her face, while the class said, "OOOOHHH." I was mad, but when I got to my seat, I looked at Carmen and smiled.

She was laughing, I said, "Okay, we gone see who have the last laugh Carmen." She just smiled and didn't say anything. The teacher watched me until I got to my seat, because she couldn't believe what I said to her. Once I got to my chair, she went back to doing what she was doing. Me and my cousins were talking amongst ourselves. We compared detentions and realized the detentions were for the same day.

That made us mad because they're supposed to give us a heads up. I told Carmen, "You need a double detention since you got mine for me." We started laughing. Carmen said, "We'll at least we won't be by ourselves, right Cashae?" During this time, Alisha was signaling me, and I kept looking back at her. As Carmen kept making jokes about me being in trouble, both twins pulled out pillows from their bags. I was looking like, where the heck ya'll get pillows from?? But I didn't say anything so I wouldn't ruin what they were about to do.

In the middle of Carmen talking, Alisha and Alicia started hitting Carmen with the pillows. They yelled, “Pillow fiiiight!!” Carmen put her head down and screamed while she smiled. Me and Cashae was laughing, our classmates thought it was so funny. The teacher got up so fast and said, “Stop that!” They kept going, until Carmen snatched Alisha’s pillow and hit me with it. I said, “I didn’t even hit you.” Alicia threw me her pillow and I hit Carmen.

The teacher started to walk fast towards us still yelling, “Stop that right now!” Cashae snatched the pillow from Carmen, and we started double teaming Carmen. She was laughing and screaming the whole time. When the teacher got to us, we stopped right away. She looked at all of us and said, “I cannot believe the way you ladies are acting right now! Put those pillows away!” We gave them back to the twins. As the teacher was lecturing us, we noticed the twins cutting the side of the pillows.

When the teacher thought she had us together, she turned her back to walk away. At this time the twins gave the pillows back to me and Cashae. They signaled us to start swinging them again, so we did. As soon as we did, there was feathers all over the place. You couldn't see us that's how thick they were. All you heard was laughing and all you saw were feathers. Some of the other students were picking them up and throwing them at each other.

All of a sudden, our teacher yelled, "Hey!!" We all stopped because she was extra loud. As the feathers fell to the floor, we noticed our teacher was covered from head to toe with feathers. The room got quiet, she turned to look at us and blew feathers from her lips. At that moment, it was all over. We all laughed so hard at her, it made her so angry. She walked to her desk and said, "Alisha and Alicia you can join your cousins in detention, come get your slips!" After the twins got the slips, we were still standing up holding the pillows. She looked at us and said, "Camille, Carmen and Cashae…get out of my classroom!"

When she said that, the bell rung. We shrugged our shoulders, dropped the pillows and said, “Oh, okay it’s time to go anyway.” We got our stuff and started to walk out the classroom. On our way out, she heard Cashae say, “That was a fun class, I can’t wait for the next class.” The teacher was holding her head as she took a deep breath. She was stressed. We all had to also place our assignments on her desk before we left, which we did. When we got out in the hallway, we were laughing at everything that happened in the classroom.

I asked Alisha, “Where did ya’ll get those pillows from anyway??” My other cousins said, “Right!” The twins laughed and Alisha said, “We was tired this morning and thought we would need them to sleep in class.” We all burst out laughing. Carmen said, “Dang, ya’ll must’ve been real tired to be that bold and plan to sleep on pillows in class.” We all laughed even more. Then I turned to Lashae and said, “At least <u>you</u>

didn't get detention Shae." She smiled and said, "I know right?"

At that moment she ran ahead of us. We watched her to see where she was going. She ran to this fire extinguisher that was on the floor and picked it up. We walked up to her as she was looking at it. Carmen said, "Where that come from?" Lashae said, "I don't know, it must've fell off the wall or something." Cashae said, "Girl put that down and come on." Lashae was still examining the fire extinguisher, as she lowly said, "I always wondered how these things worked."

Alisha said, "Shae come on leave that thing alone." Lashae said, "I think you just press…" Right before she finished speaking, the principal walked up and said, "What are you girls doing?" He scared us, Lashae gasped looking up at him and accidently pressed the handle on the fire extinguisher. The foam went all over his face, his suit and his glasses. It happened so fast. We all just stood there staring at him with our mouths open.

He was so mad, he took his glasses off. We tried to hold back our laughter, he looked funny because the only place that didn't have the foam was his eyes. Lashae was the only one not smirking, but that's because he was looking at her and she was still in shock. Once he collected himself, he said, "Ms. Lockhart!" I made a face like, dang. I have to admit, it was weird to hear someone say that and they're not talking to me. But in this case, I was happy it wasn't me for a change.

Lashae said, "I'm sorry, I didn't mean to press that, you scared me." He said, "You shouldn't have that in the first place." She said, "I'm sorry, I..." He took the fire extinguisher and said, "You can explain it in detention, after school...today." She took a breath and said, "Aww man." She was almost whining. He walked away. Cashae and Carmen started laughing so hard.

Lashae said, “I’m mad and ya’ll laughing.” Cashae said, “We sorry Shae, that was funny and now he walking around looking like a melted frosty the snowman.”

We laughed even more. Carmen said, “Yeah, he gone scare a whole lot more people before he get a chance to clean up.” We were all cackling. Lashae was still mad, so she didn’t think it was funny. I said, “Dang Shae, you almost made it, now you right along with us.” She sucked her teeth a little bit and eventually started laughing. After she got over being mad, she realized how funny it was and couldn’t stop laughing like us. She even said, “I’m glad it hit him, he gave me a detention, at least it was worth it. If I knew I was gone get in trouble, I would’ve emptied the extinguisher on his a**.” We thought that was the funniest thing, we laughed continuously throughout the school day about it.

We were having so much fun. We didn't once think about our mamas, and how much trouble we would be in if they found out what we did in school. Well at least not until the school bell rung for school release. We all met in the hallway near pick up, trying to figure out what we were going to do about our detentions. Knowing our mamas was outside waiting on us, we didn't have the guts to stay after school. We planned to make it home and pick up the 6:00 phone call the school would make to tell our parents on us.

We tried to play it safe, because our mamas by any means could not find out we got detention or the reasoning behind it. When we got home, we were so scared and hoped we would catch the phone call. It was kind of risky, because 6:00 is kind of late and our mamas would definitely be home and settled in. I didn't do anything else but watch the phone. If anyone from our school called, they would call the house phone in the Livingroom because it has a separate line. I became too paranoid and couldn't take it no more.

I snuck downstairs and unplugged the phone cord to where you wouldn't know it was unplugged. I did this around 5:30pm. Thank God my mom didn't try to use it, because I left it unplugged until about 10:30pm. That's when I was able to go back downstairs to plug it back in without my mom seeing me. I was so relieved and was able to sleep comfortably.

The next morning, me and my cousins showed up to school thinking that everything was fine. We felt good and felt like we dodged a bullet. As we started going to our classes, everything seemed normal. We ended up forgetting about the whole detention situation. That is until we got into the classroom we acted up in the day before. We walked in and went to our desks like normal. As we sat down, the teacher looked up at us.

Cashae was still standing up because she was taking off her jacket. The teacher said, "Ladies, how we doing today?" We looked at her and said, "Hi." We were a lot more calm today, we must've worn ourselves out the day before. She said, "I see you ladies didn't serve your detentions yesterday." We all took a deep breath, I rolled my eyes and shook my head as I rested my face on my hand. Carmen said, "How you expect us to serve a detention the same day you give it? You don't know what we have to do after school. We could have a show, rehearsal, interview or even a flight to catch." We all said, "Right."

The teacher sat on her desk with her arms folded and said, "Okay, you ladies have a point. So, what did you have to do yesterday?" It got quiet for a second then Alisha said, "We had an appointment at 6:00." We all started snickering but not too loud, she heard us though. Some kids in the class were laughing too. We snickered because Alisha was referring to the phone call the school made home.

Our teacher looked at us as if she was trying to figure us out. Then she said, “Well, because you skipped detention yesterday, policy states that you now have to serve a week’s detention.” We all said, “What?!” She said, “It’s not my decision…but don’t worry, you ladies have a huge heads up…it starts next week Monday.” I looked at her sarcastically with my eyes squinted and my head tilted to the side.

Cashae got mad and kicked the desk, then she sat down and held her head while she leaned on her desk. The teacher walked around to hand us back our assignments, the ones we did the day before that we put on her desk. As she walked around handing the assignments out, she was telling the students things like, great job, or very creative. When she got to us, she paused, she stood next to Cashae. As she put her assignment on her desk upside down so nobody would see it, she said, “And you can explain to your mom why you received an F on this assignment.”

Cashae mouth dropped while she looked at her paper, she didn't flip it over she was just staring at it. Our mouths dropped too. She gave Carmen her paper, Carmen looked at it, threw her arm down while holding the paper and said, "A D??" The teacher kept walking, Carmen said, "You shaped like a D." We all giggled low. The teacher turned to her and said, "I'm sorry did you say something Carmen?" Carmen said, "I'm just looking at my paper." She gave the twins and Lashae their papers.

Alicia got a C, Alisha got a C-, and Lashae got a C-. Alicia said, "A C?? I can't bring this home!" The teacher said, "And apparently, you couldn't do your work in class yesterday." Alicia said, "If I take this home, my mama gone say, you C this belt??" The whole class laughed. The teacher said, "You ladies starting up again?" Alicia said, "I'm not tryna be funny ma'am, you being real funny though with these grades you giving." Then she finally got to me.

When she came to my desk, she put my paper down and started walking away. I picked it up looking confused and said, “UH UN! What is this?!” She turned to me and said, “It’s an I.” I said, “That’s lower than an F, I can’t show my mama this?!” She said, “Well, you should’ve finished your work. You got an I for incomplete.” My mouth dropped, I pointed to Lashae and the twins with my thumb said, “They didn’t finish theirs either! …” I turned to them and said, “My bad ya’ll I ain’t tryna throw ya’ll under the bus…”

Then I turned back to the teacher and said, “But they got C’s!” She looked at me. I said, “Oh, I see. This is about that composition book…I didn’t throw it at you! If I threw it, it wouldn’t have missed!” Everybody started laughing, I rolled my eyes. The teacher said, “Excuse me?” Cashae said, “Can we talk about how you can change my grade?” The teacher laughed a little and said, “That grade is not changing.” Cashae said, “But why?? Can I do it over please?”

The teacher said, "No, your mom needs to see what type of assignments you decide to do at school." Cashae said, "And she can if I do this over." The teacher said, "That reminds me, I need your mom to sign your paper and you need to bring it back." Cashae was leaned over her desk with her arms stretched out towards the teacher, still holding her paper. Her mouth was wide open, I started laughing because the way she was looking was so funny.

The teacher looked at me and said, "Camille, I don't know why you're laughing, your mother needs to sign your paper too." I stopped laughing instantly and said, "What?!" My cousins all laughed hard at my reaction. I shook my head in a no motion and said, "No, my mama not seeing this." The teacher said, "If you do not bring the papers back signed, we'll schedule a teacher parent conference." We all said, "Oh my gosh!" The teacher smirked while she walked back to her desk. She was happy because she felt like she got us back.

We didn't even want to stay in the classroom no more. At one point Cashae got up to walk out, but the teacher threatened to give us Saturday school if we left the classroom. So we sat there staring at her looking mad the entire class. Even when she gave us work, we sat there with our arms crossed staring at her. She noticed and said, "If you decide not to do your work, that would be another bad grade." I said, "What's the point? You only gone give us the grade you want based on what we did. In my case, I don't feel like working for another I." The teacher threw her hands up like, okay.

We could not wait until that class was over. Once school was out, me and cousins were talking trying to figure out what we were going to do. This time it was more serious because we had a week's long detention and our mamas do not play that. Trust me, that school do not wana see Latoya, Trinity, Beonca, Latonya and Antwanise (Lashae's mom) at the same time and when they're mad. We were terrified. Cashae was so mad she had tears coming out of her eyes, she kept wiping them.

I said, "Shae stop it, yo eyes gone be red and you mama gone find out everything." She stopped for a minute. Carmen said, "That b*tch think it's funny too, I'm figuring out how I'ma get her a** back." Alisha said, "She made me mad too, she being real funny." Lashae said, "How can we get by a whole week, ya'll know our mamas be on to us." I said, "We'll figure it out, but let's just go before they start looking for us." We all walked outside. We straightened up our faces and our moods before we got to the cars.

When we got home, we all got on the phone with each other. We talked about a lot. At one point Carmen said, "Cashae did you straighten up or did you get in yo mama car mad like that?" Cashae said, "I tried but she asked me what's wrong." We all said, "UGH!" She said, "I told her I was sleepy." We said, "Oh." She said, "So guess who's separated from everybody and stuck in their bed?" We all started laughing so hard. She said, "Ya'll know my mama do too much."

Her mama was concerned because she really thought Cashae was that exhausted. We all spoke longer and then Carmen said, "I have an idea ya'll." We said, "What?" She said, "Maybe we can get away with this. I'm thinking we tell them we at each other's houses after school. We would switch up the location every day, there's enough of us to do it." I said, "Hmmm that just might work, detention is like two hours so it wouldn't be late. We still might be able to make it to that person's house after the detention and still have time to chill."

Alisha said, "Sounds good to me, but how would our mamas know?" Alicia said, "We can ask them before school, since we would still have time to go to that person's house, they would know we were there." Cashae said, "But what do we say for the two hours we not there?" Carmen said, "Whoever house we go to, we can tell them that we stopping somewhere first. We wouldn't tell them beforehand, we would do it after school."

Lashae said, "Oh I get it like, oh ma we have to go to the store real quick, or can we get something from our friend house or something?" Carmen said "Yeeeah." Cashae said, "Why you said ma??" Lashae said, "Because it won't be suspicious to ask or tell your own mama we going somewhere, it would be if a cousin say it." We all said, "Ooooh." I said, "So whoever house we at, that person's daughter would have to ask or tell their mom where we're going?" Lashae said, "Exactly."

I said, "We gone have to assign a day for all of us, because ya'll know my mama, I have to ask in advance like the night before." Cashae said, "I got Monday." I said, "I got Tuesday." Carmen said, "I got Wednesday." Lashae said, "I got Thursday." Alisha said, “I guess we’ll take Friday.” I said, “Okay good, ya’ll have to remember that order.” Carmen said, “Just text it to us.” I said, “Yeah that’s a good idea.” I started to text it to them while they continued to talk.

After everybody had the text and the plan was mapped out, we all got off the phone for the night. We were extra quiet in school that week, especially in that teacher’s class. We did the same thing all week, sat there when she gave us work and refused to do it. She started to be bothered by it, but she couldn’t do anything about it. The weekend came and it was a normal weekend, on Sunday me and cousins spoke again. We went over the plan and everything.

During the time we talked I said, “Oh crap, I forgot! I gotta ask my mama.” They all sucked their teeth, I said, “No, it’s okay I think she’ll say yes.” They all said, “Okay,” and decided to ask their mamas too. But first Cashae needed to ask her mom, that way we can avoid our mom’s asking if she knows that we’re coming and us looking stupid not knowing what to say. Cashae said, “Let me ask my mama…hold on.” While she went to ask, we continued to talk.

I said, “Oh shoot, it’s my turn to ask my mama next…that means I’ll have to make up something about where we at.” Soon after, Cashae came back and told us her mom said yes. Carmen said, “What you gone tell her about the two hours?” Cashae said, “Um, I’ve been saying I wanted to buy this bracelet for Canieka, so I can tell her we going to pick it up.” Alisha said, “What happens when we show up without it?” Cashae said, “I’ll just tell her they had to do some personalization’s to it, and I’ll have to pick it up later.”

We agreed she had a good alibi. She made me start thinking about what mine would be. I knew I had to come up with something good because Latoya is not easy to get over on. We eventually got off the phone and went to bed. We felt prepared for the next day.

When we woke up, we went to school. After school we found a quiet place so Cashae could call her mama.

When she called, she told her she wanted to go check on the bracelet and that she was gonna call their driver to take us. Beonca was okay with it, so she left the pickup lineup and headed to Camieka school. We were relieved it worked. We went to detention, the teacher assigned to detention was surprised to see us. I guess word got around and they all thought we would skip it this week too. Not this time, we had too much on the line especially involving our mamas in it.

We didn't act up or anything in detention, we were quiet and did the work we had to catch up on. The time seem like it flew by. When the teacher said, "Okay ladies and gentlemen, detention is over for today, I'll see some of you tomorrow. For the rest of you, enjoy your week and don't come back here." We looked at each other and whispered, "That was fast." We closed our books, packed our bags and left out of the classroom.

Cashae never called her driver, so when we got outside no one was there to drive us. Alisha looked at Cashae and said, “Please tell me you called yo driver.” Cashae said, “Hold on, I’ma call now.” After she got off the phone she said, “He’ll be here in 10 minutes.” Soon after, her mom called. Cashae said, “Hey ma…yes, we’re almost home now. I requested for them to do some more stuff to it, so I can’t get it today, yes ma’am…okay.”

After she hung up, I said, “What she said?” Cashae said, “She wanted to know why we taking so long, and we better not be nowhere we not supposed to be.” We said, “Aw!” Cashae said, “It’s fine, she gone be cool, I promise.” I said, “I’m scared now, my turn tomorrow. If yo mama checking in on you like that, I know my mama gone drill me.” Alisha said, “Well, you know now, so you better have yo excuses ready." The driver pulled up and we got in.

During the ride, Cashae requested that the driver don't tell her mom where he picked us up from. She made him think it was because of a surprise she had for her. When we pulled up, Beonca was on the porch leaning on the wall with her arms crossed. We got out the car. When we were walking up to her, we were saying, "Hey Auntie!" As we walked past her, Cashae said, "Sorry ma, I didn't know it was gone take so long." We said things like, "Yeah, that was tiring," and "For real." Beonca watched all of us with her eyes and said, "Mmm hmm."

Once we were in the house, we put our stuff down. Beonca said, "I'll get ya'll food ready while ya'll do ya'll homework. Although it's kind of late to start homework." Without thinking Alicia said, "We already did our homework." We looked at her and so did Beonca. Beonca looked curious and said, "How? I thought ya'll just came from the mall." Carmen said, "We did it in class, so we wouldn't have to worry about it when we got here."

Beonca got quiet, but she don't go for that, so she said, "Alright, I'll get the food and when I come back, ya'll have ya'll homework out so I can check it." We said, "Yes ma'am." When she walked away, we all looked at each other with big eyes. Carmen said, "Cashae…what's up??" Cashae said, "This is what she do, it's normal." Alicia said, "Camille, you have anything you want to tell us? Because if yo mama do this or is worse, I'ma tell you right now…I'm not gone be able to hold my composure. I'm scared of yo mama."

I said, "No, my mama don't do that. I mean unless she expects something…If she tell us to do our homework, just pretend to do something because if we say we did it, my mama the type that would check with the school." They all took a deep breath. I said, "Don't worry, if ya'll act normal and comfortable, she won't question it. She not gone check it either, as long as we don't act funny." They said, "Okay."

When Beonca came back, we showed her our work. We thought she was just gonna look at it to see if it was finished. But she actually looked through it all and checked it. She even had our books making sure our answers and work was correct. We couldn't believe it. While she did that, we all ate in the kitchen and whatnot. When she was done, we were able to go in Cashae's room and chill. We didn't go home until around 8:00 that night. We was happy day one was over. Things could've went left, and with the person we thought was the easiest to get over on.

Cashae was happy her day was done, but now it was my turn, and I was so nervous. When I got home, I took a shower and got ready for bed. My cousins called me and told me to ask my mama if they can come over so they can ask they mamas. I said, "Okay, hold on."

While I asked, they continued to talk. When I came back, Cashae said, “What she said?” I said, “She said yeah.” Carmen laughed and said, “What she said? How you asked her? I know yo mama.”

I laughed and said, “I said, Ma my cousins wana know if they can come over tomorrow after school, she looked at me for second and said why…yeah but why?” They started laughing. Carmen said, “I knew it, Auntie be on it, what you told her?” I said, “I told her we just wana chill like we did yesterday, but don’t want to tire out Auntie B.” They said, “Oh okay.” Alisha said, “You know what your two hour excuse gone be?” I said, “Not yet, I’m hoping it’s good enough for her to leave the lineup.”

Cashae said, “It better be because we gotta go straight to detention.” I said, “I’ll probably tell her I have to get something from my dad, that way we have enough time because he live so far.” Alicia said, “What if she call him?” I said, “I’ll call him before, he won’t catch on." They all agreed to it. We spoke a bit more and eventually we got off the phone to go to bed. The next day, we did the same thing as the day before. When it was time for me to call my mom after school, I called my dad first.

I said, "Dad, I need to get my journal out my room." We spoke for a couple of minutes. The last thing I said was, "Alright." After we hung up, Carmen said, "What he said?" I said, "He not gone be home." They said, "Aw man!" Cashae said, "We might as well give it up now." I said, "No, it'll work. If my mom call him, he'll say he wasn't home and that's the excuse I'll use." Then I called my mom, my cousins heard me say, "Mommie, I left my journal at daddy's house I need to go pick it up before we come home…yes…no Tiara said she'll take us, that way you can pick up Crystal and Careecia…nooo Mommie I really need it today, please? …okay." When I got off, Alisha asked, "What she said?"

I said, "She asked if I spoke to him and I said yes, she thought she had to take me, but I told her Tiara was gonna take us. She said she didn't want Tiara to go out her way, but I told her I need it today. So she told me to call her when we were on our way, and I said okay." They felt better about it. We went to detention. During the two hours, surprisingly Latoya didn't call me. I remembered to call her when we were on our way. When I called her, I said, "Mommie, we on our way home."

She said "Okay, did you get your journal?" I said, "No, he had to leave when I was like 10 minutes away. He thought I wasn't coming no more, and I didn't know until I got there." My cousins were looking at me on edge because they know my mama would go off quick if he did something like that to me. They heard me say, "It's okay, I'll get it another time." When we got to my house my mama wasn't outside. So when we came inside, she couldn't confirm how we got there.

She did look out the door and it seemed weird to her, because if Tiara dropped us off, she would've came in to say hi. My mom squinted at us for a minute and said, "How ya'll got here?" I said, "Tiara, remember?" She said, "Hmm mm… ya'll start ya'll homework." We looked at each other side eyed and said, "Yes ma'am." She looked at us for a second and walked away. I looked at my cousins and whispered, "Remember what I said, pretend like ya'll doing homework so she won't get suspicious."

We all sat down and took out our books and papers. We were making up work to do. Carmen goofy self almost got us caught, my mama caught her drawing a picture. She was drawing a big head and was working on the facial features. When my mama saw it, she picked it up and said, "Carmen, what are you doing?? This can't be homework." We tried to hold in our laughter after glancing at the picture. I covered my eyes and shook my head while I smiled.

Carmen said, "It's a reflection on how we would depict the character from the story we're reading in class right now." My mouth dropped, we were so shocked she came up with that reason and so fast. It was a very good reason and it worked. My mama said, "Oh okay, I thought you was foolin around." Carmen said, "No." When Latoya walked away, Carmen eyes got big as she said, "Whew!" I said, "That was a good reason, how you came up with that so fast?" Carmen said, "Girl, I stayed up most of the night getting my rebuttals together for yo mama. I knew we wasn't supposed to talk but I'm prepared. Yo mama scare me too." We laughed low.

Latoya heard us and yelled from where she was, "I hope ya'll doing ya'll homework! Don't be messing around in there!" We looked at each other scared and started to continue to fake and do homework. After we were done, we ate, and we went to my room to chill. Everybody left my house around 8:00pm like we did at

Cashae house. I was happy my day was over, and surprised we made it through it.

What we didn't know was that my mama called my dad after I told her he left his house. When she spoke to him, she said, "Camille said she came to get her journal but when she got there you was gone." Andre said, "I didn't know she was still coming, I told her I had to leave last minute." After they spoke, it seemed like everything I told my mama was true because of the way he responded to her. It was this way for the next couple of days and it worked.

On Friday, it was the twins turn. Everything was going as planned and we were happy it was the last day of the detention. After this day we would be free and not have to sneak anymore. After school, Alisha made the call, and her mom went for it, so we went to detention. While we were in detention what we didn't know, was that the school was going to call our houses being that it was the last day of our detention.

Well our moms were home and the school called about 30 minutes into our detention. Every last one of our mamas answered the phones, they received an automated call. It said, "Hello, Ms. (their last name), we are reaching out to you to inform you that your student (student's first and last name) has completed their week's detention today and will be released at 4:30pm. Thank you for your cooperation." They were livid.

My mom called Trinity, but of course everybody was calling her because we were supposed to be at her house. Eventually they all were on the line together. Beonca said, "On Monday, they said they went to the mall. But Cashae said the bracelet she went to get had to be personalized, so she had to leave it there. But I wondered why it took them so long to get here if she knew they had to personalize it. She would know that not too long after getting there."

Latoya said, "Wait, they showed up to yo house late too?" Beonca said, "Yeah a little over two hours late." Latoya said, "They did the same thing to me, and it was a little over two hours when they showed up here too. Camille said she was going to pick up her journal from her daddy house. She was telling me how bad she needed it that day before they got home. So I said okay. But when she came back home, she didn't have anything with her, and said her daddy had to leave when she was about 10 minutes away. This child told me it's okay she'll get it another time, after she was about to have a fit if I didn't let her go get it…I spoke to him that day and he said he left last minute, just like Camille said. It was weird to me that he would leave while she was on her way and not tell her, or for him to tell her not to come no more but she still go. So after that message from the school, I called him again today. It made no sense to me that she was there because she can't be in two places at once. He said he wasn't home at all that day. He said Camille called him right after school and he told Camille not to come because he wasn't home, and she told him okay. He sent me the screenshot of his call log, homegirl called him before she called me. So her a** knew he wasn't home."

My aunties was shocked and said, "Mmm!" Latonya said, "Yep, they got me too, same time frame. Carmen said she needed some stuff from the store, but they came back empty handed. She claims the store didn't have anything they needed, but she should've known that a few minutes after being at the store. It shouldn't have taken that long."

They had Antwanise on the line too and she said, "Lashae said she wanted to stop at my mom's house to check on her and say hi, but I checked with my mom after that voicemail from the school, and my mom said she never came. She didn't even hear from Lashae this week." Trinity said, "Well d*mn, they got me today too…the excuse is that the twins wanted their nails done before they got home so they wouldn't have to leave after I left tonight." Latoya said, "They been lyin to us all week. Trinity, they don't know you got that call right?" Trinity said, "No."

Latoya said, "Good, so they obviously think they gone show up to yo house and pretend like nothing is wrong. More than likely they'll show up without they nails done, and probably say the place was crowded or wasn't taking any more customers…We know where they are, I say we go out there and surprise they a**es and call'em out." All of my aunties were on board, and they all were so mad. They got ready and then headed to our school.

Meanwhile, we in detention celebrating on getting away with our plan and happy it was the last day. About an hour and 15 minutes in, the classroom door opened. We all looked up and in walked, Latonya, Latoya, Trinity, Antwanise and Beonca. All of our mouths dropped as we saw our mom walk in and we froze. We were speechless. They stood in front of the classroom staring at us with their arms crossed. We were looking back at them and terrified. The teacher did not say a word, instead he smiled and said, "OOOOHHHH." He was ready for a show.

It was quiet and our moms were still giving us the death stare, we looked at each other slowly. Carmen covered her mouth and said, "F*ck!" Of course they didn't hear her. They were really scaring us, they wasn't saying anything but they kept staring at us. We didn't know what to do. I burst out crying and Latoya was still staring at me, I knew she wanted to beat my a**. While they were standing there, our teacher walked in. I covered my mouth and said, "Sh*t!" It was like something from a scary movie. They didn't hear me either when I said that.

At first, she didn't recognize them because she wasn't paying attention. But when she finally noticed, she said, "Oh hiiii, I've been wanting to meet with you all." We knew it was all over. She told our mamas what we did the week before and how we skipped detention, she also told them how we refused to do work. She pulled out our work from that day and showed the grade we got. When Latoya saw that I, she looked at me quick. The teacher said, "These are your signatures, right?" Our mamas said, "No, we never saw these."

We was breathing hard because we were scared and nervous. She showed Beonca Cashae work thoroughly, she saw the drawing and the guide for having a fun class for dummies and everything. All we could do is shake our heads because we knew Cashae was in some serious trouble with her mama. The teacher told my mama I threw my book at her and Latoya wanted to rip my head off. I looked at Carmen, Carmen looked at me and then looked down.

We were both scared to say anything, and I didn't want to get her in more trouble. We felt that if we said anything at that time, we would get in more trouble. So we decided to wait until we got home. The teacher went on to tell them everything we said to her, even when I said it was a threat. Our moms were not amused, and I never seen Auntie Antwanise that upset before.

After the teacher told her that Lashae sprayed the principal with the fire extinguisher, that was the maddest we've ever seen her. She's normally calm, peaceful, understanding and always smiling. We knew we was all in trouble. When the teacher finished talking to them, the teacher for detention told our mamas, "If you ladies would like, you can take them with you." Latoya looked at him and said, "No, they can finish." Then she looked back at us and said, "We'll be in the car." Then they walked out.

We were more scared than we ever were. The other kids in the classroom were looking at us. Some of the kids were excited to see our moms, but the feeling was not mutual with us. That day, detention went past even faster than before. Once it was over, we all got up really slow. When we walked outside, we saw they drove two different cars. Me and Carmen were in separate cars. When we got in the car our mamas was fussing us out bad.

I told Latoya, “Ma, I didn’t throw that book at the teacher.” I was still crying, she said, “Then who threw it?!” I said, “Carmen did, you can ask her, she’ll tell you.” Latoya paused, then she got on her phone. I heard her say, “Go to my house.” Everybody pulled up at my house. When we went inside, we sat in the Livingroom. Our moms was standing up in front of us looking at us. We had our heads down, only now all of us was crying.

Latoya addressed the book throwing, she said, “Camille said Carmen threw the book to get her in trouble.” Latonya looked at Carmen and said, “Is that true??” Carmen shook her head yeah and said, “Yes, I threw it.” Latoya shook her head in a no motion, threw her hands up in frustration, while she looked away and took a breath. Latonya said, "Why the h*ll would you do that?!" Carmen said, "She was laughing at me because I was in trouble." Latonya said, "Yo a** need to be laughed at if you acting like a f*cking clown! Now you got this girl in trouble…Lord knows she get in enough trouble on her own!"

Trinity said, "That mean Camille shouldn't even be in trouble." Latoya said, "No, her a** still in trouble for f*cking lyin to me like I'm stupid!" My mama was mad, but Latonya was even madder at Carmen. Trinity looked at the twins and said, "And ya'll…ya'll do know that if ya'll showed up without ya'll nails done I would've knocked ya'll a**es out! Ya'll school called us." When she said that we all looked up surprised.

She said, "Un huh, they called us today and told us ya'll was finished with ya'll week's detention." We had no idea they did that. Antwanise looked at Lashae and said, "A fire extinguisher?? You know better!" It was quiet for a minute, then Antwanise said, "Then ya'll walk around talking about the man look like a melted Frosty the Snowman?! Shae, you know I'm not with the disrespect." When she mentioned melted Frosty the Snowman, we all laughed but they thought we were just crying more. We couldn't help ourselves.

We all got yelled at and put on punishment. When everybody left to go home, I got the beaten of a lifetime for lying to my mom. Every last one of my cousins got beatings when they got home too, which is very surprising because some of them get by sometimes. This is how we knew our mamas was mad. We thought we had it all figured out and we did. If it wasn't for that follow up call, we would've gotten away with it. Instead, we were sore, in trouble, and on punishment…again.

Chapter 9

Let's Do It

A couple weeks later, we were still on punishment. During this time, we heard about a party, and we wanted to go so bad. The only thing is, we knew our moms would say no because we were on punishment. Not only did we hear about this party, but we were personally invited to the party by the party hosts. The hosts were some guys that had crushes on us, and they really wanted us to come.

Aside from us being on punishment, I didn't mind going because I was single so the guys liking us was no problem for me. When we first got invited, we told the guys we were sorry, but we couldn't make it. They seemed disappointed and we didn't think much of it. We thought they were just playing, until we saw them two days before the party. When they mentioned the party again, they told us they were disappointed. This time it was believable, and we saw it in their faces. We felt bad and before we could say anything, Carmen said, "We'll be there."

We all looked at Carmen quick. Thanks to all of our years of training from being celebrities, we knew how to play it off and not seem surprised. We just smiled and the boys were going crazy. They were so excited, jumping around and everything. Then one guy went in his phone while he stood close to Carmen in front of her. He was giving her the information. The entire time in between us smiling at the other guys, we were still giving each other looks because of what Carmen said.

After the guy gave her the information, they walked away so happy saying, "They coming!" They were smiling and laughing. Once they were out of our view, we all turned to Carmen and stared at her. She smiled a little and said, "I'm sorry, I didn't know what else to say. That was awkward!" I said, "So now what are we supposed to do??" Alisha said, "For real, if we don't go we gone look so bad. But how can we go?? We been on one of the worst punishments ever for the past two weeks, and it hasn't gotten better yet…what would possess you to say some sh*t like that Carmen??"

Carmen shook her head in a no motion and said, "Mannn, I'm sorry. I didn't even know I was gone say something. It's better than ya'll just staring at them making them feel dumb." Cashae said, "Well, we can't do much about that now." Carmen said, "Right, so since we going now…what should we do??" We all looked at Carmen kind of upset, shaking our heads and took a deep breath at the same time. Then Alicia said, "Carmen, we all know the only way we can go is if we sneak out."

We were shaking our heads in no motion again. Lashae said, "God forbid we get caught, that's all our a**es!" We all said, "Right!" Carmen said, "I know, but we don't hang with these people, so nobody we know should be there. Of course people would know us, but at least we wouldn't be in the areas we hang out in…we can get in and get out. Our mamas won't have to know." We were side eyeing Carmen while she spoke, she can tell she had our attention. She spoke a lil bit more trying to convince us.

I said, "If you didn't get me in trouble, then maybe I would have permission to go." She said, "Camille, we all know if you went a year straight without getting in trouble, yo mama still wouldn't give you permission to go." We all laughed a little bit. Then Carmen said, "We get in, we get out…ya'll down or what?" We hesitated for a few seconds and then said, "Alright." Carmen was happy, but we all were on edge. Being on punishment my mama checked on me a lot.

I was really in my head thinking, this is stupid we not gone get away with this. But at the same time, I was thinking of ways to get around my mama in order to pull it off. I figured it couldn't be that bad because like Carmen said, nobody we know should be there anyway…we get in, we get out. The next two days, I watched my mama every move just to get a feel of how she was doing things. By the day of the party, Friday, I thought I had it all figured out.

In the beginning of my punishment, I could barely get out of her site. She checked on me constantly. But I noticed the more time I was on punishment, the less time she checked on me. Since it's been two weeks now, the last time of day she would check on me was at 8:00 at night. This could have been problematic, but she was exhausted from her week's work and planned to go to bed early. Bingo! This is exactly what I needed. I was so excited when I saw how tired she was, it was going to make my night a lot easier.

The party started at 6:00 that night, but I could not leave to make it at that time because my mama was still up. I spoke to my cousins, and we all were waiting for our parents to go to sleep, leave or get distracted. My mama checked on me at 7:00. She told me she was going to sleep because she was tired. I gave her about 30 minutes to really get in her sleep.

Once that time passed, I went to check on her. I was scared because she could've been up and if she saw me, she would've known she needed to watch me. I creeped near her room door and peeked inside. I saw her in her bed knocked out. I ran back to my room and gave my cousins the okay.

I snuck out the house the way I always do, out my window and down the outside flower wall. When I got down to the bottom, I walked out to the front on the side of my house. Alisha picked me up. She was the driver that night because Lashae got her car taken, and her mom would notice if she took it. Trinity on the other hand is not used to checking for the car, because she never really take them from the twins. Although she did this time, she still wouldn't think to check.

Soon Alisha had picked us all up and we headed to the party. Carmen said, "We don't even have to stay long ya'll, we can just show face for a little while and then head back." Cashae looked at Carmen and said, "You sound scared." Carmen looked back at her and said, "I am." I looked at Carmen and said, "Fine time for you to admit it." Carmen just looked at me and took a breath.

When we pulled up, Alisha said, "Okay ya'll I'm with Carmen, we show face for a little while and we head back. It's too early in the night and we never snuck out this early. We don't know when our mamas gone wake up or come back or check on us again." We agreed and just as we were getting out the car, I looked up and my mouth dropped to the floor.

I said, "Oh my gosh." My cousins stopped, looked at me and said, "What??" I said, "Carmen, there's people that we know here." They all looked and said, "Who??" They looked in the direction I looked in and said "Oh sh*t." We were so shocked to see Shaun, Jacoby and their homeboys at the party too. Carmen said, "D*mn! How many people they know??"

By this time the party hosts saw us and came to help us out the car. We told them we didn't wana be seen in the front, so they helped to hide us by walking around us. As we turned the corner to go to the backyard, Jacoby looked up and caught a glimpse of me. He stopped drinking his drink and stood there in shock for a second. Then he tapped Shaun and said,

"Aye man, call me crazy but I think I just saw Camille."

Shaun started looking around frantically and said, "Where??...man you playin." Jacoby said, "Naw, I just saw her. She went in the back." Shaun looked at him for a few seconds and then said, "Alright, let's go look." As they were making their way to the backyard, we were getting acquainted with the hosts. They were really cool. For each of us, there was a boy that had a crush on us, and that boy was all up on us. But we didn't mind because they wasn't aggravating and they all had good vibes.

They brought us some drinks out being good hosts. Nonalcoholic of course. They were smiling from ear to ear because they were so happy we were there. We were enjoying ourselves already. When Shaun them made it to the backyard, it was not hard to spot us. They saw us right away and did not like what they saw. So they stormed over to us without us seeing them. When they got to us, we were so into what the guys were doing to entertain us that we still didn't see them.

In the middle of the guy playfully singing me a song that likes me, Shaun grabbed my arm and pulled me up. We all gasped. When I saw it was Shaun who did it, I was confused. I said, "What are you doing?!" He said, "No, what the h*ll you doing out here hugged up with some dude?!" I looked at him squinting my eyes and said, "Shaun, we are not together no more." He said, "Yo mama know you out?!" I looked at him like, really?? He said, "Huh??...I bet she don't."

My cousins was looking confused too. Carmen said, "Shaun, why you trippin??" Shaun said, "Ya'll the ones trippin! Come on we taking ya'll home." We all said, "What?!...No!" They were pulling on us and we were resisting. They stopped for a minute and Shaun said, "Camille, I promise if you don't let me take you home right now, I'm telling yo mama you was out here." I stared at him for a good minute as he stared back at me without breaking eye contact.

Then I sucked my teeth. When I turned to tell the boys we were leaving, Shaun turned me around quick and said, "Uh un, let's go, the car over there." We all walked to the front, leaving the hosts looking and feeling crazy not knowing what just happened. All of us except the twins got in the car and because Shaun them came together the car was big enough for the rest of us to fit. Of course his homeboys did not ride with us so there can be enough room.

The rest of my cousins rode with Shaun too so I wouldn't be by myself. Shaun made sure he dropped each of us off home, he dropped me off last. When he pulled up to the side of my house, I looked at him mad. He said, "I don't care if you mad, you should be in the house anyway." As I got out, I said, "You never complained when I snuck out to see yo a**."

He leaned over to see me out the window and said, “You ain’t fina be out sneaking around with some randoms.” I was looking at him still mad and made a face at him and said, “Whatever.” I walked towards my window, and he pulled off. When he pulled off, I came from the side of my house again to check and make sure he was gone. Then I got on the phone, called Alisha and said, “Okay girl he gone, come on.”

Alisha was waiting for me down the street. She pulled up and I got in the car, she had Carmen, Lashae, Alicia and Cashae with her. She picked everybody up as he dropped them off, we had planned this through text while he was taking us home. When we got in the car we laughed because he wasted his time doing all that. Cashae said, “He got some nerve, he had a whole girl in his house but trip on you because some dude in yo face??”

My cousins said, “Right!” I said, “I know! Then use my mama to get me to listen. He made it seem like I still cared about what he thought." We contacted the boys and they decided to meet us at the guy's house who liked me instead, so we can chill some more. They gave us the address and we were on our way.

When we got there, they were in the Livingroom, and everybody was super chill. We each sat next to the boy that had a crush on us. They had their arms behind us on the couch while we all sat, talked and laughed. We liked this better than the party, because we were able to relax and could actually hear what each other was saying. Alisha said, "What happened to the party?" One of the guys said, "Oh we shut it down, it went on long enough."

The other guy said, "Yeah and after ya'll left it was no point. We threw the party just for ya'll to come through anyway." We said, "What?" Another guy said, "Don't think we creepy or nothing, but it would've been weird for us to ask ya'll to come over and chill with us on a regular day. I mean we like ya'll and we needed to break the ice." We smiled and said, "Oh okay."

We chilled for about 20 minutes, then the front door opened. We didn't think anything of it, we just figured they had some friends come over. We were still talking and not paying attention until we heard, "What the f*ck?!" We looked up quick just to see Shaun, Jacoby and a few of their homeboys looking confused. Shaun looked pissed, especially because we looked more hugged up and I was at the boy's house this time.

Our mouths were wide open, we couldn't believe they were there. We couldn't understand why they would be there either. Shaun said, "You really snuck out again to come to his house?!" I said, "What are you doing here??" He said, "Better question, what are you doing here?! I just dropped ya'll home, how the h*ll ya'll get back over here so fast?!" I said, "Stop talking to me like I'm yo girlfriend, cause I'm not!"

He got so mad, he darted at me, Jacoby tried to stop him, but Shaun snatched away. My cousins stood up. When Shaun got to me, he yanked me up from the couch so hard, and flung me behind him. He pointed at the boy and said, "Aye man, stay away from her!" While he started going back and forth with the boy, me and my cousins made eye contact with each other and ran outside.

Jacoby and his homeboys subconsciously saw us, but they were too busy making sure things didn't get out of hand with Shaun and that boy. After going back and forth with him for about 10 minutes, Shaun turned around expecting to still see me standing there. When he didn't, he started to panic and said, "Where they at??" At that moment Jacoby thought about it and said, "I think they went outside man." Shaun turned to say one more thing to the guy and then went outside.

When they got out there, they were looking for us but couldn't find us. They were calling our names and everything. After a while Shaun said, “She better not be hiding waiting me for me to leave so she can go back in this n*gga house.” He tried to call my phone, but I let it ring out and he got the voicemail. He got so mad that he didn’t care if I was hiding or not, he said, “F*ck it, I’m going to her house.”

Jacoby said, “Aye man, let it go.” Shaun said, “No, she don’t know these people, why is she sneaking out to see this dude??” Jacoby said, “That’s her business. Ya’ll not together no more come on man, she can do what she wana do now and you have to accept that. You feel me? You f*cked up…she didn’t.” Shaun didn’t like that, he looked at him and said, “Man you know how that went, Camille think I f*cked up but it wasn’t even like that.”

Jacoby said, “That girl <u>was</u> in yo house, at least Camille at his house and not hers.” Shaun looked at Jacoby for a second and said, “Man that ain’t no better! ...I’m going to her house, she just gone have to get in trouble tonight." Shaun left to head to my house. He was driving so fast to get there. At this point I had done pissed him off so bad he didn't care about anything else but getting to my house. He had to be mad because Shaun is not a snitch and he normally cover for me rather than tell on me.

I guess his feelings was involved in this one, love can make you do some crazy thangs. In his case EVERY THANG but the right thing, but we not gone get into that. After some time he got to my house, jumped out his car and headed to the front door. He straightened his self up before he got to the door, because he didn't want my mom to know he was mad. He rung the doorbell and waited. After about two minutes, he heard the front door opening.

When it opened, he saw my mom. She was kind of squinting as if she was sleep, just woke up or tired. At this point it was around 10:30 at night. She said, "Shaun?" He said, "Hi Ms. Lockhart, I'm so sorry to bother you." She said, "Hi, it's okay. What's wrong?" He said, "Can I please speak to Camille for a second, it'll be brief." She said, "Okay, you wana come in?" He said, "No thank you, I'm kind of in a rush." She said, "Okay, wait here." She closed the door and went upstairs yarning.

Shaun was at the door thinking to his self, yeah, she caught now, and I don't even have to tell on her. His plan was to act surprised when she came back and said I wasn't in the room, so he can pretend to remember a party that was going on and lead her to the guy's house. After about two minutes, he figured she knew I wasn't there by now, but he waited to hear her response to it. Finally after 3 minutes of waiting, he heard the front door opening again.

He looked up not knowing what to expect but was preparing for whatever Latoya would say. When the door opened, he looked up and saw me, his face went from straight to confused. He had no idea how I was there, how I got there so fast and was not expecting me to come to the door. We stared at each other for what felt like a long time, then his face went from mad to pissed. I smiled at him sarcastically with my mouth closed and my head titled a bit to the side, all while maintaining eye contact.

I did this because I realized what he tried to do. He tried to ask my mama for me so she can see that I wasn't there and then I would've gotten in trouble. But it didn't work, so I smiled, and my smile said everything I needed to say. We did not say one word to each other that entire time. After smiling at him for some time, he eventually couldn't take it anymore. He walked away still looking at me until he got off the porch. I closed the front door relieved and happy his plan didn't work. He got in his car and left.

I took a breath and smiled because we did it, we made it home in time. I texted my cousins that everything was okay. Right after I sent the text Latoya said, "What did he want?" I stopped quick because she scared me, I said, "Oh he was making sure I was okay, he hasn't seen me in a while." She said, "Okay." She went back to her room. I called my cousins and told them what happened. Carmen said, "Didn't I tell you??" I said, "I know, I'm so glad I listened and left right away."

Alisha said, "Yeah, I'm glad I drove, or we would've been caught." I said, "He looked spooked when he saw me come to the door." Lashae said, "Yeah, I mean he probably wondering how you got there. It's a good thing Alisha hid her car down the street, or he would've made sure you didn't leave out that house without him." Cashae said, "Camille, how long after you got home did he show up?"

I said, "Girl! He came probably like 15 minutes after I snuck back in. I was rushing to change my clothes and look like I been home. By the time I finished I was breathing so hard. I'm glad I had time to catch my breath and look relaxed before my mama came in my room. Thanks for dropping me off first, if you didn't, I would've got caught." Alisha said, "Yeah girl, it's the only thing that made sense."

We talked for most of the night, my mama went back to sleep. The thing is, if Shaun would not have showed up to that house, I probably would have gotten caught. My mama took a nap around 7:00 and she woke back up around10:00, which is around the time we ran out the house from Shaun. We ran to Alisha car, and she drove off fast to take me home before he could do anything else. We knew he was mad and could tell my mom at any given time, so they all decided we should go back home.

When I climbed in the window it was around 10:15 ish, although my mama woke up at 10:00 she was still laying down. By the time I undressed and put on house clothes it was close to 10:25, which gave me about 5 minutes to sit down and catch my breath before

Shaun showed up. He was so mad at me and at the fact that I made it back home before I could get caught.

Me and my cousins were so relieved and happy. Our mamas had no idea we had left the house. We were able to live up to our word and go to the party. Carmen learned her lesson and planned to just let us look at people stupid next time. This had all of us so nerve wrecked, we never wanted to feel this way again. One thing is for sure though, we was feeling real good about getting away with it all.

Chapter 10

You Tried It

We had about a day to recover from the rush we had from sneaking out. You would think because we was so scared and didn't get caught the last time, that we would chill and stay away from doing it again. But it was that very thing that made us think about it and figure we can get away with it again since we got away with it last time. Being out of the house after being locked in for so long, it felt great going out.

This time around me and my cousins decided to sneak out just to do random things. Even if we had nothing to do, we decided to sneak out and find something to do. There could be a stick on the ground and it's like, oh we gotta sneak out and get that stick…now that we out here what ya'll wana do? Lol. We really acted like we had no sense. We figured we can try our luck and sneak out that night. We wanted to see if we would still be as scared as we was the last time, or if we would be okay.

If we felt the same way as we did the last time, we said we wouldn't do it no more. I guess you can say it was more of an experiment, and also a bunch of teens that desperately needed to get out the house because they've been on punishment for so long. Night one approached, and I was nervous like never before. I called Carmen to calm my nerves, but we all know she wasn't gone help.

Once we were on the phone I told her, "I'm nervous, I'm not sure if I should go with ya'll." Carmen said, "Girl shake that sh*t off! You just thinking about the night of the party." I said, "You can't say you wasn't scared Carmen." Carmen said, "I was scared as h*ll, that night scared the sh*t out of me…LITERALLY! I was on the toilet most of the night when I got back…" I started laughing, she said,

"You laughing, my mama almost took my a** to the hospital, I was literally sh*ttin bricks!" We both laughed hard.

I said, "See, so you should understand where I'm coming from." Carmen said, "I do understand, but Camille, I want you to understand…that was two days ago! Come on…" I took a quick breath and said, "Okay fine." She said, "Good. I didn't want to have to tell everybody you couldn't sneak out because you was a scary party pooper." I laughed and said, "Really??" We finished our conversation and prepared for operation sneak out and not get caught.

I didn't speak to anyone else besides Carmen. We didn't even have a plan, all I knew was to sneak out. I didn't know who was gone pick me up, how long I had to wait or where we was going. Regardless of so many doubts and red flags, I went ahead and snuck out when I saw fit. Once I got in the front on the side of my house, I texted Carmen. As soon as I sent the text, I saw this car creeping up real slow.

I didn't recognize the car, so I ran back towards my house and I hid near the bush. The car stopped in a spot to where they could see me, then I heard very light whispers saying, "Camille…Camille." I was still scared to move and then I saw Alisha face. I squinted to make sure it was her and I whispered, "Alisha??" At that moment, Carmen texted me back, it read: Okay cool, Alisha should be there for you. She in her friend car.

When I read that text, I took a breath of relief and smiled for a second. Then I took off running to the car and we drove off. Alisha was in the car with one of her guy friends, Alicia was in the car too. I was wondering where the rest of them were, but we didn't really say much in the car. I guess we was still trying to process everything. Next thing I knew, we was pulling up near Lashae house.

We pulled up on the side of her house and surprisingly her and Cashae came running from behind a bush. When they got in the car, we drove on the next block over. I was looking at Cashae with my mouth wide open. When she noticed it, she said, "What?" I had a confused look on my face as I said, "How did you get to Lashae house??" They all started laughing, then Alisha said, "Cashae a** got scared and thought her mama was gone catch her, so she took her a** in the backyard, jumped the fence and high tailed it to Lashae house!"

I started laughing uncontrollably. Lashae said, "She had me coming out the house earlier than what I was supposed to, that's why we hid in the bush." I said, "Well Cashae, why didn't you just come in my yard?" Alisha said, "I told her that!" Cashae said, "Well, for one, I would've scared the sh*t out of you if I was standing there or if I walked up on you when you snuck out…" I said, "True." Then she said, "And two, if that happened, we both would've been caught by yo mama and then mine…and just like that operation sneak out and not get caught is over, because they would've called everybody mama knowing we wouldn't be sneaking out by ourselves."

We all said, "Ooh," and agreed. I told her, "Well, now I know, so if you need to, just come in my yard and text me that you would be there so I would know. That way you wouldn't have to walk so far." She said, "Okay." We pulled up to Carmen house and she darted out of the darkness from the right side of her house. We didn't even see her, she scared us. She got in the car, and we pulled off. During the ride we all got acquainted with Alisha's friend, and Alisha explained to us what we were going to do that night.

By the time we got to where we were going, we all were comfortable with each other. I mean us and her guy friend. You would not have known that we just met him that night. Anyway, we all chilled at this nighttime lounge. This lounge is mainly for teens, but after a certain hour, teens were not permitted. Since Alisha's friend knew the people at the door, he was able to get all of us in. We sat down and started to have a good time. We even played pool, ate some food, had nonalcoholic drinks and played some games.

We had to be desperate for freedom, because we was bold being out in the public like that. Anybody can see us and could potentially tell our mamas. But the night went as smooth as a baby's bottom. We stayed out until about 11:00pm. Then we all headed back home. We all thanked Alisha's friend the entire time, because without him we wouldn't have been able to pull this off. Alisha and Lashae didn't have their cars because we was in trouble, and everybody and they mama know I haven't had my car in ages because I somehow stay in trouble.

Carmen drives sometimes but her mama banned her from driving too. Let's not even get on Cashae. She don't even have access to the garage because of the last time when she stole her mama most expensive car to sneak out. The only reason she got caught is because she parked it about 2 inches off and her mama know exactly how she leave her cars. So we all were carless. The guy dropped us off in the order he picked us up in, only Cashae got dropped off with me.

She decided to take me up on that offer and see how easy it was to get from my backyard to hers. I snuck back in as Cashae made her way around the back of my house. As I was changing, Cashae texted me, it read: I got in! That was waaay easier. I'm using yo backyard from now on. I laughed and texted back: Lol okay, glad you made it.

All of us checked in with each other to make sure everybody made it inside safe, which we all did. We said our goodnights and went to sleep. Looks like we succeeded again and did not get caught, we were happy about that. The only issue was, we were doing this on school nights. It didn't hit us until it was time to get up for school the next morning. What a morning it was, I was dragging. My level of tiredness was ridiculous, but I knew I had to hide it from my mama.

If she sensed that I was that tired, she would've gotten suspicious, and I didn't want that. At one point, she did look at me and ask, "You okay??" I looked at her quick and said, "Yes, I'm okay." She said, "You yawning a lil bit too much." I said, "I was sleeping good." She looked at me a little longer and said, "Hmm mmm, you need to stay yo a** off that phone late at night." I looked at her quick and said, "I wasn't."

I was afraid to say much else because I didn't want to dig myself in a hole. She didn't say anything about it after that. When we were at school, it was obvious that we were super tired. All we did was yawn and write, write and yawn. We were making other people feel tired just by looking at us yawn. Shaun came out to my school that day. He approached me trying to explain how he wasn't really gonna tell on me that night. He also said he was just mad because he still wanted to be with me and can't handle the thought of me being with somebody else.

He was spilling his heart out to me and just as I opened my mouth to reply, the only thing came out was a yawn. He said, "Am I boring you?" Still yarning, I shook my head no and said, "No, no…" He said, "That's all you have to say? I'm trying to talk to you on a serious matter Camille." I patted his chest as I yawned again and said, "It's not that, it's not you, it's me." My cousins was in the hallway and Alisha said, "Camille!" I looked at her and then back at Shaun and walked away from him. He was confused on how to feel, and he wondered why I was so tired.

When I got to my cousins, they gave me this pass. I said, "What is this?" Alisha said, "Ms. Peterson gave them to us and said to come to her class. But we have to show our 2nd, 3rd, and 4th hour teachers it first."

I said, "Okay." We all went to our classes to show them the passes and they dismissed us so we can go. We didn't know what was going on. When we got to her classroom, she said, "I noticed how tired you ladies were today." Carmen said, "We're sorry, we didn't get enough sleep last night."

Ms. Peterson said, "That's alright, I understand it happens. A lot of you students are so busy, and I get it, you have to balance life and work. You ladies probably had rehearsals, shows and who knows what else." Cashae said, "We have a lot to do." Ms. Peterson said, "You poor babies…this is why I called you out of class…Follow me." We looked at each other confused, but we followed her anyway.

We walked behind her through the school, she said hi to a few people and even stopped to help some. But she did not let anybody stop her for more than 10 seconds, she would say, "Let me get back with you, I have to tend to these ladies." After walking for what felt like forever, we finally came up on this door. She had to open the door with a key. She kind of looked around before opening it, we noticed but we were too tired to really care. Once she opened the door she said, "Come on inside."

When we got inside, she closed the door behind us and turned on the light. We saw some nice clean unused looking massage like beds, they were arranged in a professional manner. We never saw this room before and we never knew it existed. I was squinting from tiredness and calmly said, "What's this?" Ms. Peterson said, "This ladies, is our spa slash masseuse headquarters." We all said, "Huh??"

She turned to look at us and said, "We have a program we're looking to add to the school for students that have an interest in massage therapy, but we haven't announced it to the student body yet." We said, "Cool." Alisha said, "That is pretty cool, but Ms. Peterson, with all do respect, why are we here?" She smiled, clapped her hands together once, which made us jump a little and hold our ears and said, "Well that's the best part! We needed some students to test this out, but we didn't quite know how to approach students without this information getting out prematurely."

We looked at her and she looked back at us and continued, "We haven't found anyone trustworthy enough and you ladies are tired, so I figured…why not you?!" I'm not sure if we were too tired to comprehend what she was saying or if we were just confused on what she wanted us to do. But we stared at her like she was crazy. She said, "Oh my, you ladies are more tired than I thought." Lashae said, "What do we have to do?"

She said, "Well, today, all you have to do is pick a bed and sleep for the next 3 periods." All of our mouths dropped, for the first time that day we all looked like we were well rested if only for a second. Carmen said, "So, you got us out of class to come here and all we have to do is pick a bed and sleep?" Ms.

Peterson smiled and said, "Yes." Carmen said, "And we won't get in trouble?"

Ms. Peterson said, "No, no one will know you're in here except me. I wanted you girls to feel comfortable and have your privacy. At the end of the week, you ladies would give me your feedback and I will take that information to our team that's working on this project…and that would help with our decision." She was smiling again. It sound too good to be true, but we was tired and wanted to sleep. Cashae said, "Thank you so much Ms. Peterson for choosing us, I didn't know how I would've made it through the day."

She said, "You're welcome…now, would you ladies prefer to sleep though lunch as well or leave here after 4th hour?" We all said, "Sleep through lunch!" She laughed and said "Okay, just keep this door locked and enjoy ladies." She showed us how to lock the door and then she left. We couldn't believe it, we were so happy we were able to sleep. We picked a bed, and we fell asleep almost instantly. We dimmed the light and turned on the relaxing music before laying down.

Our classmates wondered where we were because they would see us up until 3rd hour and then we would disappear until after lunch. After lunch Ms. Peterson would come in and let us out to where no one would see us. After lunch we would have so much energy and not look tired at all. Everyone wondered what the heck happened to us but couldn't figure it out, even Shaun was looking confused.

By the end of the first day, Carmen said, "Did I hear Ms. Peterson right? Did she say at the end of the week we give her our feedback, as in we'll be doing this all week??" We looked at her as she smiled, I said, "She did say that." Carmen said, "Yes! I won't have to worry about missing sleep." Cashae said, "This is the best week ever, we get to sneak out and then catch up on sleep when we get to school."

I said, “Yeah but after this week, we need to chill because we only giving our feedback for this week…and I can’t imagine being this tired through the entire day. I’ll get in trouble for sleeping in class.” My cousins agreed. Soon after our conversation, we went home and got prepared to sneak out that night. Things were like this all week long. We would sneak out and sneak back in, we would go to school and secretly go to the spa room and sleep during class and lunch.

The only difference is on the third day, they actually brought in masseuses for us to have the full experience. As soon as they started, we was out like a light. Ms. Peterson stayed in there to watch them, and she made sure they all left when she left after an hour of them giving us a massage. This was her way of still giving us our privacy, even though we were sleep the entire time.

We got massages for two days, which was for Wednesday and Thursday. Ms. Peterson was excited that we were coming up on the closing of the week, and we were too. She told us they were bringing in some people that were going to do pedicures for us, while another person would massage our heads and shoulders at the same time. We were looking forward to it.

On Thursday before our mamas picked us up from school, they all talked to each other. Beonca asked her sisters, “Has anybody else’s daughter been extra tired this week?” They all said, “Yeah!” Trinity said, “When we leave in the morning, the twins look like they be about to fall on they faces. But I noticed when they come back home…” They all said, “They so energized.”

Trinity said, “Exactly, it’s like they got a charge from somewhere. But it don’t make sense.” Latoya said, “What don’t make sense is them being so tired in the morning and at the same time.” They all agreed. They soon finished their conversation, because at that time it was time to pick us up from school.

Once we got home, we all did our normal routines. Once it was nighttime, we got prepared to sneak out. When it was time, I got the text from Cashae warning me so I won't get scared that she was in my yard. We all snuck out and had absolutely nothing to do, so we just chilled in the car and talked about everything. We didn't talk about anything too personal because Alisha friend was in the car. He rocked with us all week long, we couldn't thank him enough.

But he said he enjoyed it and that he needed to get out too. We talked about the pedicures and massages we looked forward to the next day, the guy couldn't believe the treatment we were getting in school. He thought we paid somebody for it but when we told him we didn't, he said we were lucky. Our chill session that night was everything, we were so relaxed and felt refreshed. At first, we thought we wasn't gone stay out until 11 like we did before, because we was just chillin.

But we ended up staying out a little past that time, because time fly's when you're having fun. It was Lashae who noticed, she jumped up and said, "Oh sh*t! It's after 11 ya'll." We all gasped. Alisha's friend sat up quick, he was leaned back in his chair, he cranked up the car and said, "Don't worry I'll get ya'll back in time." We didn't even go far this time, we were still in our neighborhood.

He started to drop us off as he did before, first Carmen, then Lashae, me and Cashae and then the twins. By the time me and Cashae said bye to each other, I expected to already get a text from Carmen and Lashae saying they got in the house already, especially Carmen because she was dropped off first. But I figured she wanted to change her clothes first, plus I had to worry about getting back in my house without getting caught.

I climbed up the outdoor flower wall to get to my room. I made sure I was really quiet coming in.

After I successfully snuck back inside my bedroom, I

quietly closed my window. As I turned around, I started to tip toe towards my bathroom barely making a sound. Before I could get to the end of my bed, my lights came on. When my lights came on, I think I stopped breathing. My eyes got so big and everything in me went numb.

I found myself stuck staring at my mom who happened to be sitting in a chair by my door, with a thick huge belt in her hand. She was staring back at me, but she looked pissed. She said, "So this is why you been so tired." I gasped real slow and light. She continued, "You been doing this all week haven't you?" I couldn't do anything but blink repeatedly while looking stupid, because I was trying to comprehend what was going on.

She said, "Where you went this time?" I opened my mouth and quietly said, "Nowhere." I was looking back and forth from her to the floor, back to her and into nowhere when I answered her. I didn't realize how I sounded when I answered her until she laughed a little bit, and said, "I just saw you sneak back in, and you still lie to my face." At that point, I realized how it sounded. I quickly tried to explain.

But because I didn't know if my cousins got caught and I didn't want to get my cousins in trouble, it sounded a little bit like, "No! no, that's not what I meant. I didn't go nowhere this time, we just went around the corner…" She looked surprised and said, "We??" I took another breath with my mouth wide open and said, "I…um." When I'm not prepared for Latoya, this is how bad it gets. I can't speak properly and can hardly finish a full sentence. I was terrified.

She saw my phone in my hand and said, "Give me that phone." I gasped because I didn't have a chance to delete anything, and my cousins might text me at any moment. I didn't want them to get in trouble, especially if they didn't get caught. At this point I was shaking. I don't know if it was because I had to give my mom my phone, or if it was the fact that I had to walk up to her and not know what was gone happen. Maybe it was both.

I hesitated for a second, she said, "Give me the phone!" I walked to her and gave it to her. She took it and said, "Who you was with?" I didn't know how to answer that, and she saw that in my face. After about a few seconds, she got up quick, swung that belt at me and said, "Who you was with?!" By this time I was screaming crying, those licks hurt. She just kept going, I tried to run but she was right behind me.

I fell and I knew it was all over at that point. She was talking to me while she beat me, so you know that beating was horrible. While that was happening to me, Cashae snuck back in her room. When she tried to walk from the window she turned around and bumped right into her mama. She screamed to the top of her lungs, she didn't know who it was at first. But then Beonca turned the light on, and Cashae screamed even louder.

Beonca instantly hit her with her belt and said, "Shut yo a** up!" That started Cashae's whoopin. Cashae was getting beat all across her room because she was running. She screamed extra loud every time she got hit and that made her mom madder. When Lashae got home, she got halfway through the window before her dad pulled her all the way in. It scared her so bad she screamed so loud. Uncle Gary said, "What the h*ll you doing sneaking in the house?! If you sneaking in, that mean you snuck out!"

Lashae was so quiet because she was so scared. She hardly get caught, so this was new to her. Uncle Gary called her mom in there to deal with her because he didn't want to hurt her. So Antwanise it was. She knew Lashae had snuck out, but she wasn't waiting in her room because she needed to calm her nerves before Lashae got back.

Now that she came in the room, Gary walked out after giving Lashae the worst look a parent can give a child when they're in trouble. Lashae looked down in disappointment. Her mom was giving her the stare. After about a minute Antwanise said, "Lashae what in the h*ll got into you?! I never even knew you would be the type to sneak out, this make me question everything." Lashae was looking down still.

Her mom said, "I had to leave the room when I found out you snuck out, because if I didn't…yo head would've been through that window right now." Just then Gary came back in the room and handed Antwanise a belt. She looked at him and he said, "If you don't do it, I promise you, I will!" He walked back out. Antwanise closed her eyes as she turned her head from the door, and opened them when she turned to Lashae again.

Lashae was scared, she got a beaten by her mom before but not often. Her mom said, “You forced me to do this.” Her mom started to beat her and Lashae went down, she was screaming crying too. When the twins snuck back in, they were working together. They helped each other in the window and was whispering about what they was gone do next, in order to not get caught. But as soon as they closed and locked that window, that light came on.

Before they could get a good glimpse of they mama, that belt started swinging. They started running around and crying. They didn’t see they mama good but they sure did hear her. She was cursing them out. All they heard was, “Ya’ll wana f*ckin sneak out and come back in here like ya’ll slick?!” She made one twin sit down while she beat the other one and then did the same to the twin that was waiting. I later found out that was the reason Carmen didn't text.

She was the first to get home and the first to get got. When she snuck back in, she got in her room and was happy because she didn't get caught. Then she opened her closet to change her clothes. When she opened the closet door, her mama was standing in the doorway with a belt. Carmen gasped, the light came on and her mama said, "You looking for these?" She was holding clothes Carmen had in a specific place in the closet, the clothes she planned to put on when she snuck back in.

Once she said that, Latonya started to beat Carmen. Carmen was more like me, she was stuck. So when she started getting hit, her mama got the best of her because she was too in shock to move at first. When those licks kicked in Carmen tried to run too, but she only made it to her bed, and it was over from there. We was getting our butts kicked! This really sucked because this was the last day we planned to sneak out and we messed round and got caught.

Mind you it was like 12 midnight now, so you know we was waking up the house with all that screaming and crying. This made our mamas madder because our sisters were sleeping. They felt like they had no other choice. They refused to let us get away with it, and we were still on punishment from lying to them when we had those detentions.

After my mom stopped beating me, she said, "You staying yo a** home tomorrow so you can get yo punishment!" I immediately thought about our feedback deal we had with Ms. Peterson, then I thought about the fact that I thought the beating was the punishment. I struggled to get it out, but I managed to say, "No, Mommie I…" She raised that belt again and said, "What?!" I jumped and got quiet.

She put the belt down and said, "What did you say?" I said, "I wana go to school." She said, "You just saying that to get away from me, you staying home tomorrow…now get yo a** up, change them clothes and take yo a** to bed!" I was crying a little bit more, because I didn't know what was going to happen with Ms. Peterson. I didn't want her to feel like we used her or lied to her. Latoya walked out my room.

I got up as quick as I could and started changing my clothes. I didn't want her to come back in my room just to see that I didn't do anything she told me to do yet. Lucky for me she didn't come back in my room that night. It took me at least 20 minutes to go to sleep, because I was scared that she was gonna come back in there and beat me again. The next morning, my mama and her sisters decided not to wake us up until they got back from taking our sisters to school.

So we were able to sleep in a little bit. I guess they did that so we can be rested for the punishment they had for us. When my mama woke me up, I was scared, and she didn't even wake me up in a hostile way or anything. I think it's safe to say, I'm scared of my mama too just like my cousins said they were. Once I got my morning routine done, I was told to go in the Livingroom. I sat on the couch on edge just waiting. Then the doorbell rung.

I was scared to move but Latoya came around the corner to open it, so I didn't have to worry about it. When she opened it, I saw Carmen walk in with her head down, her mama was right behind her. Once she came in, my other cousins came in with their mamas too. My cousins sat on the couch with me, while our mamas stood directly across from us with their arms folded. They were giving us the mom stare again, all of our heads were down.

Beonca said, "How long have ya'll been sneaking out this time?" We were quiet, then she said, "Alisha?" Alisha looked up fast and looked back down just as quick and said, "A week." Beonca was shocked and said, "Where did ya'll go? …Camille?" I looked up at her, took a breath, kind of looked to the side, then looked back down and said, "We went to a lot of places, it was always different." She said, "Camille?"

I looked up at her and said, "Ma'am?" She said, "I wana know where ya'll went, and I wana know NOW…every place, in the order ya'll went to them, the times ya'll arrived and the times ya'll left." I was looking very intimidated. Beonca don't get like this unless she is pissed, and I must say she was pissed. My cousins looked at me too like they was about to help me. Then Beonca said, "As a matter of fact, go get paper and a pen. I want you to write it down." I got up to go get paper and a pen.

This is what I mean by Beonca don't have to yell at you to get you, she has a way of talking to you that would make you instantly regret you ever did what you did. She was more aggressive this time than she usually would be. I wasn't gone try her because the next step would have been her going across my head. It takes a lot for her to do that and for some reason I think she was at that point. When I got the paper and pen, I came back in the Livingroom.

I was on my knees at one of the glass tables by the stairs writing. As I was writing, my aunties and my mom were still drilling my cousins. Since Beonca seem to be handling everything well, they decided to let her take over with the questioning because she was getting answers. I heard her say, "Whose idea was it to sneak out all week, Carmen??" Carmen looked up slow and back down, then she said, "All of ours."

Beonca said, "So it wasn't one or two people who came up with this, it was all 6 of ya'll??" Carmen and my other cousins all said, "Yes ma'am." Beonca got pissed, she turned around to me reaching her hand out and quickly said, "Give me that paper."

I got up and handed her the paper. She glanced at it, looked at me and said, "I need you to write the location of these places." She gave the paper back, I stood there looking confused with my mouth wide open. I said, "Auntie, I don't know where these places are…" She said, "Figure it out. You went to these places you should know…you got 5 minutes." I looked shocked and ran back to the table I was writing at.

I was holding my head looking at the paper stressing. I was able to write down a location for some of the places but not the full addresses. Soon, Beonca said, "You got two more minutes." While she started talking to my cousins again, I looked at Carmen and lowly said, "Help me." I looked like I wanted to cry. Some of my aunties heard me, my mama did too because they all looked at me.

Carmen budged, then her mama said, "Gone head and help ya cousin out, because she about to be in more trouble if she don't have that information on that paper in about a minute." Carmen hurried up to get to me. We started to talk low, she was pointing at the different locations and telling me what area they were in. She knew a lot but there was one place we didn't know. Beonca said, "Ya'll got 30 seconds." We started panicking.

They heard me say, "I don't know where that's at!" They heard Carmen say, "Well I don't either!" Beonca said, "20 seconds." Then Carmen looked up and said, "Alisha! Come here!" Alisha ran over there, we showed her the place, she thought for a second and then she told us what area it was. Right after I finished writing it, Beonca said, "Times up." She reached for the paper, I gave it to her. We sat back down. She looked at the paper and as her eyes went down the list of places, after reading it for a couple of seconds she said, "Ya'll gone get ya'll a**es beat again."

She wasn't even finished reading the list yet! Trinity said, "What happened, they didn't finish writing the locations??" Beonca said, "No, it's the places they went to!" Our mamas looked shocked and said, "Where they went??" Beonca went down the list and said,

"Well according to Camille, the first night they went to the Bar & Grill Lounge." Trinity said, "The one up the road, just past 5th??" Beonca said, "Yep…according to Camille, they got there at 9 and left at 11."

Trinity said, "You know that's after hours right? Kids can't go in there after hours." Our mama's looked pissed. Beonca said, "How ya'll got in??" We all looked at Alisha, we didn't mean to, but it happened that way. Alisha said, "My friend got us in." Latoya said, "Another teenager??" Alisha said, "Yes." Latonya said, "How the h*ll another teenager gone get more teenagers into an adult lounge after hours?!" Alisha said, "He knew the bouncers and the management working that night."

Our mamas shook their heads. Beonca said, "When did ya'll get home??" Cashae said, "Right after we left, we all got home in the 11 o'clock hour." Latoya said, "Keep going, where else they went?" Beonca looked back at the paper and started reading again, she said, "The next night, they went to the movies. They left there around the same time, 11. On Wednesday, they went to…a friend's house??" She looked at us and said, "I don't know why ya'll thought this was gone fly…who is this friend?? And they live about 20 minutes away." We looked worried.

I said, "Um…we met a couple nights before…" All of them yelled something at me at the same time, but I heard my mom the clearest, she said, "You went to somebody house you just met?!" I said, "We just met them, that's Alisha friend!" They all looked at Alisha, Beonca said, "That's yo friend??" Alisha said, "Yes." Beonca said, "How long ya'll knew each other?" Alisha said, "4 years." Beonca said, "And what is this friend's name?" The room got quiet, our mamas was tuned in because they wanted to know if it was a boy or a girl.

Then Alisha said, "Terrell…" Our mamas said, "Oh h*ll no!" Beonca said, "So ya'll snuck out to go chill at some boy house late at night?!" Trinity said,

"Were there any other boys there?" They all got quiet again, then Alisha said, "Yes." They all went crazy fussing at us. Latoya got up and said, "Where is my belt?!" We were scared. Latoya actually went and got a belt, then came back in the Livingroom and sat down with it.

She looked at Beonca and said, "Where else did they go?" Beonca said, "Last night, they were chillin in the car a couple of blocks up…" Beonca looked at us and said, "What car ya'll was in?? None of ya'll supposed to be driving, so I know like h*ll ya'll didn't take a car!" We all said, "No." She said, "Then who car ya'll was in when ya'll was chillin and who car ya'll was in this whole week?!" We all said, "Alisha friend."

Beonca said, "What friend?? What's their name??" We all said, "Terrell." Our mama's said, "What?!" We all jumped up off the couch and ran towards the stairs. Good thing we did because Beonca and Latoya darted at us. Latonya and Trinity stopped them in their tracks. Trinity said, “Wait a minute ya’ll! I know ya’ll wana beat they a**es right now, I wana beat they a**es my d*mn self! ...But let’s move on to what we need to do for the punishments while we still have the time. Remember? This is why we kept them out of school today.”

Beonca and Latoya calmed down, we were looking confused. They made us get dressed and get in the car. They drove to every place we said we went to, except the park and the movies. When we got to the lounge, they spoke to the manager. It was so embarrassing. They made sure they knew our faces and told them to not allow us in there anymore. The manager agreed because they didn’t want to get sued.

It was a big deal because they were planning to check who worked that night. They also wanted to watch the cameras to see who let us in. We didn’t want to get anybody fired and we didn’t want to mess up Alisha friend’s connection. These people were so shook, they took our pictures to give to their staff to make sure we never got back in. It was humiliating and our mamas was like, "This is what happens when you wana be sneaky."

We thought the worst was over because we came back home and had been there for some hours. But then, our mamas forced us to give them Terrell's address. Before we knew it, we were pulling up to his house after school was over. When we got there, we were like, "Oh no," and "Aw man." Alisha was crying when her mama tried to make her get out the car, she said, "Ma please…" Trinity said, "Nope, get yo a** out the car."

When Latoya told me to get out, I said, "Ma this is so embarrassing, this not even my friend." She said, "But this was yo friend when you came over here …let's go." They had a hard time getting us out the car. When we finally got out the car, we went to the door and his mom answered the door. She was shocked to see us, she didn't know us personally, but she was shocked to see us. She said, "Hi, how can I help you?" Latoya said, "Hi, we're here to speak with Terrell's mom." She said, "I am she, come on in."

We all walked in and sat down. She said, "So, what brings you ladies here?" Beonca said, "We're here because Terrell had our girls in your house two nights ago. They snuck out to come here to "chill" as they say." His mom's eyes got big, she instantly yelled, "Terrell!" We got scared because we didn't know he was there. He came running downstairs saying, "Yeah Ma?!" When he saw us, he paused as he looked around nervously.

We were so embarrassed. Our parents purposely waited until school was out, because they knew it was a good chance he was home. He said, "What's happening?" His mom said, "Did you sneak them in my house two nights ago?!" He took a deep breath as he grabbed his head and rubbed his face. She said,

"Terrell??" He said, "I brought them here, they wanted to chill so we came here because it was safer than chillin on the streets."

His mom said, "I wasn't home that night, you know better than to have people in here when I'm not here." Latoya said, "Can I ask Terrell a question please?" His mom said, "Of course." Latoya looked at him and said, "Are you the one that's been picking them up and dropping them back off home all week??" Terrell looked nervous and said, "Yes ma'am." His mom was confused. Our mamas explained the whole thing and the sneaking out.

His mama was mad and said, "Why would you help them sneak out Terrell??" He said, "If I didn't, they would've still snuck out with no transportation. I didn't want anything to happen to them, the least I could do was make sure they was safe. They were desperate, they said they would still do it even if I didn't help them."

Our mamas was livid with us. Terrell sat down and we all had to hash out the whole thing. His story matched our story about our whereabouts that week. To our mamas, he seemed like a nice boy, and they appreciated him looking out for us. But that still did not excuse what we did. They told his mama there were more boys there, he had to tell his mama who the boys were. Our mamas told him they went to the lounge and said something, he was on edge about that.

By the time we left, we were still on good terms with him, but we felt horrible. We cried on the way home because we were so embarrassed. Our mamas told us we should be embarrassed. When we got back to my house, we were sitting in the Livingroom again. This time my mama took over, when she stood up everybody got nervous. She said, "We checked ya'll phones last night…"

We took a breath while covering our faces and lowly said, "Oh gosh." Latoya said, "Ya'll was real vague with ya'll text messages, but we were still able to see enough." She stared at us for a few seconds and then said, "Ya'll have the nerve to celebrate sneaking back in without gettin caught…and then these text messages between ya'll as ya'll snuck out is disturbing!"

We were quiet still looking scared. She continued, "Ya'll really work together, telling each other when to sneak out, how to sneak out and where to go when you sneak out. This is how ya'll get away with it so much!" The entire room was quiet. After a few seconds Latoya said, "Do we need to separate ya'll and keep ya'll from each other or something?!" We all responded quick and said, "Nooo."

She looked at us and said, "That's where it's gone head if ya'll don't cut this sh*t out and I mean right d*mn now!" Latonya said, "You know what Toya, that's not a bad idea. Maybe if they separate, they'll know how to act." We all looked at Latonya hoping they didn't do that, Carmen looked like she was about to cry as she said, "Ma, nooo please." My other aunties started to agree with the idea, which scared the crap out of us.

By the time they looked back at us, we all were crying and wiping tears from our eyes. They had our attention, and they knew it. They talked to us some more, they were all mad at us especially after seeing our text threads. All we could do was listen and be quiet until we were spoken to. After getting drilled for another 5 minutes, Latoya told me, "And Camille..." She looked at me with daggers and I looked at her.

She said, "You are not allowed in your room after 6 until I say different." I pouted just a little bit and she said, "You have a problem? Because I can take you and lock you up. You won't see or talk to nobody." I said, "No, I don't have a problem." She said, "You sure??" I said, "Yes ma'am." I was so scared. She looked at me a little while longer and then said, "Good.

Like I said, after you leave from this Livingroom get what you need from yo room and take yo a** in that guestroom closest to Reci. You don't need much, get yo clothes and don't worry about electronics or a charger, because from 6 until you get to school the next morning…that phone is mine…and don't try to be slick and text anybody making plans before that time, because I'm checking yo phone everyday throughout the day."

I took a quick light breath, my cousins was looking like, daaaaaang. Beonca said, "It'll be the same for the rest of ya'll too." All of my cousins looked at her like they saw a ghost, I was shocked myself. Beonca continued, "Ya'll wana sneak out all the time and ya'll obviously familiar with ya'll rooms, so ya'll will not have the privilege of sleeping in ya'll rooms until we feel ya'll can handle it." Latoya said, "We don't wana hear nothin, ya'll know what we told ya'll, and ya'll better not f*ck up or ya'll gone have a whole lot more sh*t to deal with…ya'll understand?"

We was looking sad and said, "Yes ma'am." Latoya said, "Good…Camille go get yo stuff and head to that room." I went upstairs, me and my cousins were too scared to say bye to each other. My cousins left soon after I went upstairs. All we knew was to avoid trouble at all costs. We was in deep this time, we didn't know what to do. We had one more strike and everything to lose.

Chapter 11

No More Trouble

It had only been three days since we started this punishment, and it already felt like forever. I was on edge in my own house 24-7 since we got caught, so it was a relief when Monday came, and we could go back to school again. My mama was not exaggerating when she said my phone is hers until I get to school. She didn't hand it to me until I got out the car!

It was weird because I didn't have my phone all weekend, but I was so happy to get it back. Of course she didn't see how happy I was because I waited until I went inside the school to show it. When I got inside, I smiled so hard and yelled, "Yes!" with my knee to my elbow. As I did this, my cousins walked up on me and Carmen said, "You okay??" They scared me because I didn't see them, they laughed. I laughed and said, "Oh! Girl yeah, I just got my phone back."

They all said, "We did too." Cashae said, "I feel so lost now, we didn't talk all weekend and now we here…at school…booo." Alisha said, "I feel the same way." We started walking down the hallway. I said, "I just feel all wrong…I can't sleep in my room, I don't have full access to all of my stuff, I'm being watched 24-7…I feel like a prisoner in my own house." My cousins agreed and said, "Yes!" I said, "Not to mention, today just feel kind of off to me. Does it feel off to ya'll?"

Lashae said, "It does feel off, but I just thought it was because of how we had to change rooms and stuff." Carmen said, "Nah I feel it too, something don't seem right." I said, "Exactly…like who's Camille?? I feel off and my surroundings feel off." Alicia said, "Ya'll being weird." Cashae said, "No they not. Alicia, just stand there for a minute. Don't talk or think, just look around for a second." We all got quiet so she can do what Cashae told her to do.

After that minute Alicia body shook like she was creeped out, then she said, "Okay, yeah I see what ya'll talking bout." We said, "See??" and "Told you." It was a few minutes before the bell rung, so we started to head towards our classes. While we walked, we talked some more. Carmen said, "Did any of ya'll mamas threaten ya'll this morning?" We all laughed a little and said, "Yeah." I said, "My mama told me I bet not get in no trouble at all or that's my a**. Especially after all the trouble I been in lately."

My cousins said, "Same." Alisha said, "Well let's just enjoy this time we have out of the house and get through the day without getting in trouble." Cashae said, "Yeah, I'm trying to get my room back." As we agreed and said, "For real," a group of girls pushed their way right through us, bumping all of us. We stopped for a second in shock. We turned around to the girls and they turned to us. The girl that bumped me said, “Next time move out our way.” I looked at her like, I know you didn’t.

Carmen came near me and put her arm in front of my chest and said, “Don’t do it Camille.” She stopped me right in time because I saw myself jumping on that girl. The girl saw Carmen hold me back and felt she was bad. So she said, “Hold on, nobody gotta hold you back.” She handed her stuff to her friend and said, “Hold this.” She looked at me and said, “I’ll make it easy for you, I’ll come to you.” She started walking towards me and stopped right in front of me.

Carmen was still right there staring the girl down, she still had her arm up in front of me. The girl just stood there at first, but then she felt dumb, so she pointed her finger in my face and said, “If you don’t wana get bumped, next time move out the way b*tch.” Carmen was still looking at the girl but was shocked.

Without looking at me, Carmen said, “Camille…” Without looking at Carmen and keeping eye contact with the girl, I said, “What?” Carmen said, “Do it.” As soon as she said that she moved her arm, and I hit the girl like 6 times before she even realized she was in a fight.

Her friends of course ran up, so my cousins started fighting them. For girls who have that much mouth, they cannot back it up. I mean I know we some great fighters but were we that great? These girls made us feel like we beat up some elementary school kids. The crowd started to form as people realized there was a fight. Next thing you know, we hear whistles and security came running down the hall.

They were yelling, “Hey! Break it up! Break it up!” When security broke it up the bell rung, they were exhausted and pissed off. We looked at the girls and they were all crying. I looked at the one I fought, she was struggling to get up off of the floor. I kept looking at her until she looked at me and when she did, I said, “Who the b*tch na?” She looked back down still crying and picking up her stuff.

We looked untouched, but they looked like they needed a touch up. The security drug us all to the office. When we got in there, one security guard said, “School didn’t even start yet and ya’ll out here fighting! It’s too early in the morning for this.” Soon the security walked out, and the principal walked in. I don’t know what we were thinking, but we didn’t expect to hear the next thing that came out of the principal’s mouth.

We were sitting quiet waiting to see what would happen next. The principal sat on the desk facing us and took a breath. Then he said, “Ladies, ladies, what’s going on this morning??" We were quiet and looking down. Up until this point, we only thought about how mad we were that the girls tried us. Until of course the principal said, "Fighting is an automatic suspension for 10 days." When he said that, reality kicked in. Our reactions were so fast and loud.

We scared him with how we reacted, and he jumped hard for a split second. We all burst out with, "NO!" Then we started to cry loud like babies. We were crying so hard he couldn't understand what we were saying. He started to feel bad for us, he was staring at us still in shock for a minute. After he was over his shock, he got some tissues for us and talked us down until we were calm. When we finally got to the point of light breaths and occasional sniffles, the principal was able to ask us what happened.

We explained to him what the girls did that morning, he seemed shocked and said, "I'm gonna check in on that." He left out the room and when he came back, he said, "I believe your story, I do, but the way those girls look out there…I'm not sure how we could get past not suspending you all without it looking like favoritism." We started crying again. We begged him not to suspend us.

I said, "Just because they look like they were in a fight and we don't, doesn't make it fair for us to be suspended when they started it." The principal said, "I know." We would not give up, we kept begging him not to call our parents and not to suspend us. We spent like 5 more minutes pleading, apologizing and trying to persuade him to let us off with a warning this time.

After listening to us for so long he said, "Okay, I'll tell you what…I'll go speak to a few people about what they saw. Then I'll speak with the Vice Principal, because in situations like this we both would have to agree on waiving the suspension." We said, "Okay." He left out. He was gone for like 10 or 15 minutes. While he was gone, I told my cousins, "This is f*cked up, they not seeing our side because we don't look like we been in a fight." Carmen was talking through her crying and said, "I can't get in…trouble man."

After we collected ourselves, I said, "I say we make ourselves look like we was in a fight." My cousins said, "What?" I said, "The Vice Principal didn't see us yet, if we look like we been in a fight maybe they'll take our side." Cashae said, "How we do that?" I said, "Like this." I loosened my ponytail and made it look like it was pulled out. After that, I shifted my clothes a bit to make it look like they were stretched out. My cousins said, "Oooh."

Then they did the same thing, not the exact same thing but they got what I meant. Shortly after we finished, the principal walked back in with the vice principal. He was looking at the vice principal explaining what was going on, so he didn't see us right away. Once they closed the door, he looked at us and he tried so hard to hold his laughter. We were looking straight faced and exhausted, we knew how to act. The whole time we were talking to the vice principal, the principal put his arm up to his mouth whenever he had a minor outburst of laughter.

He laughed every time he looked at us, because he knew we didn't look like that before he left. The vice principal thought something was wrong with him, at one point she asked him, "Are you okay??" He said, "Yes, I just need some water." The vice principal spoke to us, and she believed us too. She felt bad for us. She looked at the principal and said, "I believe them, it's not fair if the other girls did this…I say waive the suspension." We got so happy when we heard her say that. The principal said, "Yeah, that was my take on it as well."

As they agreed to waive the suspension, the security guards came back in. When they came in, they saw us and paused. One of them said, "What happened to ya'll??" The vice principal said, "They got in a fight, but we can handle it." The security guard said, "Again??" The vice principal said, "What do you mean? They were in one fight this morning." The security guard said, "The one I broke up?!" She said, "Oh did you?" He said, "Yeah! …and they didn't look like this!"

She said, "Of course not, when you come to school you dress nice you look nice." He said, "No ma'am, after we broke up the fight, these girls looked like a million bucks. If they ran before we got to the fight, we wouldn't have known they fought." We was looking at him squinting our eyes, we really wanted him to shut his fat mouth. The vice principal said, "Well regardless of that, if they were left with the only option to protect themselves, they shouldn't get suspended." We were so relieved to hear her say that.

The security guard said, "But did you see the other girls??" The vice principal said, "The only thing I'm concerned about is who and what caused this conflict…" The security guard cut her off and said, "But they asking for medical attention!" The vice principal's mouth dropped. Me and my cousins looked at each other surprised. The security guard continued, "The ambulance is on the way."

The vice principal jumped off the table and hurried out the door behind the security. We were left just sitting quiet thinking. They were gone for a while. About 20 minutes later, the vice principal came back in talking on a walkie talkie. The principal came in after her, she looked distressed. She sat on the table again and took a deep breath while she looked at us.

We looked back at her. She said, "I'm so sorry ladies, we really wanted to waive the suspension. But because the security knows what happened and the girls are now going to the hospital, it would be frowned upon for us to allow you to stay at school. Not to mention, anyone, their parents, security or whoever, can reach out to the county and have us terminated for it if this gets bigger and you ladies weren't suspended." Me and my cousins were disappointed, we took a breath and looked down.

The principal said, "I do hope you ladies understand we're on your side and we were going to waive it for you, but under the circumstances we...." I said, "We understand, and we thank you both for doing that for us." The vice principal said, "I'm sorry ladies…" When she said that, the security came in the room. We didn't even want to look at security, they came in and just stood there staring at us. They would speak with the principal and vice principal here and there, but that's it.

Soon the principal said, "We need to go get the paperwork for them." They excused themselves and left out. While we sat there dazed, I said, "I don't know how I'ma explain this to my mama." Cashae said, "Security just wana see us get in trouble." Alisha said, "That, or they wana see our mamas." We all said,

"Typical." We were so upset how it all played out and at the same time we were lost for words. We were all still looking down in silence, then the door opened again. We expected we had to sign the papers for the suspension.

But when we looked up, we saw our mamas walk in there and Latoya was first! I was in the seat closest to the door, so I was terrified. Our eyes got so big, I was shaking. I leaned over resting my arms on my lap as I covered my face with my hands, I lowly said, "Oh my gosh." They didn't tell us they called our mamas already, this was bad.

As soon as they walked in, they was fussin us out. They each went to their child and stood in front of us. First thing they said was, "Why ya'll look like that?!" They got mad because in their heads they were thinking, I know they didn't sit there and get they a**es beat like that. Latoya said, "So this is what you do?? …I send you to school, tell you to stay out of trouble and you get suspended before school even start?! How the h*ll you do that?!" My cousins was getting fussed out too.

The security walked in the room just as my mama hit my hands to move them from my face. The security saw it and heard her say, "Take yo hands off yo face!" We all paused and looked at security. The security guards faces lit up when they saw our moms, they tried to hide it. They said, "Hello, how are you ladies?" Our mamas said, "Hello." Security started to explain the fight, which I'm sure they were not supposed to.

The security said, "Your girls were all over those girls, they sent them to the hospital…the ambulance just left before you got here." Our mamas looked back at us, then security felt the need to say, "And I don't know what they got going on, but they didn't look like that after the fight, they looked untouched. Not a hair was out of place. Unless there was a strong gust of wind from the hallway to the office, I don't know why they look like that right now."

We were so mad and irritated with security. Our mamas said, "Thank you for letting us know." Our mamas turned back to us looking pissed, they started fussin at us again. We tried to explain but they were mad because the hospital had to get involved. I said, "Ma, if we didn't they would've still fought us." Carmen said, "Exactly, they was all up in our faces." Latonya asked Carmen, "Ya'll know them??" Carmen said, "No."

Latonya said, "Then how the h*ll ya'll know they was still gone fight ya'll?! Why would they be fighting ya'll anyway out the blue early this morning if ya'll don't know them??" Carmen threw her arms in her lap, looked to the side and took a deep breath. I think at that point she gave up. Cashae said, "They bumped into us on purpose." Alisha said, "We even let that go,

Carmen calmed Camille down and we was about to walk away."

Lashae said, "Yeah, but the girl that bumped Camille turned around and came up in her face being disrespectful. She was puttin her hands in her face…" Alicia said, "Yeah, threatening her and calling her out her name. So when her hands got too close to Camille face, she popped off. Then the other girls ran up on us."

Latoya said, "What?!" Beonca said, "Something not adding up, why ya'll look like this?" Carmen said, "We was trying not to get suspended." That confused all of them. Trinity said, "What?!" I said, "We told the principal what happened and he believed us, but then we saw how security and other people were bias because the girls looked beat up and we didn't. So when the principal went to get permission from the vice principal to waive our suspension, we messed our hair up and stuff so they could listen to our side and not judge us off looking untouched…"

Antwanise said, “What the h*ll??” I said, “They decided to waive the suspension because they knew those girls started with us…” Then I extended my arm out toward security and said, “But <u>they</u> came in making us look like the bad guys, so the principals said they couldn’t waive it no more!” The security said, “Excuse us, just to be clear, they couldn’t waive the suspension because the girls got the hospital involved and that would look bad on the principals.”

Our mamas looked back at us pissed. “I said, “They just wana see us get in trouble.” Latoya quickly pointed at me and said, “Shut yo d*mn mouth.” Just then the principals walked in. They showed our mamas the papers and explained what happened. They went into further detail on why each girl was seeking medical attention. They explained why they couldn’t waive the suspension and then they told them we were suspended for 10 days.

When our mamas heard that, they hesitated for a second to take it all in. Latoya completely zoned out and was looking into space while my aunties continued to talk to the principals. I knew I was in trouble. She eventually started talking to them again. They gave them our suspension papers and our mamas walked over to us. Latoya lowly said, “I just f*ckin dropped you off. I couldn't even make it to Crystal school good before they come calling me about yo a**…lets go.”

We all got up and left out the school. When we got to the front of the school, our mamas stopped in front of us giving us that death stare. Latoya said, “Ya’ll better get a good look at each other…” We instinctively looked at each other confused. She continued and said, “Because this is ya’ll last time seeing or talking to each other for the next two weeks.” We gasped.

We started to tear up. Trinity said, “Gone head and say bye, give ya’ll hugs because we ain’t playin with ya'll a**es." We gave each other hugs as we lightly cried and whispered bye to each other. When we finished, Latoya said, "Phones." They all held out their hands, we slowly took out our phones and handed them to them. Latoya said, "During this suspension, ya'll will not have phones, electronics, visitors, tv and ya'll staying ya'll a**es in the house at all times."

We begin to pout but not too noticeably, then Trinity said, "Ya'll already got ya'll rooms taken away, are ya'll not gone stop until ya'll have nothing left??" At this point we knew the only thing they were concerned about was us being suspended, and we were hoping they didn't send us back to bootcamp. Beonca said, "Ya'll didn't even get off ya'll first punishment, because ya'll got in trouble again after that and ya'll just keep adding to it."

Latonya said, "It's just gone keep getting worse every time for ya'll." Antwanise said, "Ya'll have to realize that we not lettin up on ya'll until ya'll cut the foolishness." Latonya said, "All this trouble ya'll been in back to back is ridiculous, it needs to stop now." Latoya said, "If ya'll didn't learn by now, ya'll gone learn today…let's go."

We all went with our mom and went home. They really meant what they said about not seeing or talking to each other. Normally they would all meet at my house and then go home from there. But I guess that's why they spoke to us in front of the school, because they knew we were not meeting up afterwards. When I got home, I had to get what I needed from my room because I was told to stay in the other room fully for now.

My mama knew I couldn't climb out the window in that guestroom, and if I came out that room, she would hear me because I would have to pass by her room. I was stuck. I had no other options but to listen and be on punishment. I eventually fell asleep. When it was time to pick up my sisters, my mama woke me up. She said she was not leaving me home by myself. When we got back home, I was told to go back in the room.

My sisters wasn't even allowed to purposely interact with me, like to play or come in the guestroom to talk. I was bored, miserable and helpless. I imagine my cousins felt no different than what I did. This punishment straight up sucked! Although the fight wasn't our fault, our mamas don't do suspensions, detentions, expulsions, nothing, they are no nonsense parents especially when it comes to school. This is why we make it worth it whenever it happens.

But they never did us like this before, separating us and not allowing us to talk or see each other. We started to feel like bootcamp wouldn't have been so bad. Our mamas were dedicated to this punishment, they didn't see each other either just so me and my cousins wouldn't see each other. I guess they hoped that being apart like that, would make us act right when we got back together again and appreciate that privilege.

Not sure how that's gone play out but for now it's affecting all of us terribly. We were on close watch and lockdown for real this time and all we had was time to think.

Chapter 12

Not Again

After ten long days, fourteen if you count the weekends, the day had come for us to go back to school. We were happy to go back to school, not only to see each other, but to also finally get out of the house! For fourteen days all we saw was those four walls in the guestrooms they put us in. Not to mention we got a beaten everyday of our suspension…yeah getting suspended dealing with them is on a whole different level.

We NEVER wanted to experience that again. As we left the house, we hid our excitement because we were scared we would get in trouble. When I got to school, I slowly got out of my mama's car. After closing the door, I slowly walked up to the school's door. Although I was happy to be out of the house, I have to admit I was kind of reluctant to go in the school.

Once my mama drove off, I was stuck standing right in front of the door looking down at the ground. I was in deep thought, until I heard, "Camille!!" I looked up quick and saw Carmen running up to me smiling. I smiled and said, "Carmen!!" When she got to me, she jumped in my arms like a toddler lol. She gave me the biggest hug and I gave her one back. We were so happy to see each other.

As I put her down, Cashae dramatic behind walked up looking and sounding like she was crying. She had her arms spread out. We embraced her when she got to us, then we realized she really was crying. She made us cry, although me and Carmen was lowkey wiping tears from our eyes from when we first saw each other. When we stopped hugging, Cashae said, "I missed ya'll so much, I never been on a punishment like this before." We said, "We miss you too."

Then we heard, "Oh my gosh!" We looked and both twins was running towards us. We all screamed and gave each other hugs. I looked around and said, "Where Shae at?" Then I heard from behind me, "Hey ya'll!!" I turned around and saw Lashae running to us from the opposite direction. We all said, "Shae!!" We gave her hugs. After our hugs, I said, "Aw man, it feels good to see ya'll again." They all agreed and said, "Yeah for real." I said, "Did any of ya'll get ya'll rooms back yet?"

It was silent for a couple of seconds, then we all burst out laughing loud. Carmen said, "Yeah right!" After the laughter died down, I said, "I just hope those girls don't come back with the foolishness today." Alisha said, "Forget them h*es, if we fight again, I'm dragging them off campus." Cashae said, "For real." Lashae said, "I'm just happy to be out of that house!" Carmen said, "Yeah…" as she rubbed her butt she continued, "I'm <u>too</u> sore."

All of us said, “Me too,” as we rubbed a body part that was sore from those beatings. Alicia said, “Well, now that we have a second chance at this, let’s just get through school so we can start hanging out like we use to.” We agreed. Then the bell rung. I said, “Let’s go so we won’t be late, it’s best for us to start off on the right foot today.” Cashae said, “Yeah, let’s go.” We walked inside the school and headed to class.

We all have the same first hour, so we were able to walk together. People who knew we were suspended was staring at us, but we ignored it. We finally got to class. As we walked in everybody including the teacher couldn’t keep their eyes off of us. It was like they were shocked to see us there. The teacher said, “Ladies! Welcome back!” We said, “Thank you,” and took our seats.

The final bell rung shortly after we sat down, and class started. We begin to do our work given to us by the teacher, we were extra quiet trying to be on our best behavior. We did not want to get in trouble with our mamas no more. Everything was going well, we even finished all of our work right before first hour ended. Since everyone was finished, we were able to chill and talk for the rest of the class period. It was only five minutes of class left but we still did not talk.

Everybody including the teacher noticed. Once the bell rung, we got our stuff and got up to leave the classroom. When we got in the hallway, we were about to separate because we had different classes next period. As we were walking down the hall, the girl who I fought was walking in our direction. Cashae and Carmen was supposed to turn off at the hallway we passed by right before.

But when they saw the girl, they were on edge and wanted to stay with us in case something went down. When the girl got to us, she tried to not to look at us as she walked past us. We all were side eyeing her until she was out of our eyesight. Once we couldn't see her no more, Carmen said, “That’s what I thought.” Then Carmen and Cashae turned around to watch the girl.

They were still walking with us but because they turned around, they were walking backwards. After a minute they heard me say, “Carmen.” Right after that, the other girls who we fought was walking past us. But they kind of walked through us again this time! Some of them tried not to touch us but one girl did not care. She walked right between me and Carmen. Her shoulder bumped Carmen hard enough for Carmen to jerk forward. Carmen looked at her and then at us confused.

The girl kept walking. I looked at Carmen confused, pointed at the girl and said, “Did she just…” Carmen said, “She did.” I started walking in her direction fast, my cousins didn’t try to stop me either. They walked right behind me. The girl knew what she did because as soon as we started walking in her direction, she took off running. Our mouths dropped, she started running without even looking back. We didn't know how she knew we were behind her. This is how we knew she was aware of what she did.

I said, "Oh h*ll nah!" Carmen put her arm in front of me and said, "Camille wait." We all stopped and watch her as she ran up to the girls she was with. When she reached them, they didn't ask questions, they all started running. Now we felt like it was planned. While they ran, we heard one girl say, "You did it for real?!" Cashae said, "Ya'll heard her??" Alisha said, "Them scary slick b*tches, she did that on purpose!" The girls started looking back at us as they ran a little further.

As soon as they looked back, they tripped and fell. They tore that floor up! The sound was so loud, everyone in the hallway got quiet and turned around. We instantly started laughing uncontrollably loud. The girls heard us and saw us laughing, which made them mad. They were really hurt from the fall and struggled to get up. By this time everybody in the hallway was pointing and laughing at them. They got so embarrassed they started to limp towards the front door. They wanted to get out of everybody's site. We watched as they cried and limped towards the door.

When they finally got out the door, I told my cousins, "Ya'll come on!" We ran to the doors and saw the girls looking at their wounds and checking themselves. But they were standing right in front of the doors, they didn't go far. While me and my cousin were running towards the doors, Lashae said, "What are we doing?" I said, "Let's lock them out." Carmen and Cashae smiled and said, "Yes!" When we got to the door, we looked to see where they were.

Cashae and Carmen locked the first set of double doors right away. The girls heard it and looked. They saw us and realized what we were doing, so the girl who bumped Carmen ran to the second set of double doors where I was. She pulled it open. I pulled it back closed. The second time she pulled it open, the twins and Lashae came to help me. In the middle of what seemed to be tug of war, I said, "Wait!" My cousins let up on the door. When the girl pulled the door open again, I pushed her, she flew backwards and fell on the ground. When she fell, we pulled the door closed and locked it.

She was still on the ground looking at her friends confused and checking her hands. We started laughing amongst ourselves and peeking through the window laughing and pointing at them. Alisha said, "Okay, that's enough. Let's head to class now." We were still laughing as we all said, "Okay." We turned around to head to class. When we turned around, the principal was standing there with his arms crossed looking at us. We all gasped, and our eyes got so big.

He said, "Did I just see what I think I saw?" We were looking around with shifty eyes. We were speechless. Cashae said, “Uh…that depends…what did you see?” The principal said, “I hope I’m wrong, but I saw you girls push some girls out the door and locked them out…am I wrong?” There was a slight pause, then Carmen said, “Oh you’re way off, completely wrong.” The principal said, “Excuse me,” as he made his way to the door. We moved out of his way.

He looked out the window and said, “Then why are there girls outside?” We all looked at each other. He opened the door and asked the girls, “Why are you ladies out here?” They said, “They locked us out.” He asked, “Did they push you all out?” The girl said, “I got pushed.” The principal turned to us and said, “I thought you said I was wrong?” Carmen said, “You still are.” He looked at her and said, “How so Ms. Rogers?”

We were not prepared for what came out of Carmen’s mouth next, but we knew it was about to piss him off. Carmen said, “You said you saw us push some girls out the door and lock them out…” He said, “Yes, they are the girls, and these are the doors that were locked." Carmen continued and said, "But you loud and wrong though." We all looked at Carmen, at this point the principal crossed his arms and zoned in on Carmen and said, "Is that so?"

Carmen said, "Yes, you said we pushed some girls out the door and locked them out…we didn't push nobody, and Camille only pushed one girl. If you ask me, she saved her from getting hurt because she was about be smashed in the door." The principal took a deep slow breath as he rolled his eyes up towards the ceiling. At this point I started to whisper to my cousins.

Once the principal collected himself, he looked at us and said, "I tried to save you last time because you were innocent. But you just got back from suspension, and you do this. It makes you look bad, it makes you ladies look like the aggressors." We all talked at the same time saying, "But we not!" Cashae said, "She bumped into Carmen first!" Carmen said, "Yeah, she started with me!" I said, "We was only trying to get rid of the problem, to make yo job easier!" The principal had to laugh at that remark, he laughed so hard. When he stopped laughing, he looked at us still smiling and said, "I really do like you ladies, I do but you can't do stuff like this."

We stood there quiet. Then he stopped smiling and said, "This is considered an altercation on top of other things that are not permitted in school. You cannot lock someone out and you cannot lock the doors that are supposed to be open. That is a safety hazard…I'm sorry ladies but, I'm afraid I'm going to have to suspend you again for this." Our mouths dropped. I said, "I knew it!" I tapped Alisha shoulder with the back of my hand. When I did that me, Lashae, Alisha and Alicia took off running in the opposite direction.

Carmen and Cashae immediately jumped in front of the principal and started asking him questions.

He said, “Wait a minute, where are they going?!” Carmen said, “Why are we getting suspended?” Cashae said, “Yeah that’s not fair, are they getting suspended too?” The principal said, “They’re the ones that got locked out.” Carmen said, “But she bumped me.” The principal said, “Where did your cousins go??”

The principal was unaware that I whispered to my cousins while he was collecting himself. I told them I felt like we were going to get suspended again, but I’m not letting my mama find out this time. I told them if he says we getting suspended, me, the twins and Lashae are going to go to the office to change our parents contacts. I also told Carmen and Cashae to stay and distract the principal while we get it done.

When Carmen and Cashae questions stopped working, they darted towards the door pretending to try to fight the girls. They were trying to distract the principal and he took the bait. Carmen and Cashae are so funny. While the principal grabbed Carmen, she was running in place with her head down like she was trying to play football. Cashae tried not to laugh, then Carmen made this funny face and started repeating, "Let me at her, let me at her!" Cashae said, "Yeah!"

She ran on the other side of the principal, so he was forced to grab her too. She did that because he was about to call security and they didn't want him to, because they were pretending. But he didn't know that. Now he had both his hands full and couldn't use his walkie-talkie.

As we made our way to the principal's office, we bumped into the office staff. We were breathing so hard and did not expect to see them. They stopped us and one lady said, "Excuse me! What are you ladies doing?!" We stopped and then I said, "The principal needs help! He can't call anybody!" The people in the office got worried. They said, "Where is he?!" Alicia said, "Come on, I'll show you!" They ran behind Alicia, leaving the office empty and vulnerable.

Alicia really played the part because this was not planned at all. While they were gone Lashae closed and locked the door. I said, “Alright, they have about 3 different files with the same information on’em, find them. Find them and change them. Ya’ll look over there, I’ll look in the principal’s office.” They said, “Okay.” They started to go through the files quickly as I made my way in the principal’s office.

Meanwhile, Alicia was taking the office staff on a wild goose chase to buy us time. She purposely took them to a hallway on the opposite side of where the principal was in the school. When she got there, she said, “Aw man where did he go! We have to find him, he’s in trouble!” Alicia did this about 4 times before the office staff got tired and started questioning her.

They were about to go back to the office, but then Alicia said, “No wait! ...Um where is the art class?” One guy from the office staff said, “The art class is in the front of the school on the west end.”

Alicia calmly said, “That’s where he is.” The lady said, “Why didn’t you so, we could’ve found him sooner, let’s go.” Alicia pretended to be lost in the school but knew exactly what she was doing. As she headed back to the principal, she looked back hoping we got what we needed.

Back in the office, we were finding our files. Lashae and Alisha had all but one. As I found the last of our files, they found the last of theirs. We put them all down. Lashae said, “What do we do now?” I said, “Let’s change the contact numbers, that way they can’t call them.” Alisha said, “What numbers should we put?” I said, “Whatever numbers don’t work.” Alisha said, “I got you.”

She gave us some numbers that were not in service, and we changed all of them. We even changed the backup contacts numbers, like my God mom and our grandmas. We had to change a lot of numbers because they were all on each of our files.

Alicia finally made it to the principal with the office staff. They saw him still struggling with Carmen and Cashae. When the principal saw them, he was so relieved, he said, "Oh thank God someone came I was unable to call." Alicia had no idea this was going to happen, it just worked in her favor. Once the office staff helped him grab Carmen and Cashae, they were shocked to see that it was Alicia's cousins. Carmen and Cashae looked up and saw Alicia and was confused. The lady said, "Wait, aren't these your cousins??" Alicia said, "Yeah."

The lady said, "You told on your own cousins?" The principal said, "Wait what?" The lady said, "They came running to the office saying you needed help and couldn't call for anyone." The principal was so spooked, he looked at Alicia and said, "How did ya'll know that? I wasn't in distress until about 10 minutes ago." Alicia just looked at him, Carmen and Cashae was calm and looking as well. Then he said, "Where are your cousins?" The lady said, "We left them back by the office." The principal said, "By themselves?" The office staff looked surprised and took off running back towards the office.

Alicia, Carmen and Cashae ran after them. The principal was yelling, "Hey! Hey!" He couldn't leave that spot because he had to get the other girls back in the school. As the staff, Alicia, Carmen and Cashae approached the office the lady said, "We have to find them, where did they go? Are they inside the office?!" When they got to the office they immediately stopped because they saw us standing against the wall outside of the office. They were confused while my cousins secretly smiled knowing we succeeded. I said, "Did ya'll find him?"

At that moment, the principal got on the walkie-talkie and told the office staff, "Please keep those ladies in the office, they're suspended." The office staff looked extra confused, the lady responded, "10-4."

Then she took us in the office. We sat down as we waited for the principal to get to the office. When he got there, he looked worn out. He stopped to look at us, shook his head and said, "Why didn't ya'll come back with the office staff?" I said, "We needed to catch our breath." He said, "Why did you even run away?" Alisha said, "The same reason we didn't come back."

The principal got quiet. He was so confused and said, "Ya'll deserve every single day of this suspension." We gasped as our mouths dropped. He said, "Pull their files, I'm calling their parents." As he walked away, we all smiled, because we knew they didn't have the right numbers on file. The principal called number after number, and soon got frustrated because he couldn't reach anyone.

He walked out his office to ask us about it. When he got out there, he said, "None of the numbers are working, did your parents get new numbers?" Carmen said, "No they're the same." The principal said,

"I need all of you to call your parents from your phones." We slowly picked up our phones and pretended to call our moms.

After a few seconds we said, "It's not working." The principal said, "I'm going to finish the paperwork, when I come back someone needs to be available to pick you ladies up. If not, we'll keep you here until someone comes for you." After he walked back in his office, we sat there talking and filling each other in on everything we did in the office.

About 15 minutes later, the principal came back out to us. He said, "Alright ladies, the paperwork is all done. Did you get a hold of your parents?" I said, "We were able to reach our auntie." He said, "Great! Is she coming to get you guys?" I said, "Yes, she's on her way." He said, "Is she on your contacts list in your files?" I said, "Yes." He said, "What's her name?" I said, "Tracy Jackson." He said, "Okay." He went to check our files and found her name in them. Like 10 minutes later, she showed up.

When she walked in the office, we all had our heads down a little. The principal couldn't wait to tell her everything we did. He reached his hand out to shake her hand and said, "Hello, and you are?" She shook his hand and said, "Hi, Tracy Jackson." He said, "What's your relationship to these ladies?" She said, "I'm their aunt." He started talking to her normal but then he really started to unleash.

We looked up at him so confused, like he really did a 360. One of the last things he said was, "They put me through h*ll today! They've become a nuisance to the school, staff, and student body. I don't know what else to do with them." Our mouths were to the floor. I lowly said, "What?" Alisha tapped me to signal me to be quiet, so I didn't say anything else. Tracy looked back and forth from him to us the entire time looking pissed.

After he said that last thing, she said, "Oh really?? Okay, well I'm sure you won't have that issue out of them anymore." He said, "Can you please inform their parents? I couldn't reach them." She looked at us and back at him and said, "Oh most definitely, their parents will be informed today. I'm sorry on their behave." The principal said, "Thank you so much." Tracy looked at us and said, "Let's go."

She watched as we walked out the office door, then she walked out. The principal felt so fulfilled and was happy he got through to someone for us. When we got outside, we stopped in front of the building to wait for Tracy to come out. When she came out, she pointed around the corner and said, "Walk this way." We went around the corner, still in front of the school.

When we got around the corner, we all paused looking at each other. Then we burst out laughing. I said, "Whew! Thanks Tracy, I don't know what I would've did if we had to call our parents." Tracy said,

"Oh girl it's not a problem, just don't out me if ya'll parents find out." Alisha said, "You saved our lives just now, we would never out you." Carmen said, "Right, besides we might need you again."

Tracy laughed and said, "Alright, well I'll be on my way. Ya'll ladies enjoy ya'll day and stay out of trouble." I said, "Wait a minute." I pulled out a wad of cash and broke her off. She said, "No, Camille I can't take your money." I said, "It's yours, we gave you a job and you executed it." She smiled. I said, "You deserve every penny of it. If my mama was in there and he said that stuff to her, I would not have been able to walk out of there. We all would've been knocked through a wall."

My cousins agreed and said, "For real." Tracy took the money and said, "Well when you put it like that…thank you." I said, "You're welcome…tell your cousin we said thanks again." She said, "Okay." Then she left. Tracy is not our aunt. When we were switching the numbers in our files, we knew we would have to have someone come pick us up. So we called our friend, and she came up with the idea for us to use her cousin to get around calling our parents.

We put her name and number in our files as a contact that can pick us up. Her cousin did a great job and was very believable, her name isn't even Tracy Jackson. She has a fake ID and uses that for certain things. Her real name is Avery Johnson. Now that we got that out the way, we needed to be on our way.

While we were in the office, I was already texting our ride so they could be on their way. About 5 minutes after Avery left, our ride pulled up. I had one of our homeboys come pick us up. When I saw his car, I said, "Come on ya'll he here." We all got in the car and left. While we were in the car, he said, "What's up ya'll?" We all said, "Hi." I said, "Thank you." He said, "Oh you know I'ma look out…where ya'll wana go?"

I said, “We still gotta figure it out, I didn’t plan this far in advance. We still gotta figure out where we gone go for this entire suspension.” He said, “Alright, how bout ya’ll kick it at my crib today until school out…and if ya’ll need more time to figure things out, ya’ll can come back to my house tomorrow.”

I looked at him and said, “Really?” He said, “Yeah, I mean ya’ll can crash at my place for the full suspension if ya’ll need to.” We were so relieved. I smiled and said, “Thank you so much, we really appreciate it. We’ll still try to figure things out, so we won’t invade your space too much.” He said, “Ain’t a problem, just let me know. I can scoop ya’ll up from the school after ya’ll get dropped off in the mornings.”

Alisha said, “Yes! Thank you because I had no idea how we were gonna get past our parents.” He said, “I got ya’ll.” He drove us to his house. Although we had to leave school at that moment, our suspension didn’t start until the next day.

We could not believe we got suspended the same day we got back to school! If our parents found out, we would be in even more trouble than we were the first time. We definitely were not going to let them find out. We wasn't worried about the school calling them, because they no longer had their numbers in their files. When we got to his house it was still early, we came in quiet.

He managed to get us in his room without his parents knowing. He still lived with his parents. He didn't go to school because he graduated. He is 19. His parents don't check his room and he said we could roam the house after his parents left for work, which was around 10 o'clock.

We all chilled in his room until 10. His parents left exactly at that time. We would have rather been somewhere we could feel free, but in our situation we really had no choice. We hate to have to sneak around, although it happens a lot, we rather not do it. After his parents left, we started to roam the house and we felt free. We realized we just have to get through the early morning when his parents are there and then we'd be fine for the rest of the day. His parents didn't get home until well after 6pm and by that time, we would be long gone because our school got out before 3pm.

We got hungry and asked him if it was okay for us to order food. He said it was fine, so we ordered food for us and him. He loved it. He realized at that moment, he would eat good the entire time we would be there. We had no problem buying food for him because he was helping us out a lot. We all had a really good time at his house, he kept us entertained. When it was time to go back to the school, we got our stuff and left his house.

He pulled up in the lineup at the school. We looked around to make sure our mamas cars were not near his. This way they wouldn't see us get out his car. We had to wait for the bell to ring to get out the car so nobody would see us. We sat in his car ducking. When the bell rung, I said, "Thank you again for everything." My cousins said, "Yes thank you." He said, "No problem, same time tomorrow?" We said, "Yeah." He said, "Alright, I'll be here after ya'll get dropped off." When the students started to come out, we got out the car and mixed with the crowd. We saw the school staff outside, so we hurried to our mamas cars.

When I sat down in the car, I immediately rested my head on my hand. My head was facing Latoya, I had my jacket over my hand too. I was trying to hide my face so the principal wouldn't see me. Latoya looked at me and stared at me for a minute, then she said, "What's wrong with you?" I said, "I'm tired." She stared at me a little longer but didn't say anything, then she drove off.

I was so nervous, it made me feel sick. After we pick up my sisters from school, we went home. When we got there, I was still nervous. I went to open the car door, Latoya said, "You shaking, what's wrong with you?" I slowly looked up at her and said, "Huh? ...oh I don't feel good." She said, "I'ma have to call yo school and keep you home tomorrow." I was scared but didn't show it and said, "No ma it's okay. I think I just need some rest."

She said, "Okay, stay off that phone then and go to bed. If you still feeling and looking like that in the morning, I'm keeping you home and calling you out of school." I said, "Okay." We got out the car and went in the house. That was a close call, I knew I had to clean up my act by morning. I texted my cousins telling them I couldn't be on the phone for the rest of the day, and I would see them in the morning.

They were confused but replied, okay. Since my mom was keeping an eye on me, I did lay down. I laid down for so long I eventually fell asleep for real. I was mad I gave that excuse, but I didn't want her to catch on to me. I had to play the part. I wasn't about to play with her because I didn't want her to take my phone. After I went to sleep, she left me alone and made sure my sisters didn't bother me either.

I stayed in bed for the rest of the day. When I woke up, it was morning. I was surprised I slept through the entire night after sleeping all day. I guess I was too scared of my mom to be bold enough to get out of bed. I woke up a few minutes before my alarm went off. It's a good thing I did, because my mama came in my room to check on me. I had to get my thoughts together quick. I knew I had to act like I was completely fine.

She came in, sat on my bed, and felt my head. She said, "Are you feeling any better?" I said, "Yes, I feel fine." She said, "I don't know you slept all day and night. I probably should still keep you home today. I'll just call the school." I said, "No Mommie, I'm fine. I just needed sleep." She said, "Okay, well get ready." I said, "Okay." She left out my room, I took a deep breath of relief. I got up and got dressed.

My mama dropped us off to school, she normally drop me right in front of the school. I got out the car and immediately put my jacket over my head. I started walking in the opposite direction, my mama didn't notice because I was walking through students. She drove off to take Crystal to school. I saw my aunties in the lineup and saw my cousins getting out the cars.

They had a reason to run my way because I was standing there, so when they did their mamas didn't find it weird, because they mamas saw me. Once they got to me, we watched until our mamas left the lineup. As soon as they left out the gate, we ran to our homeboy car. He was waiting for us in the lineup the entire time. Once we got in the car, he drove us to his house.

We snuck in per usual and roamed the house when his parents left for work. He entertained us, we had fun, we ate and when it was time to leave, he dropped us back off at school. It was this way the entire suspension. We never found anywhere else to go, so we took him up on his offer and crashed at his place for the 10 days.

The last day of the suspension, we were excited because we got through the entire suspension without our parents knowing. Or did we? While we were at our homeboy's house, our mamas got a call for a last minute gig they had to do. The gig was going to take a while, so they decided to pick us up early from school. After talking about it amongst themselves, they all decided that Latoya would pick up the big kids. Beonca would pick up the little kids and Latonya would pick up the tweens. They all headed out to our schools.

When Latoya walked into the office, the office staff were surprised. They thought she wanted to speak with the principal about something regarding our suspension. The lady immediately yelled, "Sir! We have a parent here for you." Latoya said, "No, I just want to…" Before she could finish, the principal came out of his office. When he saw my mama, he was shocked and said, "Ms. Lockhart!" She jumped a little as she looked at him.

He said, "Please come in my office." She shook her head as she followed him. When she got in there, he said, "Please have a seat." She said, "Okay but I'm in a huge hurry. I just came to pick up the girls, because I have to be somewhere in less than an hour."

The principal's mouth dropped wide open, he was just stuck and lost for words. Latoya said, "Is everything okay? ...did they do something else?" The principal finally said, "I'm sorry, forgive me, I know you're in a rush…um didn't Tracy talk to you?" Latoya was so confused, she said, "Tracy?" He said, "Yes, Tracy Johnson." Latoya said, "I'm sorry I'm confused,

I don't know a Tracy Johnson." The principal's eyes got so big as he took a breath. Latoya said, "I'm sorry, I just really need to sign them out so I can be on my way."

The principal looked at her spooked, because he was still trying to figure out what was going on. Latoya said, "Are you okay?" He said, "Ms. Lockhart, the girls are suspended." Latoya said, "No, they were but they came back from suspension. They're not suspended anymore. That was a month ago." The principal said, "Ms. Lockhart, the girls came back, and they got suspended again, the same day they got off of suspension. They haven't been in school for the past two weeks. Today is actually the last day of their suspension."

Latoya squinted her eyes with her mouth wide open, her head titled to the side and said, "What?!" The principal softly said, "Yes, we tried to reach you but none of your contacts worked. The girls were able to get ahold of their aunt and she said she would let you all know about the suspension." Latoya was livid. She said, "Which auntie?" He said, "Tracy Johnson?" Latoya stared at him, she had him scared.

Then she said, "My daughter and nieces do not have an aunt named Tracy, and what do you mean you couldn't reach us?? We recently updated our contacts with you guys." The principal said, "One second." He got up quick and pulled the files out, he had the office staff to pull up the files they had too. Once he had them all on his desk, he said, "I would like you to take a look at these Ms. Lockhart."

As Latoya looked through the files, she looked more and more confused. She noticed that the emergency contacts like our grandmas, dads, aunties and my God mom was not listed. She saw all of the numbers were completely wrong and that her name and her sisters names were not on everybody's files like they were before.

The principal said, "See? Besides the parents, the only other contact listed is Tracy Johnson." Latoya said, "I don't know what's going on, but we do not know who this person is. If it wasn't for me seeing my daughter every day, I would flip out right now because it was that easy for a stranger to sign them out of school." Latoya was so mad she had tears in her eyes.

The principal felt bad and said, "I'm so sorry Ms. Lockhart, there was so much ciaos going on and we only were able to go off of our files. We couldn't reach you." Still looking down at the files, Latoya said, "This is not even our numbers, they're far off. I don't understand how this changed." As the principal started to explain what happened that day, a few tears fell from Latoya's eyes. He gave her tissues and consoled her with words.

She was so upset, she couldn't fathom how she would get through the gig they booked that day. The principal calmly told her everything he told Avery that day. Latoya couldn't believe what she was hearing. She said, "We dropped them off every day and picked them up every day." The principal said, "They never made it in the school." Then she thought about how I stopped her from keeping me home from school.

She was pissed, embarrassed, and lost for words. The principal said, "Ms. Lockhart, I'm so sorry, are you okay?" Latoya said, "I'll be fine…just please take her out of their contacts, we'll update ours later." The principal said, "Okay." She said, "Thank you for the information." The principal said, "You're welcome." She put her shades on and walked out the office. The principal couldn't believe that she didn't know, and to find out that Tracy wasn't our auntie he was completely baffled.

He removed her name from all of our files. When Latoya got to her car, she called her sisters. They were all connected to the call. When she told them what happened, they were all shocked and upset. They decided to meet up. When they got together, they found out that their gig was going to be no more than a couple of hours. This was perfect for them because they wanted to done by the time school was out. After dropping our sisters off to our grandmas houses, they took a minute to talk.

Latoya said, “Just text them and tell them to come to my house after school, I’ma tell Camille we have a gig and have Lexi pick them up.” Trinity said, “Ooh you gone have Lexi there too?? Lexi gone beat Camille a**.” Latoya said, “I know, that’s exactly why I chose her to pick them up. But I won’t tell her until she get to the house.” Beonca said, “Yeah, let’s text them then.”

Latonya said, “We don’t even know where they at.” Trinity said, “If they respond we know they okay…I can’t believe they pulled this sh*t.” They all sent us text messages. The messages came to our phones almost at the same time, we thought we were caught. Then we read the messages. I said, "Ya'll mamas told ya'll about a gig?" They said, "Yeah." I said, "Oh good, I thought this was a trick or something."

Cashae said, "Camille, how we supposed to get to your house?" I said, "My mama said Alexi gone pick us up." Cashae said, "Okay good." Carmen said, "Good thing it's our last day of suspension." Alicia said, "Yeah and the best part is, we get to spend it together." We didn't think anything of it and was happy.

Meanwhile, our mamas went to their gig. It was difficult for them to get through it because they were all pissed. They couldn't wait to get a hold of us. They did some great acting because nobody noticed anything off with them. After they were finished, they didn't pick up our sisters. Instead they went back to my house to get prepared for our arrival. While they waited, Latoya was able to fill them in on everything the principal told her.

When she told them about Tracy, they were all confused and said, "Who is Tracy??" Latoya threw up her hands and shrugged her shoulders as in, I don't know. Latonya said, "Where are they now, and where have they been the entire suspension?" Latoya said, "That's what we gone find out when they get here…and if it's what I'm thinking, Camille gone get her a** beat." They knew what that meant.

She planned to beat me regardless but if she hears more stuff she don't like, she was really gone jump on me. So it was like she was saying she was gone beat me worse than she planned. Beonca said, "Girl, you and Alexi gone be fighting over who get to her first." Latoya said, "Oh I'ma get to her first, I'm too upset not to. Alexi would just be finding out. Once it sink in, then she'll get her." They talked for a while and just sat in the Livingroom waiting. They did not leave that Livingroom.

Once school got out, our homeboy took us back to school. We thanked him for everything. Before we left from his car I leaned over, looked in the window, smiled and said, "Oh yeah, I left something for you under your pillow." He smiled and said, "Nah Camille, you ain't have to do that." I said, "I wanted to. We really appreciate what you did for us, so thank you." He said, "Alright, ya'll welcome anytime and thank you." I said, "You're welcome." Then we walked from by his car.

I left him money under his pillow. We knew we didn't have to be too discreet coming from his car, because Alexi is not used to picking us up. She wouldn't know which way we normally walk to get to the car. We were feeling good and happy. When we got to her car we jumped in with smiles. I said, "Hi Goddie!" Alexi smiled and said, "Hey ya'll!" We were so excited, we talked all the way home. When we got there, we all got out of the car.

As we walked up to the door, we were talking about what we were going to do when we got inside. I opened the front door with my key, and we all came inside. Once Alexi closed the front door, we looked up and saw our mamas staring us down with a death stare. Our smiles faded quick as we stopped in our tracks. It was clear that we were scared. Carmen was bold enough to ask, "What happened?"

Latoya looked at Carmen with her arms folded and said, "You know, that's a good question Carmen…But we need to be asking ya'll that." We started looking at each other, Alexi said, "Uh oh." Then she walked next to where my mama was sitting. Now they all were staring us down. Alexi looked down at Latoya and lowly said, "What happened?" Latoya gave Lexi her phone. Lexi started to read something. Latoya wrote down everything so Lexi can read it before she can tell us what they knew.

Lexi started pacing while she was reading, this was getting scary. We sat there waiting while our mamas didn't take their eyes off us. After Lexi finished, she gave the phone back to Latoya. Then she started looking at us the same way they were. We looked confused. Latoya said, "Don't look confused now…we know ya'll suspended." When she said that we all gasped, our eyes got big, we immediately dropped our stuff, screamed, and started running.

As soon as we ran, all of them jumped up and ran after us. I couldn't get up the stairs quick enough, I tripped on the second stair and my mama caught me. Carmen couldn't get past the Livingroom table before her mama got her. The twins got caught by the back door, I don't know where they thought they was going. Cashae got stuck by the door, because she tried to go back out but couldn't unlock it fast enough.

Lashae got caught by Alexi because she tried to run down the guest hallway. That hallway was literally behind where Alexi was standing. Alexi didn't beat Lashae, but she did bring her to Latoya, because Lashae parents wasn't there. When she brung her to Latoya, Latoya redirected her attention to Lashae and said, "Oh yeah, yo a** too!" Latoya started to beat Lashae and as soon as that happened, Alexi snatched me up from the stairs and started beating me. They did a swap!

I couldn't win for losing, I always managed to get beat multiple times in situations like this. We were screaming still trying to get away from them, but they had a good grip on us. After what seemed to be forever, they finally stopped beating us and threw us on the chair by our arms. We were left sitting there crying and looking up at them as they stood over us in front of us. Then the questions started.

My mama knew the perfect time to question me, she knew right after I got beat, I would be too scared to beat around the bush with her. She wasted no time. She said, "Who is Tracy??" We all looked at each other scared. We remembered the girl said don't out her if we got caught, we knew she would be in a lot of trouble. Latoya again said, "Who is Tracy Johnson?!" I said, "I don't know who that is."

Latoya said, "Apparently, you do! She signed ya'll out of school and her name is the only emergency contact in all ya'll files! It's funny how all of our names including Alexi was removed…now I'ma ask one more time, who is Tracy?" I opened my mouth and said, "I don't…" Before I could finish, Latoya snatched me off the couch and started beatin my behind again. I was screaming so loud. I couldn't take it no more and said, "Okay, okay, it's a lady I paid…"

Latoya stopped and said, "What?!" I was on the floor looking up at her with my hands up, trying to block any future hits coming my way. She had me by the front of my shirt with the belt in her other hand. I was boo hoo crying and said, "A random person…" Latoya looked up at her sisters and said, "Did she just say she paid somebody??" They said, "Yep." Trinity said, "A random person."

Latoya really started tearing me up with that belt. While she beat me yet again, she started talking to me. She said, "You paid a stranger to take ya'll out of school?! And she in ya'll files, so you must've switched them! You took every body names off and put some stranger on there?!" I was screaming, "Ow!" and "Ouch!" and "I'm sorry Mommie! I'm sorry!" My cousins were so scared, because they knew they mamas wasn't too far from doing them the same way.

By the time she stopped, I was crying so hard I just knew my voice was gone be gone. I was still on the floor shaking. She looked at me and said, "Get yo a** to that couch!" I made my way to the couch and sat back down, but I couldn't stop crying. I was crying so hard they couldn't ask me anything else for the time being, because they couldn't understand me. My cousins were happy that I didn't tell on Avery, they were amazed at how I covered it up.

I got the worst beating ever but at least we kept our word. My mama had more questions and so did my aunties. So they started questioning my cousins. They were terrified, nobody wanted to get snatched off the couch like I did. Latonya stood up next to Latoya and Carmen almost had a panic attack.

Latonya said, "There is a lot going on here, I had questions but now I have new ones…first of all who made these changes to the files, because it's real ironic that Camille paid a random person to sign ya'll out and that person was the only person listed on ya'll emergency contacts." Trinity stood up and said, "Right! How could that person's name be on all ya'll files if that person was so random??" Latoya said, "Somebody had to change 'em because ain't no way that was on those files, our numbers were just on the files from the first suspension."

Trinity said, “Who changed them?!” We all jumped. I knew I was screwed. Latonya said, “Carmen you got two seconds to answer.” Carmen didn’t wana tell on us but had no choice. She quickly but lowly said, “Alisha, Lashae…and Camille,” as she pointed at us. We all looked up, I looked at my mama like, mama please! But she said, “Come here.” When I got off the couch, Trinity pulled Alisha off the couch and started tearing her up with that belt. Latoya looked at Lashae and said, “Come here.” Lashae got up and went to Latoya too.

When we got to her, she said, “Ya’ll two again! Don’t ya’ll know the severity behind changing those contacts?! That’s for ya’ll own safety and whoever came to pick ya’ll up would be in jail right now if I knew who it was!” We looked at each other and was really happy we didn’t tell on Avery. Then Latoya said, “Why would ya’ll do that?! ...ya’ll need ya’ll a**es beat!" Latoya started beating Lashae without warning. I gasped and backed up.

Then I heard Latoya say, "Lexi!" Next thing I knew, Lexi was over there beating me again. I was already sore, and I knew it was far from over. After those beatings we sat back down on the couch. Right after we sat down, Latonya said, "Now who house was ya'll at, cause we know ya'll had to be hiding out somewhere." When she said that, I said, "Oh my gosh!" while I covered my face and cried some more. Lexi signaled Latoya because of my response.

Latoya looked at her and said, "Hmm mm, "as she shook her head in a yeah motion while she side eyed me. This time Beonca stood up and said, "Yeah, where did ya'll go Cashae?" Cashae let out a little gasped and then said, "To our friend house." Beonca said, "Who??" Latonya said, "Boy or girl Cashae?" Cashae was looking down. Beonca said, "Look at me."

Cashae looked at her mama, Beonca can be intimidating when she does this.

Without breaking eye contact or even blinking, Beonca said, "Was this friend a boy or a girl?" With tears in her eyes Cashae lowly said, "A boy." Trinity said, "I figured it was." Beonca said, "How do you know him?" Cashae said, "Camille." I put my hand on my face with my eyes closed, my mama zoned in on me. Beonca said, "Whose idea was it to go to his house?" Cashae said, "It was his idea." Beonca said, "Okay well, whose idea was it to contact this friend?"

Cashae said, "Camille." My hand was still over my face. Then Beonca said, "Okay, and how old is this friend?" Cashae looked up at them and said, "16?" Our mamas gasped a little bit in shock and then Cashae said, "Oh no! He 19." At that point my head went all the way down, all of our mamas gasped so loud and started talking at the same time. Then I heard Latoya yell, "Camille!" I looked up at her, she pointed towards the guestroom downstairs and said, "Bring yo a** on here!"

I got up already crying. She looked at Lashae and said, "You too! Ya'll ain't got no business at some boy house!" As we walked past by her, she said, "19 years old, that's a grown man!" She took us in the room while my cousins got beat out in the Livingroom. This time Latoya beat us on her own without Alexi and she got us both good. While we were in there with her, she found out that we was in his room and how we navigated from school to his house and back.

Everybody wondered why she was taking so long. Trinity said, "I don't even take that long, and I beat the twins all the time." When we came out the room, Trinity asked Latoya, "You was struggling?" Latoya said, "No, I found out some more stuff and had to beat they a**es until I felt satisfied."

My aunties asked her what she found out and when she told them, they started beating they kids again. These beatings was nothing compared to what we got the first suspension. After they finally stopped beating us, they threatened to homeschool us if we didn't stop getting in trouble in school…that's the last thing we needed.

Chapter 13

Déjà Vu

After getting all those beatings we couldn't go back to school the next day. We were sore and bruised up by those belts, so our mamas kept us home for another week. Once we did go back to school, our mamas came with us. We showed up after the bell rung because they had to speak with the principal. When we were in the office, our mamas told the principal what they found out. The principal was bewildered, and we were embarrassed. He pulled out the files and we watched as our mamas updated the contact information again.

Once they were done, my mama said, "Do ya'll have anything to say?" We all said, "Sorry." The principal said, “Thank you ladies, we all make mistakes, you’re forgiven.” Beonca said, “I’m sure you won’t be having an issue out of them anymore.” The principal said, “Thank you Ms. Knight, thank you all for coming out to fix everything and I’m sorry again. I’ll look further into things from now on.” Our mamas said, “No problem.”

Once they left, we went to class, and we were the quietest things. We got through school just fine, we didn’t want no smoke from our mamas. The principal started to go outside after school to tell our parents, “They’ve been good today, no problem!” We really wasn’t trying to mess up now. After school we all went to our own house. While I was doing my homework, I got a text.

I looked over my shoulder towards the kitchen to make sure my mama wasn’t around. My mama make me do my homework in the Livingroom, this way she is able to check up on me and make sure I do it. I’m not allowed on my phone at all while I do my homework. I didn't see her, so I looked at my phone and saw that I had a text from my homegirl.

At first, I looked at the phone saw her name and put it back down. But then my phone beeped again. I didn't want my mama to hear it, so I picked it up again and opened the text. The first text read: Camille, can you talk right now? The second text read: I guess you can't…send me a video saying it's me real quick. I was confused, but I quickly did a video putting up the peace sign smiling and whispering, "It's me." Then I sent it to her.

She replied: Okay good, oh you doing homework? I texted back: Yeah. She texted: I'm sorry to bother you but I thought you needed to know that Michelle is looking for you. I admit I was lost, I texted: Michelle who? She texted: Michelle… Shaun…

remember? I took a deep breath and texted: Oh my gosh…for what? Me and Shaun not even together no more.

She texted: Idk but she going around telling everybody she looking for you, so word can get back to you. I texted: Well I guess it just did. She texted: The way it sounds is like she wana fight you. I texted: Ugh! Why can't this girl leave me alone? She didn't learn from the last time?? What I look like fighting over Shaun, he's not my boyfriend anymore.

She texted: I think that's her problem, he so up on trying to get you back, he not paying her the time of day. I texted: Well she need to go fight him then, she so irrelevant. She texted: I just wanted to let you know. I texted: I appreciate it. She texted: I wish we could've spoke on the phone, erase these messages so yo mama won't see them. I texted: Okay.

Before erasing the messages, I took screen shots and sent them to my cousins. This way I still had them as proof in case of anything. When my cousins got the texts, they were livid. They started calling my phone back to back, but I was scared to answer because I would get in trouble. Then they started texting me, I texted them that I would call them when I finish my homework.

I finished my homework quick because I knew their blood was boiling. When I did call, we all were connected to the call. Carmen said, “Camille fight that h*e! I’m sick of her a**.” Alisha said, “Camille already fought her Carmen, this is harassment.” Carmen said, “Well I’ma fight her, she made me mad now. Tell her Carmen lookin for her a**!”

Cashae laughed and said, “Carmen calm yo a** down.” Alicia said, “Cashae you know if Carmen fight, you gone be right with her.” Cashae said, “I never denied that I’m just saying save the hype for later.” We all laughed.

A few more days past and more people were contacting me telling me the same thing about Michelle. Some messages were more in detail than others. On that 3rd day, this boy texted me: Michelle talkin bout, where yo homegirl at? She gone get her a** beat. I texted: What? I didn't know if he was hyping it up or if he was for real.

He texted again: Yeah man I told the lil b*tch to get away from me and stop worryin bout my homegirl and her dude. I texted: You know we not together no more right? He texted: Word? Oh my bad I ain't know but the lil b*tch was still bold, I wish you would beat her a**. I texted: I already did. He texted: Please do it again. I thanked him for telling me.

This time she was putting out threats and that did not sit well with me. I called my cousins and told them. Carmen said, "Alright, I'm ready to whoop some a**! Camille tell me when." Alisha said, "Carmen…" I said, "No she right, this b*tch wana dish out threats now and over a n*gga that don't want her!" Cashae said, "Talk yo sh*t Cee Cee!"

I said, "I'ma give her what she want." Lashae said, "So what's the plan?" I said, "I need to figure out where she stay." Alicia said, "You finna go to that girl house?" I said, "No, I'ma be in her neighborhood." Carmen said, "Oh sh*t I'm loving this." Alisha said, "How we gone pull this one off?"

I said, "F*ck that, she bout to get all this frustration! All them beatings, this breakup, school, I'm about to take it all out on her." Alicia said, "Don't kill her na Camille." I said, "She asked for it…and Alisha, I'll worry bout my mama later. But for now, I need her address and I know a lot of people willing to give it to me." Lashae said, "D*mn Camille, you mad huh?" I said, "She brung it all back."

Once we got off the phone, I started to do my research on Michelle. I was looking for her whereabouts, her neighborhood, her friends, her school, anything I can find in order for me to find her and put an end to her rant. I found out a lot of details on my own. But I had to reach out to some of my friends, in order to verify my findings and find out where she lived or what neighborhood at least.

A person can talk real big when they're in hiding and no one knows where they stay. By the end of the week, I had everything I needed on Michelle. Before I knew it, me and my cousins were back on the phone talking about it. I said, "I have the information on her neighborhood, and I know what street she stay on. I just don't know what house."

Cashae said, "Well that's good enough, you said you wanted to know what neighborhood she stayed in and now you even know the street." I said, "Yep, that's all I need." Alisha said, "So what now?" I said, "I'ma go to her neighborhood Friday evening and pretend like I didn't know she stay there. I'ma let her see me as if it was on accident and see if she try to fight me." Carmen said, "How you gone do that?"

I said, "My mama gone be with my daddy Friday night remember?" Carmen said, "Oh yeah, they going to a basketball game, right?" I said, "Yeah, so I'm supposed to be at yo house anyway." Lashae said, "So we can just go to Carmen house then and leave from there…Carmen where yo mama gone be?"

Carmen said, "You know my mama never stay here the whole time, she gone step out for something. We'll have time." Cashae said, "Okay, well I'll see ya'll there." Soon we got off the phone. On Friday my cousins checked in with me to make sure I still wanted to go through with the plan. I told them yes, because I was tired of Michelle mouth and her foolishness. Everything was going as planned.

My mama and my daddy dropped me off at Carmen house, then they headed to the game. Eventually Cashae, Lashae, Alisha and Alicia showed up. Like clockwork, Latonya checked on us and then headed out. As soon as she left, Carmen said, "Now it's our time to get out of here." We got up quick because we didn't know how much time we had.

Carmen got her car out the garage and we all headed to Michelle neighborhood. Once we got there, it was dark which was a good thing. I chose a house to stand in front of as if I knew the people living there. I looked like I was by myself, but my cousins were nearby. I was pretending to just chill or play in the yard, but I made sure I would be in Michelle's eye view if she saw me.

After waiting for a good 10 minutes, Michelle finally saw me. I saw her first, she got out of a car, I guess she was getting dropped off. As she was walking up to her house, she looked over and saw me. At first, she thought she was trippin, but then she realized it was me. She started to walk down the sidewalk so fast towards me, just to stop across the street.

I pretended not to see her and was looking down as if I was too into what I was doing. Then I heard her laugh and say, "I'm staring at the b*tch right now! …No for real…" Then she yelled out, "Camille!" I looked up at her, then she said, "Yep! It's her, she just looked at me when I called her name. I'm about to fight this h*e bout my man."

I said, "Girl, he don't want yo ole dusty a**." She said, "I bet he do!" I lied a little just to piss her off and said, "I guess that's why he be at my house huh?" She got so mad and said, "B*tch come say that sh*t to my face!" I laughed and she got back on the phone saying, "Nah she wana talk sh*t but won't come out the yard. I'm not gone fight her in her people yard. She over there laughing like the sh*t funny, she the reason why he don't wana f*ck with me nomore!"

I said, "He never did." She put her hand and arm down, that was the hand she had the phone in. She was frustrated, she said, "Uggggh! But you still talking over there! Come say it to my face Camille!" Then she got back on the phone and said, "She being so scary, she keep talking sh*t but won't come over here…no she by herself!"

I said, "You the scary one." She said, "Camille come over here!" Then I heard her tell her friend on the phone, "No, look at this sh*t!" She facetimed them and had the phone on me and said, "She just standing there! She scary as f*ck!" At that time, I happened to say, "Girl, ain't nobody scary, I'll come cross the street!" I started to walk towards her, her friends said, "Oh sh*t." Michelle said, "Oh now she wana come."

As soon as I got across the street, I was near her but not too close, all her friends saw was her phone flip up in the air. Then they heard scuffling and was saying, "Oh sh*t they fighting!" and "Why yo phone flew?!" Then they heard her say, "They jumpin me!" Her friend said, "What?! That girl by herself!" They started laughing at her and saying, “She getting her a** whooped and think she getting jumped.”

They could not be her real friends. Her other friend said, “I heard Camille fought her before and beat her a**. I don’t know why she started with that girl.” What they didn’t know was, when I walked across the street Carmen jumped out from the side and punched her dead in the face. This is why her phone flew. I didn’t even fight her at this point yet.

When she said they jumping me, Carmen was literally the only one fighting her at that time. I guess she thought that we was about to jump her. But Carmen was just mad and wanted to fight her, especially after hearing what the girl was saying to me. So we let her. When Carmen hit her, Michelle lost her balance. Carmen was tearing her up. Then Michelle tried to fight back, that’s when Cashae, the twins and Lashae jumped in.

When Michelle managed to get up, she took off running towards her house and my cousins ran after her. I ran too, we left her phone on the ground. As she got closer to her house, I ran faster. I didn't want her to go in her house because I wanted this to end now. When she got to her house, she was halfway inside but then I caught her.

I ran in her house a little bit and pulled her back out. At this point I was fighting her by myself. Her mom came outside trying to break up the fight, but I hit her by mistake. Then she tried to pull her daughter out the fight which didn't work. After about a good 5 minutes, Alisha pulled me and said, "The police coming."

So we ran back around the corner and went to Carmen car. We got in and drove back to Carmen house. She put the car back exactly how it was before we left, and we went back to her room. We made it back just in time. Latonya came back home about 10 minutes after we came back.

We had time to catch our breath and talk about it a little bit to get it out our system. When she checked in on us, it looked like we been chillin all day. About 20 minutes later, my phone rung. I looked at it and saw that Shaun was calling me. I rolled my eyes and said, "Oh my gosh." Carmen said, "Ain't no way…maybe he don't know." I picked up the phone and all of them heard, "Camille, what the f*ck happened?!" Then Carmen said, "Or maybe he do."

I took another breath and said, "Shaun, what are you talking about?!" He said, "Camille don't pull that sh*t with me, tell me the truth! You went around there fighting Michelle?!" I said, "What the f*ck you calling me asking me about that b*tch for?!" He said, "I'm not calling for that!" I said, "Yes you are, you checkin me about the b*tch you let break us up!"

Shaun said, “Camille that’s not true stop it! Answer my question or I’m coming to yo house.” I quickly said, “Yes.” He said, “What?” I said, “Yes, that’s the answer to yo question.” He got so mad and started yelling and fussing at me. He said, “Why would you do that?!” I said, “She was lookin for me! I don’t see you doing nothin to stop her from fighting me over yo a**!”

He said, “I can care less about her, I’m mad with you because you allowed her to pull you in this bullsh*t!” I said, “What was I supposed to do? She was looking for me!” He said, “And apparently, she still is!” Me and my cousins looked confused. I said, “What?!” He said, “That’s why I’m mad, she calling me trying to find out where ya’ll live at to get ya’ll arrested!” I said, “What?!”

He said, “What I look like?! I told her a** not to call me no more and then I blocked her a**! The f*ck she think this is? Everybody know ion play bout you or yo ppl… You know if she give them ya'll names they can find out where ya'll stay." I said, "Oh, I thought you was mad because I fought her."

He said, "Man nah, she deserved that sh*t! She messy as f*ck! I ain't speak to her a** since you left me for good. I'm still mad about that sh*t, after all these years nothing could break us up. Then a nobody come a long and come between us, and she wana call me?!" I said, "She said you her man and I'm the reason you don't wana f*ck with her."

He said, "F*ck outta here! I was never her man, she got one thing right though…Ion wana f*ck with her as a person, because she made me lose the best thing that ever happened to me. I never wanted to f*ck with her as girlfriend or on that level." When he said that I knew he was in his feelings, he made me start to get in my feelings.

I took a breath while I closed my eyes and rested my head in my hand. I said, "Shaun…" He said,

"I miss you. Can you <u>please</u> take me back? I don't feel right without you." At that point, I dropped the phone and covered my face with both hands while I cried silently. Carmen grabbed my phone and said, "Hello?" Shaun said, "Who dis Carmen?" She said, "Yeah…"

He said, "Where yo cousin?" She said, "She had to do something real quick. But what happened with that girl?" Shaun said, "Oh ya'll sent her to the hospital, so she real mad." Carmen said, "That's what she get, she was asking for it. She kept looking for Camille and the way she was talking to her was just crazy." Shaun said, "Yeah, that's why I called so ya'll can be up on game." Carmen said, "We appreciate it."

Shaun said, "Yeah…tell Camille to stop crying and get back on the phone." Carmen and my cousins mouths dropped. Then Carmen said, "How you know she was crying?" Shaun said, "I know my baby." Carmen smiled and said, "Shaun stop! She already crying…here she go." Carmen gave me back the phone. I had my head in my shirt at this point.

I started to talk but I was talking low, I said, "Hello?" Shaun was calm and said, "I'm sorry I didn't mean to make you cry. I know it's a lot to take in and deal with. I just want you to know I had nothin to do with it. Can we talk about us? I don't want to let go and as much as you fight it, I know you don't want to let go either."

I talked through the tears and said, "Well talk later." He said, "Okay that's fair, Camille?" I said, "Yeah?" He said, "I love you." I choked up, my cousins looked at me and then they heard me say, "I love you too." I tried to hold back but the tears came out, this time he heard me crying. Carmen started to rub my back to console me.

He said, "It's okay bae, see this why we need to talk and get everything together. I don't want you walking around hurtin like this. I do it and that sh*t sucks! Listen, please stop crying, know that I'm on your side I always was and I always will be. You the one I love and the one I wana be with forever."

He noticed I kept crying as long as he was talking, so he said, "I'ma let you go, but make sure you call me later." I said, "Okay." After we hung up, I sat there for about 5 minutes crying my eyes out. I told my cousins what he was saying, they felt bad for me and wish things were different for me. Clearly, we were not over each other.

About 10 minutes later I got myself together. Cashae said, "Ya'll might as well get back together Camille, ya'll so sad without each other." I said, "I don't know. I do miss him, and I want to be with him, but I'm not sure if it's a good thing for us to be together." Carmen said, "Why?" I said, "Because it hurt so bad. That break up was terrible and I don't want to go through it again with him. I think it's best for me to deal with getting over him." Alisha said, "I understand that. It's hard but you'll be glad you did."

I said, "Yeah, exactly." After getting off the phone with Shaun, we were a little afraid, because they <u>can</u> find out where we live if she told them who we were. Back at my house, my mama came back home, and my daddy left. About 30 minutes after she got home, someone rung the doorbell. Latoya thought it was one of us or her sisters.

As she walked to the door she said, "I told them not to bring them back until I called." She looked out the peep hole and her mouth dropped. She opened the door to see the police standing there. The guy said, "Hi, Ms. Lockhart?" Her heart sank a little as she said, "Yes?" He said, "Sorry to disturb you but we are looking for Camille Lockhart, Carmen Rogers, Cashae Knight, Alisha Tyler, Alicia Tyler and Lashae Lockhart…are you familiar with these ladies?"

Latoya was so confused and said, “Of course, they’re my daughter and my nieces…why are you looking for them?” The guy said, “Well, we received a report stating that these young ladies are guilty of battery and trespassing. The victim in question was sent to the hospital.”

Latoya was so shocked and said, “When did this happen??” The guy said, “Tonight around 8:00pm, the victim and her mom made a statement.” Latoya said, “Her mom? Who is the victim if I might ask?” The guy said, “Her name is Michelle.” Latoya looked confused because she knew the name sound familiar, but she couldn’t figure out why. The guy said, “Are they here?”

Latoya said, “No, but if you can wait, I’ll call them to have them come.” The guy said, “Were they out this evening?” Latoya said, “No, they were just around the corner at my sister’s house.” The police said they’ll wait in their cars. Latoya called me saying, “Camille, why the h*ll the police at my door talking about battery and trespassing charges??" Me and my cousins almost panicked, but then remembered to keep our cool.

I said, "What? For what?" She said, "They have all ya'll names. Apparently ya'll went to fight some girl named Michelle, now her and her mama trying to press charges according to the police. What the h*ll going on?!" I was too scared to admit it to my mom, especially with pending charges against us. So I did the only thing that seemed logical at the time, I lied.

I said, "What?! Michelle?? Mommie that's probably that girl Shaun had around, she don't leave me alone. If it's her, she probably got beat up and wanted to blame me for it. That girl got issues!" Latoya said, "I need ya'll to come here so ya'll can let these people know that. This is ridiculous." I said, "Okay we on our way." I told my cousins what happened.

Meanwhile Latoya called her sisters and told them, so they were on their way too. I told my cousins to delete everything out they phones before we got to my house. Latonya took us to my house. When we pulled up we saw the police cars in front of my house. When we got out the car the police started to get out of theirs. It looked like they came prepared to take us because they had three police cars there.

My mama opened the door for us as the police walked up. The police introduced themselves to us and filled us in. We gave him the same story I gave my mama. Latonya backed us up and said, "I'm not sure who this is, but the girls were at my house all night and never left. I was there with them the entire time." She wasn't but we didn't say anything. The police questioned all of us by ourselves with our mamas.

They were trying to see if our stories matched and they did, because we made sure we had it together before we even got in the car with Latonya. While the police spoke to us, I asked them certain questions about Michelle to pretend like I didn't know, but wanted to be sure who it was trying to file charges against us. He tried to verify who she was without giving away too much information.

I said, “Do you have a phone number for her on file?” The policy said, “Yes.” I said, “I had a run in with a Michelle before over a guy and she kept stalking me. I want you to match the numbers to see if they’re the same, that way I know it’s her.” The police said, “You have her number?” I said, “She got a hold of my number from the guy’s phone while he was sleeping and started to harass me.”

The police said, “Okay what’s the number?” I read the number to him and he said, “That’s a match!” I gasped, looked at my mama and said, “Mommie I told you!” She rolled her eyes and took a deep breath. She explained to the police the things that happened in the past with her. Then the police asked for my phone. I gave it to him with the text thread from her open. All he saw was threats and her cursing me out.

The last thing he saw was her texting: I'ma get you one of these days, you not getting away that easy. That's all he needed to see. He called all the police officers over, told them to stop questioning us and showed them the text messages. Then he asked if we would like to file a harassment and false accusation complaint against her.

We knew in our hearts this girl was telling the truth, so we didn't want to file charges, we just wanted to get out of ours. Besides, our mamas spoke up for us and said, "No that won't be necessary. We would just like for them to leave us alone." The police said, "We'll make sure of that." Our mamas said, "Thank you."

When the police left, we went inside the house. The police went to the hospital to meet with Michelle and her mama. They thought everything went their way, but when the police turned them tables on'em, they was looking crazy. Her mom was yelling saying, "How can you tell me?! I saw them with my own eyes!" The police said, "No ma'am, the girls were at their aunt's house all night and they have plenty of receipts. What we did find however, was a series of threats in one of the girl's phones, from your daughter."

Her mom said, "What?!" The police told her they're lucky we didn't file charges against <u>them</u>. He also said that if Michelle text or call any of us anymore, she will have harassment charges filed against her. She was so mad as she sat in that hospital bed. She knew we pulled something slick.

Back at my house, me and my cousins were upstairs, and our mamas was downstairs. They were talking about what just happened. Latonya said, "That was real random tonight." Latoya said, "A little too random," as she looked out the side of her eye up at my room door with her arms crossed.

She continued, "But we can't do nothin but believe them this time…they had receipts." Our mamas knew us well, but they took our word for it. We got lucky and actually got away with it this time!

Chapter 14

Cased Up

A few weeks later, me and my cousins were chilling with our friends. Our homebody came over by us and said, “Hey Camille.” I said, “Hey.” He was smiling and speaking softly as he smiled. I looked confused. He said, “You alright?” I said, “Yeees.” He said, “How you feeling?” I said, “Good.” He said, “Where Shaun at?” I said, “I don’t know, we not together no more.” He put his fist over his mouth and said, “Oooh, oh okay I’m sorry my bad…aye if you need anything let me know.” Then he walked off.

Me and my cousins looked at each other, I said, “That was weird.” They said, “For real.” We went back to doing what we were doing. Not even 5 minutes later a girl came over to us, she stopped in front of me and bent down to my face level. I looked at her, while she smiled and said, “Hey Camille.” I said, “Hey.” She said, “How you feeling?” I smiled looking confused and said, “Good.” She said, “Oh good, I’m so excited for you!” I said, “What?” Then her friends walked up, as she asked me, “Hey, where’s Shaun?” I laughed a little and said, “I don’t know, why’s everyone looking for Shaun?”

Then she said, “Well, where’s Jacoby?” I happened to know where Jacoby was because he recently texted me. In an upbeat voice, I said, “Oh Jacoby’s on his way.” At that moment, the girl smiled with her mouth closed, her eyes were open wide and glistened as she looked back at her friends. Then she said to them, “Oooh…Jacoby.” They all started to shake their heads in a yeah motion smiling back at her. I was looking like, what the h*ll?? The girl said, “Okay I’ll see you around Camille.” After they walked away, I said, “Let’s go somewhere else, people out here acting weird as f*ck.”

Me and my cousins got up and went in the building, we found a spot with hardly any people. We were able to chill for a good 20 minutes before another person we knew came over to us. When he got to us, he spoke and sat right next to me. He pushed his self in between me and Carmen, then he whispered in my ear. My cousins saw me look at him confused as I lowly said, “That’s not true.” He said, “It’s not?” I said, “No, who said that?” He said, “That’s the word but I had to come check on you.” I said, “Okay, thanks.”

After he walked away Carmen said, “What happened?” I said, “He told me there is a rumor that I got beat up and he wanted to make sure I was okay.” My cousins said, “What?!” I said, “Exactly! ...That’s why everybody been acting weird??” Alisha said, “Who said that?” I said, “He don’t know, he just said that’s the word.” As we were talking Jacoby walked in and came by us. He said hi to us and gave me a two way kiss, then he sat down. After he sat down, he said, "Camille…what's with yo friends man?" I said, "My friends?" He said, "Yeah, these girls came to me congratulating me and I don't know what for?"

I said, "You talking about the girl in the pink top with bout 6 friends?" He said, "Yeah." I said, "She did the same thing to me, then she asked where you were. When I told her you were on your way, her and her friends got weird and started smiling. Then she said Jacoby." Jacoby had a confused look on his face at this point.

He said, "What the h*ll?" Next thing you know, we heard, "Aww they're sitting together." All of us looked confused, turned to see who said it, and saw that it was the same girls. I said, "See I told you." Then Jacoby homeboy came over by us and shook his hand. He said, "Aye congratulations my boy!" Jacoby laughed a little bit and said, "Thanks but for what?"

His homeboy laughed and said, "Come on man…aye we'll talk later!" Then he turned to me and said, "I'm happy for you Camille." I was looking around with my eyes sarcastically and said, "Thanks?" He laughed and said, "Ya'll funny." After he walked away, I told Jacoby, "It's been this way all night."

Lashae said, "Let's just leave Camille, they not saying it to me, but it's getting on <u>my</u> nerves." I said, "Yeah, let's go." Jacoby got up and said, "Yeah, I'ma leave too. I'll walk ya'll out." As we were leaving out the building, we walked past by those girls. Jacoby was out the door already. As me and my cousins was about to walk out the door, the same girl said, "Bye Camille! Make sure I get an invitation to the shower!"

Me and my cousins stopped in our tracks. We walked back towards her as I said, "What?!" Lashae said, "What you talking about??" The girl looked confused as she started to explain herself to us all while pointing at me. She said, "You're pregnant, I just assumed you'll have a shower." We were shocked and you can see it on our faces. I said, "Who??" She said, "You're pregnant right?" I said, "No!"

She said, "That's what everyone is saying, I'm sorry I thought it was true." Just then Jacoby came back in there pulling me away. He thought we were about to fight. I tried to stop him so I can talk to the girl, but he kept pulling me. While he pulled me, I said, "Who said that??" She said, "I don't know, it wasn't me." Jacoby got a good grip on me and said, "Come on!"

Once we left out, the girl's friends said, "Do you think she was telling the truth? Or do you think she's mad that we know?" The girl shrugged her shoulders slow and said, "I'm so confused." By the time we got to the car I was so mad. Jacoby said, "Camille, don't be out here fighting." I said, "I wasn't trying to fight nobody."

Jacoby said, "So what was that?" Cashae calmly said, "Apparently Camille's pregnant and you the pappi…" Jacoby looked at her so quick and said, "What?!" Cashae said, "Congratulations." He said, "Camille you pregnant?!" I rolled my eyes and said, "No dumb a**… apparently that's why everybody been saying congratulations…it's a stupid rumor."

Jacoby said, "From who??" I said, "That's what I was trying to find out before you snatched me out of there." Jacoby said, "Mannn that's one h*ll of a rumor…that's the last thing we need." I said, "I'ma just go, I had enough for one night." We said our goodbyes and we all left to go back home. When I got back home, I was enraged that someone started these rumors about me.

I knew I could get in a lot of trouble if these rumors hit my mamas ears. I was on edge and determined to find out who started them. I was hoping that by telling those girls the rumors wasn't true, that they would spread the word and that would be the end of that. At school that week people was staring at me whispering. I tried to ignore them, until somebody I didn't know approached me.

It was a boy, when he came to me, he said, "Um Camille?" I said, "Yes?" He said, "I'm sorry, but I think this is for you." He handed me a sticky note and said, "It was stuck to my backpack, I'm not sure how it got there." Then he walked away. I watched him walk away and then I read it. It read: Why are you hiding your pregnancy? At the bottom of the note it read: Give this to Camille Lockhart.

My mouth dropped, I couldn't believe it was addressed to me. Whoever was pushing these rumors wanted me to know that they were doing it, but didn't want to expose who they were. I decided to save the note so I can show my cousins. By the time I got to my next class I got two more sticky notes from random people at my school. This was embarrassing. At lunch I told my cousins and showed them the sticky notes.

As they read them, they said, “This has to stop.” I said, “It really does but I don’t know where this is coming from. we don’t know anybody at this school like that.” Alicia said, “Then it has to be an outside source.” I said, “But who? Nobody know what school we go to.” Lashae said, “Camille, we’re famous. Somebody might talk.” I said, “That’s true, but that makes it so much harder for me to narrow it down.”

Lashae said, “Just keep those notes in case you need’em later.” I said, “That’s a good idea, I just don’t want my mama to find them.” Cashae said, “Just keep’em in yo bag until we can figure this out.” I said, “Yeah, I think I will.” Just then somebody else walked up to the table and said, “Camille?” Without looking at them, I held my hand out looking straight forward sarcastically.

After they put the note in my hand I said, “Thanks.” When they walked away, me and my cousins shook our heads. By the time school was over, I collected about 15 sticky notes. They were all based around the same thing, pregnancy. While I was at school I got notes, while I was at home I got texts, and I was tired of it. I was determined to find out who was behind this if it was the last thing I did.

The next day at school, I got about 10 notes before school even started. People were saying, "This was on my locker," or "This was on my books" or "This was on the back of my shirt," someone even said, "This was stuck to the wall in the hallway." I just took them all without saying anything. I was just sitting there mad and confused. The rumors were bad enough, but to know these people were reading them before giving them to me was even worst.

They didn't even say much, all they did was stare uncomfortably. I wasn't even reading the notes at this point, I just collected them and stuck them in my bookbag. By the time school was over I collected 30 more sticky notes! At this point I wasn't even bothered by them no more. I was so used to collecting them, it became a part of my day. A couple of days later, I decided to look at the sticky notes because I had time.

While I was going through them, I said to myself, “Dang, I wonder whose doing this…whoever it is have no life or just dedicated to making mines worst.” Right after I said that I picked up a random sticky note, this note had the most writing I’ve seen so far. When I looked at it, it read: Why don’t you tell your mom the truth? You fought me that night over Shaun. You’re mad because he stepped out on you as soon as you got pregnant, and now you’re stuck with his baby.

When I read that note I paused for a moment. Once I snapped back into reality I said, “Michelle! It gotta be her!” I ran out of my room quick. I wanted to tell my cousins but needed a private place to do it. I ended up in one of the guest rooms downstairs. The one that was the furthest back in the hall. When I called my cousins and read the note, they were livid.

Carmen said, “How we didn’t know it was that b*tch??” I said, “Right! I should have immediately thought about her.” Alisha said, “I guess she know what school you go to now.” Cashae said, “It all makes sense now, she can’t text Camille no more or she’ll go to jail. So she felt like she can send her notes…this b*tch living in the stone ages!” We laughed.

I said, “Cashae stop making me laugh I’m mad right now.” Lashae said, “What are you gonna do?” I said, “Well, I for d*mn sure wana keep these away from my mama. The last thing I need is to get in trouble for some foolishness this girl done cooked up again.” Just then my mama came home, I heard her say, “Camille!” I looked up surprised with my mouth open.

Then she said it again, “Camille!” I could hear her throwing her purse and everything she had on the couch. She was walking around kind of fast, I heard her heels. I didn't know what was going on. While my cousins were still talking, Carmen said, "Camille, that's yo mama calling you?" My cousins stopped talking. I said, "Yeah, you can hear her?? She looking for me I'm not in my room."

Carmen said, "You better go see what she want." I said, "Yeah, I'ma do that…I'll call ya'll back." They said, "Alright." After I hung up, I was terrified because my mama kept calling me. I opened the door and started walking down the hallway. When I got to the end of the hallway I said, "Yes Ma?!" She looked like she was about to go upstairs, but when she heard and saw me, she stopped.

She let out a quick breath and batted her eyes a little. Then she started walking towards me. As she was walking towards me, she said, "What were you doing in there?" I said, "Oh, I was talking to Carmen them and didn't want Reci to come bothering me." Latoya looked a bit agitated. She looked down for a second, took a deep breath, put her hand on her hip, looked back at me and said, "Why are people coming to me asking am I ready to be a grandma??"

My whole face dropped. She looked like she was ready to knock me out or ready to faint one. I said, "How would you be a grandma??" She gave me a stern look, I quickly said, "Mommie, I have nothin to do with it." She said, "Oh really?? Because multi people who don't know each other came to me with the same story…" She stopped to breathe again, you can tell she was holding back from spazzing out.

Once she caught her breath, she said, "I've been told by multi people, that you're expecting a baby that you been hiding…and it's you and Shaun's baby?" I took a deep breath, closed my eyes and put my hand on my head. My mama started taking off her shoes while she stood in front of me. Then she said, "Talk to me, talk to me quick." I said, "It's not true, there is no way I could be pregnant. Those are rumors."

She sat there for a few seconds thinking, then she said, "Don't lie to me." I said, "Mommie, I'm not lyin. I don't who started those rumors, but they far from the truth. I'm not hidin nothin. That's embarrassing." Latoya said, "It is embarrassing…so you don't know nothing about this, it's just rumors??" I said, "Yes, it's just rumors. I don't even know why people are saying that."

She said, "Okay, I just needed to address it." She took her stuff and went in her room. She needed to lay down. I went back in the guest room and called my cousins back. When we got on the phone I said, "Oh my gosh, the rumors got back to my mama!" I told them what people were saying to her. Lashae said, "Why would you go to somebody, thinking you know their kid is hiding a pregnancy and say are you ready to be a grandma??"

Alisha said, "Right! That's dumb as h*ll!" I said, "Man I know it's Michelle, it gotta be her, that note proves it." Cashae said, "Did you get in trouble?" I said, "No, everything went well. She just questioned me." Cashae said, "Good, you have nothing to worry about." Just then I heard my mama yell, "Camille!!" I was looking so crazy and immediately started walking out the room.

On my way upstairs she yelled again, "Camille!! Get in here now!" My cousins heard her. Carmen said, "I thought you didn't get in trouble." I said, "I didn't…let me see what she want." Carmen said, "The way she calling yo name, it sound like you in trouble." Alicia said, "You wana call us back." I said, "No, ya'll fine, I told ya'll I wasn't in trouble."

Cashae said, "Good! I wana hear what's about to happen." I heard her voice coming from my room. As I opened the door I said, "Yes??" I saw her standing over my bed looking at the sticky notes. I said, "Oh my gosh." My cousins said, "What??" I said, "She found the sticky notes! I forgot to put'em up." They said, "Oh my gosh Camille." When she heard me say that, she looked at me and said, "So you did know what I was talking about." I said, "Mommie, I heard the rumors too. But I didn't wana tell you because I know they're not true."

She said, "Or yo a** wanted to be slick and hide it like people are telling me…why wouldn't you tell me when I asked you?!" I said, "They all lies! I just found out who started it right before you got home. That's why I was downstairs. I was telling Carmen them who was writing these notes to me!" My cousins started saying, "Put us on speaker!"

I put them on speaker, and they started talking to my mama telling her what had been going on. I'm glad I had them to talk to her because I didn't know what would've happened. When she found out about the note passing and about how everybody was telling us stuff too, it was kind of hard for her to believe it.

At first, she thought that I was downstairs getting my story together, so my cousins knew what to say. But after we explained more, she believed what we were saying. She continued to go through the notes, then she noticed the one in my hand and said, "Give me that." I gave it to her, and she read it out loud. It was the same note I read to my cousins.

She said, "Why don't you tell your mom the truth? You fought me that night over Shaun…" Latoya looked up at me with her eyes. I was looking intimidated. She continued, "You're mad because he stepped out on you as soon as you got pregnant…" She took a breath and closed her eyes for a second, then continued, "…and now you're stuck with his baby."

Latoya looked up at me, she was pissed. She held up the sticky note and said, "How much of this is true?" I was quiet for a second and then lowly said, "Just the first sentence." She said, "We figured ya'll a**es found a way to fight that night." I was so quiet and so were my cousins. Then she said, "So, the first sentence is true." I said, "Yes."

She said, "I don't know Camille, ya'll just confessing now to a lie ya'll told a few weeks ago and now this. This right here is serious and it's hard to ignore!" I said, "I understand, I couldn't ignore it either but it's not true!" Latoya said, "I feel like you tellin me the truth about this, but you just admitted to lyin about fighting. The police were in your face and everything and you still lied so convincingly."

She was looking at me with her eyes squinted as if she was reading me. I said, “Ma, we only did that to stay out of jail, because she was going around looking for me to fight me. She started that and apparently, she started these rumors too, I promise you they are not true.” She was pissed. Then she said, “You know what Camille, forget it…until I figure out what’s really going on here, I’m putting you on a strict lockdown.”

I said, “But Ma!” She said, “Like I said! …You staying yo a** inside this house. You not allowed to have no company and no contact with anyone except yo cousins, and you definitely cannot have no boys over or calling and texting you. I’ma get to the bottom of this!” I said, “But Mommie, I didn’t do anything, it’s all lies!” She pointed her finger at me and said, “You hear me, but do you understand me?!” I pouted and said, “Yes ma’am.” She said, “Give me that phone.”

She took my phone while my cousins was still on it and started pressing buttons while she went through it. She told my cousins, “Hold on ya’ll.” They said, “Okay.” After about 5 minutes, she said, “Okay, ya’ll can talk to her again.” She gave me back the phone and said, “Everybody in that phone is blocked, except yo cousins, yo aunties, yo grandmas, yo God mom, yo daddy and us…if anybody else reach you outside of that or you reach out to somebody else, that’s yo a**, because I’m monitoring yo phone. I’ll be able to see everything you doing while you doing it.”

My eyes got big, I was shocked she was able to do that. I said, “Okay.” She said, “I ain’t beat yo a** yet in case it’s true, but I’m gone find out.” She stared me down. I was looking scared and didn’t say anything back, so I won’t get hit. Then she walked out my room. After she walked out, I got back on the phone and said, “Hello?” Carmen said, “Hello?” I said, “She left out, but did ya’ll hear that?” They said, “Yep, dang.”

Alisha said, “Dang, yo mama done blocked everybody.” Lashae said, “I’m just happy she said we can still speak and come over.” They all agreed and said, “Yeah.” Cashae said, “She managed to get you in trouble again Camille.” I said, “I know, that’s messed up. But once my mama know for sure for herself, everything will be fine again…I hope.” Me and cousins talked until we all fell asleep on the phone.

Chapter 15

Snitch

After that night nothing was the same. I can tell my mama wanted to believe me, but as everyday past by I can tell she was being pulled more and more away from believing me. The fact that I couldn't fully convinced her, kind of hurt my feelings. But I knew she had all the right to think how she was thinking. We did get caught in a few lies before and our track record wasn't the cleanest with them. My mom had me on such a strict lockdown, I wasn't even allowed to go to school.

She left me home by myself during the day when she had to take care of some business. She didn't think I had the guts to try her, and she was right I didn't. While I was home more rumors surfaced that day and they were even worse than before. The rumors even got around to Shaun and Jacoby. By the time the rumors got to them, people were saying I didn't know who my baby daddy was, but it has to be Shaun or Jacoby.

They were taken back by it, especially Shaun because this was his first time ever hearing anything like this. The craziest part was, they couldn't confirm anything with me because my mama had them blocked from my phone. The whole blocked thing didn't go so well with them either. Once they figured out they were blocked, they spoke to each other on the phone.

Shaun said, "Aye, what Camille got going on? We was just kickin it and now I'm blocked??" Jacoby said, "I'm blocked too…man when I first heard this Camille was right in front of me. I asked her was she pregnant and she said no she's not…but now she got us blocked. I'm starting to believe she hiding something. I don't know." Shaun said, "It's weird for her to block me, she won't do that…something gotta be up. I just hope these rumors ain't true man. Something ain't right."

They soon got off the phone but had a hard time functioning throughout the day, because they had no idea what was going on. I was able to keep in contact with my cousins throughout the day, this is how I was able to find out that the rumors were still happening and that they got worst. I dealt with the rumors silently while I was home alone. I was nervous as the rumors were coming in, so I kept in contact with my cousins to calm my nerves.

People were trying to pass notes to my cousins while they were in school, but they refused to take them. They were mad and over it. We already figured out who started the rumors and didn't care to read them no more. After the 10th person tried to hand one to Carmen, she was resting her head on her hand as she slouched. She looked at the person with her eyes and said, "Do I look like Camille?"

Alisha hit her and then Carmen smile, sat up a bit and said, "I'm sorry, I mean thank you but we're not talking notes anymore. You can put it in the trash." They tried not to be rude to people but they nerves were wrecked. Carmen said, "I don't see how Camille dealt with this all day every day." Alisha had to remind her, "Let's suck it up and get through the day. The last thing we need is for people to start saying we mean or rude."

Carmen let out a deep breath as she rubbed her hand across her face and said, "Ugggh…. okay." Lashae picked up her phone and said, "Uh un, this making me uncomfortable. I'ma call auntie and ask her if we can come over after school." Alicia said, "No, don't do that! What if she say no?" Lashae said, "Look, we've been talking to Camille all day and even we drained and lost for information. I can't imagine what Shaun and Jacoby going through because they can't even reach her…the last thing I'm worried about is hearing auntie say no."

They all got quiet and made expressions as in, well that's true. Lashae called and all my cousins heard was, "Hey auntie…" Latoya said, "Hey Shae, what you doing on yo phone in school?" Lashae said, "We on lunch, but I had to call you." Latoya said, "What happened?" Lashae said, "I don't wana bring it up, but with all these new rumors going around today we are drained. Now we have our own questions for Camille and we starting to feel lost a little bit…Can we please come over after school? This is just too much."

Latoya said, "It really is, but if ya'll have questions for Camille I know something is off. That's a good idea, yeah ya'll come over after school. That would actually be perfect." Lashae said, "Okay, thank you auntie." When they got off the phone, my other cousins asked Lashae, "What she said?" Lashae said,

"She said yeah, that would be perfect." Cashae said, "Wow and you wasn't scared to ask her?"

Lashae said, "She beat my a** just like she beat Camille a**, she a second mama to me. I be just as scared to ask her stuff as Camille be, but I'm not too scared to not ask." Cashae smiled and said, "Well, I guess we going to Auntie Toya house then." Carmen smiled at Cashae and said, "It's bout to go down today, I'm scared." After school my cousins made they way to my house, they mamas stayed with them.

We didn't go upstairs because my aunties wanted to know what was going on with the rumors too. We talked for a while about the rumors but when it came to the new rumors, Lashae looked at me and said, "I'm not gone ask you what I wana ask you until yo mama get here. She know I wana ask some questions and she gone wana hear'em." I squinted at her and said, "Okay." I was telling my aunties the same thing I told my mama, that the rumors were not true.

Beonca said, “I can see why yo mama having a hard time believing you…a lot of things sound logical but a lot is not adding up.” I took a deep breath while I played with my nails. Trinity said, “Especially now that ya’ll done caught in a lie from that night of the fight. This could be another lie if all we know.” I said, “Auntie I won’t play like that, those rumors are not true.”

Latonya said, “Yo mama believed you for the most part Camille, but something <u>is</u> missing…is there something you’re not telling us?” I looked up at her and she said, “Anything at all?” I said, “No, it’s that girl again. She’s messing with me.” Cashae rubbed her face and said, “We on yo side Camille, but I ain’t gone lie…we feel like something missing too.” I was shocked and said, “Are you serious??” She shook her head yeah and gave me a soft smile.

I looked at my other cousins and said, “Ya’ll feel like that too?” They all shook their heads yeah. I took another deep breath and looked back down. Lashae put her hand on my shoulder and said, “Camille, we believe you we do…it’s just that, some things are not making sense at all and that’s what we need to ask you about.” I said, “Okay.” Alisha said, “Camille don’t be mad at us please.”

I said, “I’m not mad, I’m just kind of disappointed. Nobody believe me fully. I thought ya’ll out of everybody would have no doubts, because ya’ll know where the rumors came from and ya’ll know me. We together most of the time.” Lashae said, “You know what, I’m just gone say it…this girl started giving dates.” I was confused and said, “Dates??”

Lashae said, “Yeah, one of the rumors that came through was from May 20th…” I curiously said, “Kayy…” as I squinted my eyes at her in deep thought. She said, “That was around the time you and Shaun broke up right?” I said, “Yeeeah.” Lashae said, “Well the rumor was, that you and him was together that day and ya'll made up, if you know what I mean." I laughed a little bit and said, "Oh my gosh…"

Then Carmen said, "And another rumor came through from May 24th. The rumor was that you were seen leaving <u>his</u> house. It didn't say who <u>he</u> was, but it said you were leaving his house." I looked like I was thinking, but I was still confused. Lashae smiled and said, "So, our question to you is…where the HECK you was at?? Because you wasn't in school those two days, and you wasn't responding to nobody!"

My mouth dropped. I quickly put my hand over my heart as I smiled a little and said, "What?!" Alisha said, "Sorry Cee Cee, we had to do our research. We got the calls and text threads from those two days specifically. You wasn't in school and you was not responding to none of us on those two days." I was looking crazy, my aunties were tuned in. I said, "Ya'll sure I wasn't with ya'll, I don't believe ya'll."

Alicia said, “Ya’ll show her.” They all showed me the text threads and phone calls from that day. Their texts and calls were definitely left unanswered. I pulled out my phone to double check, because I told them the calls and texts probably ain’t come through. When I pulled up my calls and text threads, they all were right there. I was so shocked.

I smiled, gasped and said, “No! Wait, Wait!” While my cousins were screaming, “Oooh! Oooh! Told you!” We were all standing up at this point. Lashae jokingly crossed her arms and said, “Yeah Camille, now explain!” My cousins were all around me and in front of my face. I looked at Lashae smiling and said, “This is what you was gone ask me in front of my mama??”

Lashae said, “Yep.” I said, “You tryna get me killed?? I can’t think back that far.” Latonya said, “Well you better try yo best.” I said, “I wasn’t with him, I don’t know what happened that day. I see the messages and calls now, but I don't know how I missed'em." Cashae lowly said, "Do not disturb." My cousins laughed loud as I smiled at Cashae and said, "Stooop!"

Alisha said, "But we really asked because Shaun ironically missed those same two days." My mouth dropped and so did my aunties. As I put my fist to my mouth, I said, "Ooh I just got chills." Carmen said, "That's where we at with it." I said, "So ya'll do believe me, ya'll was just confused about that part?" They said, "Yeah."

I said, "I don't know how we ended up missing the same days of school, but we were not together trust me. Shaun and I wasn't even talking after the breakup, and I was hiding from him, so I know." My cousins said, "Okay." Lashae said, "That clears it up for us." Trinity said, "But you still wasn't in school." I said, "There were some days I stayed home sick. It's weird that he missed the same days, but we were not together. We wasn't even getting a long at that time."

After we all talked, everybody in the house was feeling a lot better about the whole thing. As soon as everything was calm, my mama walked in the door. We all looked up at her, she was walking fast and said, "Hey ya'll." Everybody said, "Hey." She went upstairs straight faced to put her stuff up. My cousins looked at me scared. Cashae even mouthed, "She look mad."

I agreed with her and shook my head yeah. She came back downstairs in under a minute, she looked at me and said, "Camille I'm sick of this sh*t. There's more rumors coming out and they all connecting making sense. But what you're saying don't seem to be adding up and there's gaps in between."

I was looking around confused as I pulled on the front of my shirt. Everybody thought maybe she was talking about me missing those days. I said, "Well Mommie, I don't understand…" Latoya done had it at this point and started going off on me, she said, “You don’t understand…well what I understand is that these rumors, sound a lil bit too real to be some f*ckin rumors! How the h*ll I walk out the house and there is a flood of people coming to me so sure about you? Some apologizing, other’s congratulating me and then you got the few weird ones that just stare and judge from a distance!”

She pointed her finger at me and sternly said, “Camille, this is not a f*ckin game, do not play with me!” I was looking at her as she spoke to me. She did not break eye contact and continued, “I know you better than anybody including yo self…and you and I both know there is something you not telling me…” There was a pause, I was scared. Everybody was zoned in on us.

Then she said, “Whatever it is you tight lipped about, I’m gone find out and you better pray to God it ain’t what I’m thinking…” I was so scared because she was calm but yet so mad, plus I didn't know what information she got a hold of. I couldn't do anything but sit there and look scared. Right before she walked away to the kitchen area, she quickly said, "I called Shaun and Jacoby, I told them to come over so I can figure this sh*t out." As she walked away me and my cousins gasped.

My aunties didn't hear what she said, they said, "What happened?? What she said?" Before we could answer them, the doorbell rung. I lowly said, "Oh my gosh." My mama came back out the kitchen to open the door. She opened the door and said, "Hi, come in." They said, "Hi, Ms.Lockhart." When they came in the house, I instantly put my head in my shirt. This was my first time seeing them in a long time, especially Shaun. I was so embarrassed.

They looked right at me when they came in, and was still staring at me when they sat down. Latoya said, "Oh don't be embarrassed now! Take yo head out ya shirt!" I took my head out and the look on my face made Shaun and Jacoby nervous. Latoya turned to Shaun and started drilling him about the rumors. He denied them all like I did. He told my mama, "I just found out about the rumors a couple days ago. But Camille got me blocked so I couldn't find out what was going on."

I tried to point to my mom to let him know it was her who blocked him and almost got caught. I stopped pointing at her just in time. Latoya told him, "I blocked everybody from her phone until I could find out what's going on." He said, "Oh." I was relieved she admitted that to them. Latoya said, "Something is not adding up."

Beonca said, "Well Toya, I don't know if this is the same thing that you're confused about but it cleared things up for us…the girls said Camille missed school May 20th and May 24th. They confirmed with Camille that, she wasn't answering their calls or responding to their text messages that day. Some rumors came back about her being with Shaun and coming out of some boy's house on those two days. It just so happens, Shaun missed those same two days and everybody said they were together. But Camille said they wasn't."

Latoya looked back at me so quick, then she looked back at Shaun and said, "Were ya'll together those days?" Shaun said, "No, me and Camille was on bad terms at that time, we wasn't even speaking." Beonca said, "That checks out, Camille said the same exact thing." But this made Shaun think a little, he zoned in on me. While talking with his hands he lowly said, "Aye, who you was with on those days cause it wasn't me?"

He was bothered by it. Latoya heard him and shut that down quick. She said, "Uh un this ain't about that." At the same time I replied to him saying, "I was probably home sick, I wasn't with nobody!" He wanted to say more, but Latoya shut him up and started drilling

Jacoby the same way. Jacoby denied it to the fullest. At one point he said, “When we was at the party I asked Camille was she pregnant and she said no, so I believed it was rumors.”

Latoya squinted her eyes at him and said, “Why would you ask her if she was pregnant?” He looked guilty and slowly said, “Oh uh cause it was…people was congratulating us and uh…” At this point, he stopped talking when he saw Latoya lean over holding the back of the couch with her arms spread apart. Her head was down, and her eyes were closed. She shook her head for a second.

She said, “Jacoby, Camille, Shaun…If I find out ya’ll done…” She stopped and took a deep breath. Jacoby realized what she was talking about at that point and got scared. Now that he saw how serious things had gotten, he said, “Oh nah Ms. Lockhart! No, no, no, no, no…” My mama picked her head up, stood straight and looked at Jacoby. He made eye contact with her and by the way he was talking, she can tell he was being truthful.

He said, “It wouldn’t be mine or Shaun’s…” Shaun chimed in and said, “Nope, uh un.” Jacoby said, “It can’t be, that’s impossible! It would be impossible…” He looked at Shaun and said, “Right Shaun?? Would it be impossible for you?” Shaun said, “Waaay too impossible!” At this point my mama was looking back and forth at both of them. They were nervous but seem to be telling the truth.

Latoya looked like she was beginning to calm down because she was believing them. Jacoby looked back at Latoya and said, “That would be impossible it wouldn’t be mine or Shaun’s.” Latoya said, “Okay.” Jacoby said, “Yeah, if she pregnant…that gotta be Anthony baby!” My mouth dropped as I let out one single loud breath. I put my head down with my hands covering my head.

My mama, Shaun, my cousins and my aunties looked at me so quick and confused. My cousins looked so shocked. Their eyes were so big, and their mouths were wide open as they stared at me. Jacoby said, "What?" He looked around confused and then said, "Oh, she ain't tell ya'll about Anthony??" I looked at him shocked and confused. I calmly said, "Jacoby really??"

My mama, Shaun, my cousins, and my aunties all said at the same time, "Who is Anthony?!" Jacoby crossed his arms and said, "Gone head tell'em! …Who is Anthony Camille?" All eyes were on me. I managed to take a deep breath, but not a word came out. I could feel myself about to hyperventilate as I struggled to breath, while looking around the room at everybody.

Was this really happening?? Why would he do this to me?? Oh gosh…

What has Camille gotten herself into?

Who is Anthony??

Are the rumors true??

Find out everything!

in

Camille

-Code Red, Abort!-

Series 1 Book 3

Meet the Author

Kelonda Isom is a college graduate with a degree in Broadcasting for television and radio. She graduated top of her class with a perfect 4.0 grade point average. She is listed in her college's Hall of Fame for her many accomplishments after graduating. She had the highest scores on all writing tests in school growing up. She has been writing Camille stories since the age of 12.

www.ingramcontent.com/pod-product-compliance
Lightning Source LLC
Chambersburg PA
CBHW070610310726
48982CB00001B/38

* 9 7 9 8 9 8 6 3 2 2 4 1 4 *